A DEATH TO SEEK

thornes & roses

DANI RENÉ

Dear Reader,

As we come to the end of this series, it's a bittersweet note that I introduce Finn's story with. I wasn't expecting it to be MMF, but as I started with chapter one, Finn was adamant that's what he wanted, and I had to obey.

Even though this isn't a particularly dark story, there are some elements that some might find upsetting. This book touches on suicide, so if that is a trigger for you, please don't continue on.

I hope that you fall in love with Finn, Jarred, and Zaria, as much as I did while I spent the past few months with them.

Mad love,
Dani, xo

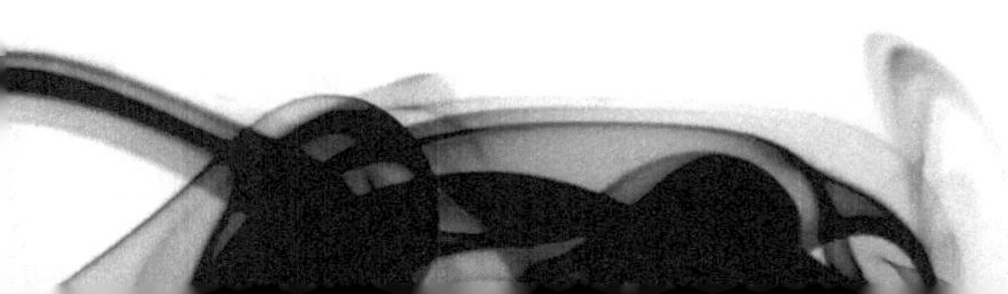

Let me take your pain
Erase thunder from the sky
Wash away those tears
Be there when you cry

Slay your every demon
Championing the night
Take my hand in battle
Together we will fight

_Hydrus

More from Hydrus at www.hydruspoetry.com

Dedication

To those who wanted to give up, but didn't.
To those left behind who stay strong.
And to those who have gone, we miss you.

Playlist

Better than Drugs - Skillet
Heaven Sent - Hinder
If You Met Me First - Eric Ethridge
Immortals - Fall Out Boy
Echo - Jason Walker
Lonely - Nathan Wagner
Death is in Love with Us - HIM
Proud of You - Georgiou Music
That's Her - Georgiou Music
Bedroom Ceiling - Citizen Soldier
The Ones Left Behind - Martin Rapide

Find the full playlist on Spotify

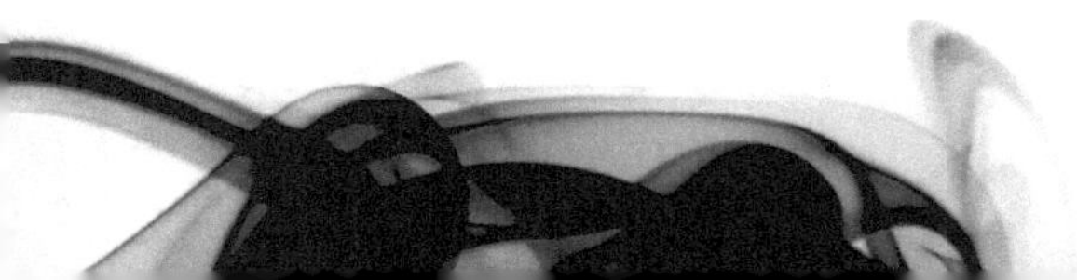

PROLOGUE
Zaria

Sixteen years old

IT ISN'T SOMETHING ANYBODY CAN UNDERSTAND. The pain is hidden down inside me, burrowed deep in my bones.

It's as if I've been tattooed with this invisible agony that will haunt me for the rest of my days. The itch to do something about it lingers in my mind. Most times, I shove it into the box with all the vicious words—*fake, liar, spoiled, slut, whore*—my followers spew at me, and I lock it up tight. In that hidden box, I've included my broken heart as well, because I

1

lost it a long time ago.

It may sound silly, but I recall the moment I gave it away. He was someone my parents would never have agreed to let me date, let alone marry. I have all of that set out for me, it's been that way since I was thirteen. I've seen the contract, my father signed it and told me one day, I'll be given to a family, and it will strengthen our foothold in America. I don't understand it, but I have to obey because it's my duty as a daughter to the Abadi name.

I break my focus from the mirror on my vanity and glance at the phone screen again, wondering if I should do some research on the family my father mentioned that day. But the moment I unlock my device, I realize it was a mistake to do so. The apps that lead to my social media always draw me in, but as much as I smile looking at my friends' photos, I have to see the comments on mine. Notifications that remind me of why I've decided to do something about the state of my life.

Useless. Ugly. Stupid.

I shake my head to clear my mind of the negative thoughts that instantly attack me. The house is empty as I pad from my bedroom to the staircase heading down to the entrance hall. I'm alone with the morbid and unrelenting thoughts as they swirl through my mind. And I willingly go into the darkness. It's where I'm comfortable. Even though my thoughts hurt me both physically and mentally, I can't stop them from consuming me. No amount of medication will ease it, no amount of talking can ever stop the voices.

Nothing you do is right.

You're a burden on them.

They don't really love you.

Even when my parents wanted to sit down and talk to me, I couldn't explain it. There were no words to explain just how broken I felt. There was no way to explain the constant negative thoughts that plagued me. No encouragement or positivity, just a barrage of destructive words.

They were convinced I was just being a *normal* teenager.

I had to be *perfect* in the public eye since my father is one of the most prominent senators in California, which means he's constantly in the news, his face on every post from the East Coast to the West. My mother runs her own import and export company. Seen as a confident woman in the business world, she's obsessed with keeping up appearances.

Convinced that portraying the picture-perfect family would only elevate her popularity.

In the bright lights of the media, I'm the princess of the Abadi family. I'm already well-known at sixteen, which means I'm followed around, hounded by paparazzi, and have been on the front of tabloids across the country. But even when I make the news, it's always for something good.

They've labeled me the Abadi princess.

The up-and-coming role model for girls my age.

But my parents don't believe the hype, because they see what I want them to. As does the public. I allow them to glimpse the perfectly-polished persona that I've been given and crafted accordingly. My reputation has been built to perfection. It cements my place in society once my parents marry me off to some rich asshole who will keep me around as merely eye candy.

I lift my phone, tapping the camera to selfie mode. Once it's focused on my pretty smile, I tap the screen a few more times, offering the world the face they want to see. After taking a few photos, I select the perfectly posed one and open Instagram.

Once I've edited the fuck out the image, making sure that it shows exactly what I want it to, I smile and post with a caption I know will lure the followers, the likes, and the comments. Most times, they're positive, but then there are times I find myself in tears from the bullies who think being behind their screens safeguard them. It makes them more confident in their slander, becoming nastier, ruder, than they would be in person.

My parents don't know about what I deal with when it comes to being in the public eye. I'm alone in it. I don't tell anyone it bothers me. I simply grit my teeth and smile.

Showing off the perfect veneer, allowing those who taunt and torment to watch you shine bright is the only thing I've been taught. So, instead of allowing the pain to take hold of and crush me, I slide on a mask, and allow the public to see the lie.

But there are times, like tonight, where I'm alone with my thoughts, and anything could set me off.

Sighing, I stand before slipping my phone into the pocket of my shorts, and I make my way down the staircase which leads to the entrance hall. From there, I pad barefoot into my dad's office and find the bottle of shimmering, copper-colored liquid and pour a double shot into one of his tumblers.

You're so fucked up.

Why do people even like you?

I choke down the alcohol and pray it helps just a bit. Most times when I steal my father's whiskey or brandy, I can quiet the voices that bring about negative thoughts, but tonight, they're particularly evil. They're all real, though, every opinion, each declaration that plays like an echo in my mind comes from an actual person on the other side of a screen.

Every comment has turned into a voice, a vocal wound hitting right through me. Their words have become my normal. I've come to believe what they say. And I can't stop it because they're right. I am convinced they are. Perhaps that's what they're trying to do, and I'm allowing them to win. Fighting it is no longer an option; it's too difficult.

You should just stop breathing.

You're nothing but a fucking waste of space.

I fill the glass once more and slowly sip on the fiery liquid. It burns its way down my throat, twisting in my stomach like a tornado about to explode through every inch of me. And I welcome it. I flick open my screen, opening the app that's brought me the pain, the heartache, the agonizing knowledge that I'm whatever they call me. I scroll through the comments. It's something my shrink told me to refrain from doing, but I can't stop myself.

Fake princess.

Pretentious bitch.

Gag, you're so fucking fake it's gross.

Disgusting whore.

Why don't you come show me what those lips can do?

Just die.

Kill yourself already.

The words blur into nothingness, and the pain grips my heart, more fire licking against my throat as I swallow the last of the drink and make my way upstairs. The memory of my father lying to my face is still fresh in my mind, and that piled on top of the words from my so-called fans, all takes a toll.

I want to fight the dark thoughts which attempt to take over me.

But I also want to hide and never come out.

If they don't see me, perhaps they can't hurt me. But I know there's no way I can disappear, because my mother will never allow it. She enjoys the attention, craves it. It's as if she basks in it because it's her way of being validated for who she is. But I'm not the same.

We've always been different. Even when I was younger, I would want to stay in while she preferred going out. At times, it feels as if I was born into the wrong family because despite the fact that I'm lucky enough to have a good dad, one who loves me, my mother and I, we've never seen eye to eye.

I turn from the office, leaving everything as I found it, and head back upstairs. The silence of the house is deafening. There are times I enjoy it, but tonight, it's particularly lonely.

When I reach my bathroom, I pull open the cabinets to find what I need. *Just die.* The words ring in my ears as my heart thuds against my chest.

I stare down at the little bottle that I set with trembling hands on the counter. The smooth marble below the bright orange container is a stark contrast to each other. Just like me and mom.

Tears burn my eyes as the alcohol sloshes inside me. It's as if I can feel every drop as it mixes with my blood. The burn of it still in my throat. For a moment, I think I'm going to puke, but I don't.

Thankfully, I swallow back the lump in my throat and focus on what I need to do. I've toyed with the idea for so long, and now it finally feels like the plan is falling into place. I've read up on the heartbreaking stories of teens who chose death instead of life. I've never been one to seek it out, but over the past while, it's been playing on repeat in my mind.

I don't blame those who've taken their own lives.

I can see why they did it. The only thing that's held me back for so long was leaving behind my parents, who would have been hurt. Even though my mother may not really be hurt, it was more my father I was concerned about.

But now I know the truth.

It's no longer an issue.

I looked right into his eyes and asked him why the kids were talking about me not being his. And he lied. He hid the truth from me and now that it's finally free, I want to be as well.

There's nothing left for me in this house, and in this life. Nobody loves me enough to give me a straight answer. They're not keeping me safe; they're only breaking me further. The people who are meant to love me, have lied to me. And I can't take it anymore.

It's time.

I flick the bottle cap and empty the contents into my hand.

With tears streaming down my cheeks, I swallow them one by one.

Finn

Present Day – Two Years Later

THE SKY HAS TURNED TO DARKNESS. I FIND it fitting actually. As we head closer to Halloween, I know the gala will soon be upon us, planning has already started. Each year, it becomes more elaborate, but this year, my father has something up his sleeve. And that's why we're here, standing beside a six-foot deep grave.

The earth smells of rain. The grass is soft underfoot, and the trees are losing their leaves as they flutter to the ground. Heaviness is rank in the air around us, but it's not because of the weather.

I think back to my childhood, as I get lost in the words of the priest as he speaks. Death comes to us all, some run from it, some seek it. Others wait patiently, and when it arrives, they smile, knowing they've fulfilled their lifelong dreams. They've ticked off everything on their bucket list. There's nothing left to do but close their eyes and sleep soundly.

But nobody knows where we go after this. There are religions who tell us about heaven and hell, each recollection slightly different from the other. But the common thread amongst them is that hell is the bad place. And heaven, that's where you want to end up. It's bright and sunny; it's filled with gentle music and angels.

Most people I know won't end up there though. They have their names already carved in hell's door, where Cerberus and Hades await them. Their souls forever damned. My mind flicks to my mother, and I wonder if her soul is at rest.

"Our Father," the deep gravely tone of the pastor interrupts my thoughts, and I finally flick my gaze up. The man is dressed in deep red and crisp white, with his hand hovering in the air, as if he's trying to bless the coffin as he says the Lord's prayer.

The corpse doesn't know what's going on. Funerals

aren't for the dead; they're for the living. It's meant to ensure you've said your goodbyes, and then, once you're done, you lower the casket into the ground and walk away.

Some people may visit, bring flowers, but others, they'll forget about the rotting dead, the gravestone that may tell the story of who is buried here. But it would be lies. We can't be sure that those engravings are true. The man may have had an affair, but that won't be written on the stone forevermore. It will be hidden in the closet like every other family secret.

I take in the procession that slowly starts moving. Men holding onto the shovels, awaiting the order from the priest. People surround the gaping hole all dressed in black. There are tears, sniffles, and the crisp white button-up shirts against the black suits are a stark contrast.

When I've taken in each of the mourners, I look up to the charcoal gray skies threaten, rainclouds hang heavily above us.

Pain.

Heartbreak.

Masks.

All these bastards here have masks on, hiding how they truly feel—frustrated, annoyed, perhaps even bored. They show their sadness, but most of them probably didn't even know the man who we're here paying our respects to. It's all for show. The enormous cathedral that looms over us reminds me of a king, overlooking his lands.

The gothic scene makes my chest light, carefree.

Usually, I'm the joker of the three Thorne sons, but my brothers don't know who I really am. Not through any fault of theirs. I've kept to myself, hidden my secrets deep inside. I'm more like my brother Cassian than he likes to believe, or perhaps to admit to himself.

I'm the youngest.

The most immature.

But at twenty-seven, I feel as if I'm all grown up now and I have to be responsible. I'm the same age as Damien—my eldest brother—was when he met Nesrin. It's been three years since he announced his love for the exotic beauty. They're happy and far away from the shitshow the next month is about to bring about.

I lift my gaze from the casket before me, and I find the women standing on the other side. One is older, her hair still the color of a raven's wings with a small smattering of silver. She hasn't got a wrinkle, even though she's nearing her fifties. The other one, she's younger, just turned eighteen. The surprise baby that wasn't planned. She was their pride and joy when she arrived though. Even when they didn't know what to do with her. Their careers were the focus, but the princess has had a perfect life.

And as I look at her, I can't deny there's something intoxicating about her pain.

Her cheeks glisten with tears as she watches her father's body, incased in expensive wood, get lowered into the earth. His final resting place. I want to smile, but I don't. There is a time and place for everything.

The part of me, the one I've hidden all this time, rears its ugly head. It's sadistic with its needs. As if a monster resides in my soul, and each time I think about that one night, the one moment I found out about my parent's non-existent love, I realize it's always been there.

My father steps forward, making his way over to the grieving widow and her daughter. He doesn't know my connection. At least, not yet. He'll learn. His hand takes the older woman's, holding it as if he's about to kiss it, but he doesn't. That would be sacrilege, kissing a widow while her husband is lowered into a hole in the ground. Another smile threatens to break free, but I fight it again.

The girl, she glances up quickly, but when she spots Cassian and me, she lowers her lashes and hides behind her curtain of sleek black hair. Just that one split second, I recognized something in her eyes, a darkness that sings to my soul.

They say, like sees like, I think that's what I've just found. Lucky for me, I'll have time to learn all her secrets. And I cannot wait. My father continues talking, his eyes never leaving the woman's, it's almost as if he's enamored with her. There's a familiarity between them, and I wonder briefly if they're more than business associates.

My stepmother isn't here. She is visiting her daughter, Nesrin, and Damien in London. To be honest, I would rather be anywhere than here right now. Cassian's hand on my shoulder offers a squeeze. I can't look at him. Not right now, because my focus is on my father. He knows I'm watching them. But my older brother doesn't see what I do. He doesn't know what I know.

Secrets in Thorne Haven have a way of burying themselves deep in the recesses of the mind. My thoughts are still plagued with the lies and fake smiles that I've witnessed. Damien, and Cassian, don't know why my mother left, and they certainly don't know I was witness to it all. They think our father is a good man. A bit of a tyrant, but all in all, a good man.

I know better.

I've seen the other side.

Suddenly, my attention is caught on movement in the distance, and when I flit my gaze over to the parking lot, I notice a figure partly hidden behind a tree. His watchful gaze is on me as it usually is. This time, my mouth quirks, and I wonder if he can see it.

I have my own secrets. Things I can't tell anyone about. And even though I know they constantly eat away at my soul, I can't stop myself from keeping them. When passion ignites, there's no stopping it. He shifts out of sight, and I offer a look to Cassian to tell him I'm leaving. I can't stand here any longer.

But as I make my move, Father turns to regard me, then he calls me over as the priest invites everyone to filter around the hole in the ground. Men lift their shovels to fill with dirt before they start the process of covering the wooden box that houses a dead body.

Without question or debate, I head toward my dad, who I know will have something to say about my almost escape. It's as if he has a tracker on me lately. But when I reach him, and the woman who's still sniffling beside him, my gaze is dragged back to the girl in black.

Her long hair is sleek straight, like a dark satin curtain. Her black Kohl-rimmed eyes are wide, chocolate brown, and her tanned skin is just a shade lighter than how I like my milky coffee.

Her lips are full, plump with a shimmer, and I wonder if she tastes like the mocha-flavored drink I enjoy. The moment she looks at me, her mouth parting slightly, I realize why she looks so familiar. She's a pristine princess that enjoys documenting her life on social media. Everything about her is perfect. At least, that's what she shows the world.

That is the problem with perfection, it's never real.

Anger surges in my gut at the lies she keeps hidden in those perfect almond-shaped eyes. They dance like flames, taunting me closer like a moth, wanting to singe itself. I should be afraid to go near her, because I know her type. The girl who needs and craves the attention.

I can't deny she's beautiful. Breathtakingly so. However, I'm no longer in need of someone who can't be real. I've spent my life hiding in the shadows, and if my father thinks I'm going to marry her, he has another thing coming.

"Finn." My father's voice drags my attention back to him. "This is Zaria and her mother, Amira. I'm sure you know them." He doesn't need to tell me why I'm here, meant to smile at the two women because I already know. He informed me last year what he wants from me, and now it's coming to fruition. I'll fight him every step of the way. And I hope before the month is up, he changes his mind. I don't care what I have to do, but I will not take this lying down.

"Hello, lovely to meet you," I greet the older woman first, offering her my hand, which she accepts. Being a gentleman was ingrained in me at a young age. And as I grew older, it runs through my veins. "I'm sorry for your loss."

"Thank you, Finn," Amira says, while offering me a teary smile. She truly is heartbroken. Most times we attend funerals, especially those of men who my father works with, their widows fake the tears. Amira is different. There truly was love between her and her husband.

"Unfortunate that we had to meet in such terrible circumstances," I tell her, trying to make an impression. I don't give a shit about my father, or the young girl beside me. When I find a person who is real, I will offer them the truth in return.

"I appreciate that," she says softly. I press a kiss to her knuckles before releasing her hand. With the soft rosy hue on her tear-stained cheeks, I know I've made my impression. The moment I do, panic sets in because I don't want to look at her daughter. But I can't refuse to, it would only bring on questions I don't want to answer.

My father's glare burns into the side of my face. If I don't move quickly, he'll lose his shit when we get back to the house. So, instead of starting a war at home, I turn toward *her*. When my stare lands on Zaria, I can't bring myself to touch her. Fury burns through my veins at the sight of her. This is the woman I'm meant to marry. We will be engaged by Halloween, if my father has his way. But there is no love between us. She's nothing more than a vapid stranger. I would never choose someone like her as my wife.

Not because she isn't beautiful.

But because she can never love the monster inside me.

Zaria

I DIDN'T EXPECT THE FUNERAL TO PASS BY SO quickly. But it did and now that I'm home, in my bedroom, safe from Finn Thorne, I can replay our meeting. He's handsome. More than I could have imagined. I've seen photos of him on social media, in the press, and from my mother after Dad's passing. She explained that soon, I'll have to go to Thorne Haven, to live with the Thornes in their home and to get to know my future husband.

The idea is ridiculous.

But there was something about Finn that had me intrigued. Closing my eyes, I lie back on the bed, and

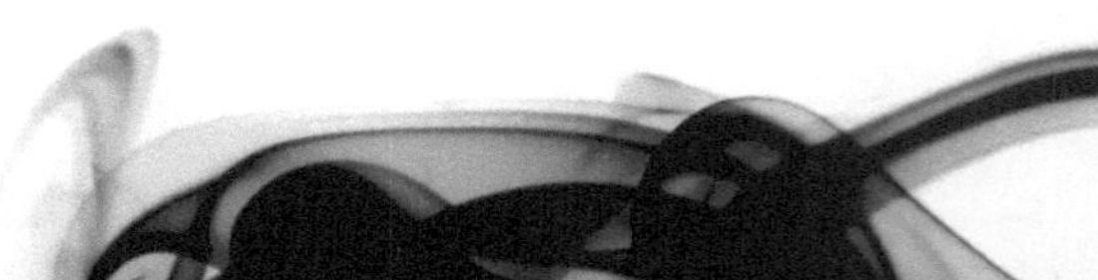

picture him once more. His brown eyes that are so dark, they're almost black. His tousled inky hair that looks like he just ran his fingers through it countless times, along with those perfectly-shaped lips that couldn't say more than one word to me.

In photos, he's handsome, but in real life, that sharp, angular jaw with his tanned skin makes for a breathtaking man. And I want to know more about him. There's not much in the papers about his personal life. He does like to party, but for the past year, he's gone almost radio silent. And that makes me wonder just what happened to have him change so drastically.

When I open my eyes, I stare up at the ceiling, taking in the perfectly chiseled roof. The way the corners are carved into tiny cherubs has always offered me a sense of solace, but tonight, it causes my stomach to churn. The patterns make it seem as if they're threatening, looming over me. A sense of foreboding twists in my stomach, and I have to shut my eyes tight to calm my erratic heartbeat.

I wonder what my bedroom will be like when I get to Thorne Haven. There is no chance I'm sharing a bed with Finn. Even though we're meant to be getting married, sleeping beside a stranger is not what I agreed to.

But I no longer have a say in the matter, not that I ever did. My thoughts bring me back to the present where sleep eludes me once more. It's always like this. The night steals my exhaustion, and I lie awake, overthinking everything. My therapist used to tell me to stop worrying about things out of my control. But what she never understood was that my entire life is out of my control.

Pushing off the bed, I race for the window, shoving it open and leaning out, I inhale the fresh, biting air that's taken hold of the night. The moon hangs above me, the silvery glow illuminating our garden, which is far too big for just my mother and me. But she won't leave this house. It holds memories of our lives, of my father alive and well as he commanded the attention of guests at parties. The laugh, the smile, the happiness he exuded had always been infectious. That's why he was loved by his employees and family alike.

I still don't understand how he could do what he did. But it's just more evidence that, at times, we don't know what's going on in someone's mind. It's a dark, twisted place, even at the best of times. A smile doesn't always portray happiness; most times, it hides sadness.

I've learned that over the years. Hiding the pain, the heartbreak, with a smile, is the only way to keep enquiring minds at bay. People don't ask if you're okay when you offer them a grin. And even if they do, they don't really want to know. Polite conversation is what we're taught as we grow up. You may ask how someone is, but how many times do you actually care?

Once the panic attack subsides, and my knuckles are no longer stark white as I grip the windowsill, I step back from the cool breeze chilling my body and shut the window. The glass reflects the shimmering light, and for a moment, I wonder what the Thorne mansion is like.

My feet sink into the soft carpet as I head to the door of my bedroom and pull it open. Silently, I move to the staircase that leads down to the office my father would work from, and the rest of the living space. The kitchen is empty, dark, and cold when I walk into it. I grab a bottle of water from the fridge before heading back to bed. But as I pass the hallway leading to Dad's old office, a soft whisper comes from somewhere inside the room, stalling my movements. My ears prick when it comes again, and

I realize it's my mother's voice.

It doesn't take me long to reach the cracked doorway, and I peek inside to see her sitting in his chair. Her back is to the fireplace as she stares out at the garden beyond the French doors. She's dressed in a negligee, which I've never seen her wear, and she's on the phone. I'm not sure who she's talking to, but her whispers are urgent, as if she's trying to get the other person to understand something important.

"It's time," is all I capture when she hisses louder than before. Then, silence from her end as she listens to whoever it is. "This is no longer a game." Her tone harder now and more demanding as she speaks. I've seen my mother angry before, but this is new, this is... different. "Fine. I'll call you tomorrow."

I make my getaway. If she caught me spying, there would be repercussions, and I've already got my future set out before me. I have no choice; I have to marry Finn Thorne, and my mother seems to have something more up her sleeve. If I can get a hold of her cell phone tomorrow, perhaps I can figure out who she was talking to.

Back in my bedroom, I settle in the chair at the window that overlooks the garden. Usually it's a place I can think, but today, I'm tense.

The silence of the evening hangs heavily in the room. An ominous cloud covers the bright silver light of the moon. And I'm not sure if it's a sign of doom, or one of promise.

Darkness has always been a comforting companion. It's where the demons that plague your mind disappear into the shadows and you're able to just be yourself. Nobody can see your pain, or the fake happiness you put on for show.

In two days, I'll leave this house for a new home. And after meeting Finn at my father's funeral, I'm not sure he's at all happy about having a wife he doesn't know. Granted, my concern has twisted in my gut making me anxious, and if I could, I'd refuse my mother's wishes. But I can't. My fate has been sealed.

I think back to the conversation with Mom, trying to pick apart her words to find the reasoning behind her decision.

"It's for the best," she says as she shuffles pages on Dad's desk. He used to be so proud of his office. He would ensure it was a place of work and a space for solitude. "This is the only way we will keep our family business afloat."

"But we have the money to survive without—"

My mother's glare cuts me off. "If your father we're here, he would be so frustrated at your lack of concern." Her voice cuts through my chest, lancing my heart along with my soul. I was Daddy's girl. He loved me unconditionally and my mother knew it. At times, I would wonder if she was jealous because their relationship seemed strained at the end. Before Dad killed himself.

The funeral is tomorrow, and even though I don't want to go, I have to. It's not that I don't want to pay my last respects to my dad, it's because I don't want to say goodbye.

I still don't understand why my father would seek death over a life with his family. Watching me grow up and live my life.

And I'll never get the answers.

"Okay," I finally acquiesce, because I can't fight anymore. I'm exhausted. She will never understand the heartache I feel, and when the news of her husband's death went public, how draining it was to keep up appearances on social media. The strength I thought I had, has slowly ebbed away.

My mother's anxiety was palpable when we had the conversation about my upcoming nuptials. Not because I would be getting married, but because she was afraid I would refuse, and that makes me nervous. There has to be a reason she's so hellbent on this union, and I will find out what it is before I walk down the aisle to marry a stranger who doesn't know me at all.

The glow of the moon appears as the clouds float away, and once the silvery light illuminates my window, I take in Los Angeles in the distance. I've done my research on Thorne Haven, it's a town that's surrounded by darkness, by a forest that leads off to a lake. I'm sure it's beautiful, but I'll miss the view of glittering lights from my window.

Tomorrow, I have to pack my life up and make the journey to my future. I lift my cell phone and open Instagram. Scrolling through my notifications, I try to ignore the vile words that people spew at me. Even when I posted the image of a gray, rainy day at the cemetery, I was vilified for it. My heart had broken into a million pieces. Losing a parent isn't easy, but the people behind their keyboards don't care.

They find strength in their vicious comments. I'm almost certain that if I were to see them face to face, they'd fake a smile and attempt to be friendly. I'm about to close the app when a message pops up in my inbox. I shouldn't answer, I shouldn't even look at it, but curiosity gets the better of me.

Tapping the icon, I gasp at the name that greets me—FinnT. It can't be him. But when I tap on the profile, it is indeed my future husband. I've scrolled through his profile before, careful not to heart one of his photos, so he doesn't know I've been stalking him.

When I open the message again, I read his words.

You're up late princess. Shouldn't you be getting your beauty sleep?

I wonder if he's trying to goad me. When we met at the graveyard, he didn't seem interested in talking to me. He was polite, but there was ice in his tone. I ponder my response for a moment before I tap out a reply.

Beauty sleep is only for those who need it.

I have a feeling he thinks I'm like all the other girls who show off their perfect side. Maybe he knows I'm hiding pain behind the smiles and the filtered images. Maybe that's why he seemed aloof when we met. If I'm going to spend the rest of my life with him, I would want him to feel something for me, something other than disdain. Maybe this is the way we'll connect.

Like I thought, a perfectly poised princess. I wonder… Is there a humble core to the over-confident veneer?

His question confirms my suspicions. He thinks I'm like every other influencer out there. I'm far from over-confident. I was taught to never show weakness, so I don't. But I can't trust him to show him the real me. Not yet.

It will take time, but when I finally arrive at his home, Finn will find out I'm nothing like the profile he's clearly been stalking. A small smile tugs at my lips when I think about him scrolling through my photos.

Never judge a book by its cover, Mr. Thorne.

I hit send and shut off my phone. I'll leave him with that to ponder for a while. I should get some sleep. Once I slip under the covers, I close my eyes and nuzzle into my pillow. This will be the last time I sleep in this bed. And starting tomorrow, I'll be in an entirely new home, with a new family.

And I'm not sure I'm ready.

Finn

MY FRUSTRATION FROM LAST NIGHT HAS kept me up. I couldn't sleep, and as the sun rises on another day, I'm tense. Stalking into my attached bathroom, I turn on the shower and strip off my sweatpants. The moment I step under the spray, I close my eyes and drop my head forward. The pinpricks of warmth massage my shoulders and neck, but it does nothing to ease the tension that's taken a hold of me.

I shouldn't have messaged her last night, but as I scrolled through those perfect photos, I couldn't help myself. I'm angry at the world, but more at

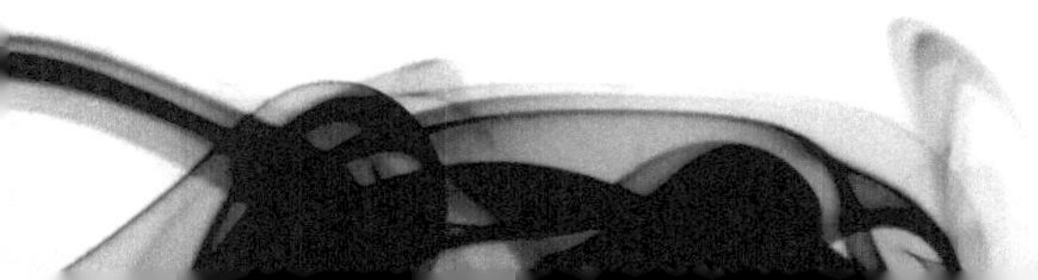

my father, who's forcing this on me. I should go to London, let Cassian deal with the princess when she arrives, but that wouldn't be fair to my brother.

I may be a dick most times, but I love my family. The question is, *can I love a girl I've only just met?* No. There's no way I can do this, and she's... special. There's something about her that intrigued me when we met. It was as if she was hiding behind a mask. Her gaze locked on mine, but in those dark eyes, I recognized demons. The same darkness that she may find resides in Thorne Manor.

I reach the kitchen to find it empty, and I'm thankful for the reprieve from people. The house is generally busy with staff, but today, it's as if they've left the house to the ghosts that dance down the hallways in the witching hour. I grab a mug and set it under the drip, flicking on the button, I wait until the machine stops.

"I didn't think I'd see you awake so early." His voice comes from behind me. The voice of a ghost that has haunted my every waking minute, and one that has appeared in my dreams since we first met seven years ago.

"I didn't think you'd be in the house," I tell him as I turn to face the boy who became a man before my very eyes. My father would call him *the help*, but he isn't just staff. And that's what dad, nor my brothers know. I've kept it a secret for so long, I don't know how to be anything else to him than a hidden truth.

His black hair is buzzed short against his scalp. Smooth, tanned skin is darkened with ink from his shoulders to his wrists, and the one on his neck that matches a dying rose, reminds me of why he got it only a year ago. It was when I told him we could never be public.

His lips are perfectly pouty, just like Zaria's. His silver eyes pierce me as he watches me for a long, silent moment. They hold so many secrets. Even mine. He's never forced the issue about us, and he hasn't ever given me an ultimatum. But he has watched me traipse in and out of this house, as well as every fucking party with a girl on my arm. And even so, he never once acted as if he was jealous.

He came to me at a time I needed someone. My brothers were always there for me, but I needed a distraction. My mind craved something more, something darker. And that's when Jarred Beaumont walked into my life and brought his demons to play with my own.

"I needed to see how you're doing after meeting

your wife." There is a biter edge to his tone I've never heard before. His eyes shimmer with unsaid emotion. My chest tightens involuntarily because I wasn't expecting it to hurt. I've had my heart broken before when I lost Eloise. She was my best friend, and I loved her more than I ever expected to. When she died, I lost myself. Nobody knows the truth of what happened to her. They blamed Creed Haven, my brother Damien's best friend. But it wasn't him. He took the fall for something that was never his doing.

"She's not my wife," I finally bite out as I clench my teeth. My jaw tightens when the corner of Jarred's mouth tips upward. He stalks into the room, making a beeline for me. When he reaches the counter where I'm standing, he leans forward, his face in mine, our mouths inches apart. The heat of him blazes across me, and his lips part on a sentence shocks me.

"She will be, and when you're fucking her one day, I know you'll be thinking of me." He steps back after delivering the truth in a harsh whisper.

"Jealousy doesn't look good on you, Jarred," I tell him, attempting to school my features, and I pray it works. I don't want him to be angry with me. This isn't my choice. If I could decide, I'd tell my father that I'm bisexual. I wouldn't hide the truth because I want the world to know I'm in love with Jarred Beaumont, but I can't. Not when I know what Father will do, he'll send Jarred away.

"And lying doesn't look good on you, Finn," he sneers as his top lip curls with disgust, and the glint of his lip ring sparkles in the light that shines from the kitchen window. It bathes him in a soft, yellow glow, which only seems to make my little monster shimmer with intent. "Perhaps I should leave." His words are low, nothing more than a breath, but I feel them right down to my soul, as if he's taken a blade and stabbed me right through my core.

"Are you threatening me?" I take a step toward him, but he doesn't cower. Instead, he straightens. We're the same height, similar build, with lean muscle in all the right places. The only difference is my hair is much longer and my eyes are almost black. My mouth is a hairsbreadth away from his; I can almost taste the minty freshness of his toothpaste.

"What if I was?" Jarred challenges, those steel eyes shimmer with confidence. His tongue darts out, teasing my lips as he licks along the seam, sending heat shooting through every inch of my body.

"Don't fucking tempt me, Jay," I warn, leaning in

closer, so our lips are locked in a burning kiss. But I don't touch him. That's one thing I've learned about him, Jarred *wants* me to touch him. He craves the connection, but I'm a bastard, and I don't give him what he needs because he's going to bring up the upcoming nuptials.

"Why? Because you're going to run to your fiancée and tell her just how much you want to suck my dick?" His words burn right through me as I grip his neck in my hand, tightening my fingers around the column until his sinister grin tilts his perfectly pouty lips. "I thought so."

I can't stand it anymore, so I allow my fingertips to cut off his breath. A smile tugs at the corners of my mouth as I take in his eyes as they widen. His pupils dilate, and I know if I were to touch his cock, he'd be rock hard right now. And how I'd love to do that. I swipe my tongue along his parted lips, first the top, then the bottom. When he taunts me with his own tongue, I suck it into my mouth, before grazing my teeth along his lower lip. A groan of pure bliss vibrates through his chest, and just as he's letting go and falling into the desire that's swirling between us, I release him.

"Don't ever fuck with me," I tell him with a bite

to my tone. But Jarred knows me. And I know him. We're one and the same, and when my little princess gets here, she'll either learn who I truly am and run, or stay and watch the show.

"Is she pretty?" he asks as he picks up my still full mug and takes a sip of my drink. The coffee must be cold by now, but he doesn't seem to mind. We've always been like this. When my brothers were at home, he didn't come near me. And if he did, it was friendly, nothing more. Damien and Cassian never paid any attention to him. And I was thankful for that.

Our relationship is different when we are in private, it's so much more than two friends hanging out.

"She is." I haven't told him much about Zaria. Not because I don't trust him, but because I'm not sure where this puts us. Jarred is the one person who knows all my darkness, all my secrets, and he's accepted every sinister part of me.

"So, are you ready to play house yet?"

"No." This time, I turn to regard him as I lift another coffee cup to my lips, which is steaming, blurring my vision of the man who's made me feel after my heart had given up. "This isn't my choice."

He sighs. We've had this conversation so many times. Since I found out about my father's decision to marry me off to some wench, I sat Jarred down and explained my situation.

We came up with a solution, marry the girl and then tell her to find herself someone to please her when she needs it. But there is another option, one I didn't want to consider, one that even Jarred didn't voice.

Jarred's gaze locks on mine, and he asks, "Do you think she would accept us?"

"What makes you think someone who's so perfectly poised on social media is going to want a bisexual husband? Also—"

He holds up his finger to interrupt me. "She's the daughter of an influential family. They won't take kindly to having their daughter slumming it with two men who want to bone all the time."

That makes me laugh. It's not a lie. "But also two men who like to watch the other fucking some pretty pussy," I add on, reminding him that there is more to the equation than just the two of us.

Jarred considers this for a long moment, then nods. "True." We've enjoyed playing voyeur, and we've also enjoyed playing our game—The Burning

Roses—with a number of girls in the past. Even though he's not a Thorne, or a Haven, he's mine, and I introduced him to the cat and mouse game that the two families enjoy.

There are three Haven siblings—Creed, Keirin, and Brody. And that's where the game originated, from Creed Haven's diabolical mind. One summer when Damien was home on break from college, he and Creed needed to entertain themselves. And that's how the little seed of darkness was planted within the forest of Thorne Haven.

It's also how I lost my best friend and my first love—Eloise.

"Don't you dare go down that dark path," Jarred warns, and I realize my expression must have turned because his stare is vicious. Whenever I've lost my mind to the memories of seeing her dead, my depression would take a hold, and it's a task for him to draw me back to the here and now.

"I don't know how else to get through this," I admit. "She's coming here tomorrow. I don't trust her. I don't want her here, and yet, there's nothing I can do but obey my father's rules."

"You could walk away," Jarred offers. It's a gentle nudge, one we've spoken about before, but it's not an option. My life is with Thorne Industries. My loyalty lies with my brothers, but my heart, that's another story altogether. "I'm not leaving you." There's a promise in his voice that I can't ask him for. I can't expect him to live a life in secret.

"And what happens when you get tired of being *the other man?*" This time, I swallow my pride and look directly into those steely gray eyes. They're watchful, taking in my demeanor. I'm so thankful the house is empty; it's given us time to talk.

But the moment I think it, Joy flourishes into the kitchen. Her happy smile is bright and friendly, but her gaze is shrewd as she regards Jarred and me standing at opposite ends of the breakfast bar. It's as if there's a canyon between us. A large, open gap that can't be filled.

"Hungry, boys?" Joy asks, arching a brow as she takes us in and moves to the fridge. I'm sure the tension in the room is heavy, and it must be noticeable. But she doesn't make mention of anything other than what's for breakfast.

"I need to get to the shed," Jarred announces suddenly. "I'll see you later, Mama Joy," he tells her, offering her one of his bright smiles. It's one of those that could break hearts. But there's nobody here for Jarred to break, because I'm already shattered. "Have a good day, Finn." With one last look, he turns and leaves the kitchen.

I can feel Joy's questioning gaze on me, but she doesn't say anything. I want to tell somebody about him. The confession sits on the tip of my tongue, but I can't bring myself to utter a word.

"Nice boy that one," Joy says, as she readies herself to cook for the entire staff as well as the Thorne men who are currently home. My stepmother will be back from London tomorrow. And then, it's time to plan two big parties—Halloween and a wedding.

Zaria

THE LAST OF MY SUITCASES ARE TAKEN TO THE car. I should be more nervous than I am, but when I woke up this morning, it was as if I was resigned to my new life. Also, leaving the home where I last saw my father has gifted me a sense of peace. I'm not sure I would want to live here when his memory lingers. The reminder of what he did, taking his life haunts me.

I haven't touched my phone since last night's interaction with Finn. And as I slip the device into my purse, I don't turn it on; instead, I leave it off for my trip. It's meant to take me four hours in our

private plane to get to Thorne Haven, and I intend on reading, perhaps even studying, instead of allowing myself to dwell in the darkness that is the bullies online.

When I get to the front door, Mom stands at the threshold. Her arms are folded across her chest as if she's angry, or, she could just be holding herself together. Losing Dad, then sending me away must be taking its toll on her. But like my mother always says, *don't show your emotion.* She's convinced this is how people can break you down and use your pain for their benefit.

And as much as I want to cry, knowing I won't see her for at least six months, I don't allow myself to do so. I stop when I reach her, shrugging my jacket on, and swinging my purse over my shoulder.

For the first time in months, she reaches for my face and cups it gently. Her thumb swiping across my cheek, as if wiping away the non-existent tears that I haven't allowed to fall.

"Remember everything I've taught you, Ria," she tells me. "There are people out there that will gladly hurt you for their gain." It's the same warning each time we're about to leave the house. I am certain my mother thinks that the ugliness of the world cannot penetrate the walls of our home.

Little does she know, it's everywhere.

And it has been for a very long time.

"I know, Mom," I tell her with a nod. She then shocks me by pulling me into her arms. She wraps me warmly into her embrace, and for a long while, I'm unsure of how to react. My mother isn't the maternal type, and this might just be the first time she's held me like this since I was a baby. I don't fight it though; I allow her to hold me, and then, when she's had enough, she steps back.

"I love you," she tells me. "Thank you for being strong enough to do this. Our family name is important, the business will be yours one day," she whispers, her voice lowering as she leans in close. "And don't allow the Thornes to take advantage of you. We may be signing ourselves over to a union with them, but there are things at play you don't know about. I need you to be the woman your father and I brought you up to be."

My chest tightens at the mention of Dad, but what has me speaking is her previous statement. "What do you mean things at play?"

For a second, she looks like she's about to spill the beans, but then Mom shakes her head. "Don't worry about that right now. Soon, we'll rule over the IT world with our name, nobody else's." There's a warning in her tone, a threat of something I am not privy to, and yet, I'm the one about to step into the line of fire.

"You need to tell me what's going on? Why am I marrying Finn Thorne? What are you talking about ruling the IT world?" Even though I know my father's business was in the IT sector, it was never my passion. And he accepted that. He allowed me to have my dreams, without forcing his on me.

But my mother seems to have something else in mind. A small smile dances on her lips. "It won't be long, give it two months," she says then, before straightening as if she hasn't just divulged a secret that I'm sure I shouldn't know. It's clear my mother has a plan, but what that is still isn't clear to me.

"I don't understand."

Mom presses her finger on my lips to silence me. "You will soon. Just go, learn about the Thornes, enjoy your time there, and when everything falls into place, it will all make sense."

"Enjoy my time?" My incredulous tone is clear. She's sold me off to the highest bidder and she's asking me to have fun as if I'm going on vacation.

"Ms. Abadi," the driver, Winston, calls to me. "The plane is going to be waiting on us if we don't leave now." He offers a curt nod when I smile and leaves to wait at the back door of the luxury sedan.

"I'll see you soon," Mom promises before shooing me out the door. And then, once it's shut behind me, I'm left staring at the bright sunlight glinting off the sleek black metal. With a long sigh, I make my way to the vehicle where I slip into the back seat when Winston holds the door for me.

Inside, it's air-conditioned. I know the weather will be ghastly when we reach Thorne Haven due to the time of year. A shiver trickles down my spine from my neck to my butt. I sit back and watch as the grounds of the Abadi estate disappear behind me, and all I'm left to look at is the road ahead. Even then, I'm left with a sense of foreboding instead of excitement. Not that I would be looking forward to living with the Thornes.

The more we weave away from my childhood home, the tighter my chest gets, and the more my stomach churns with nervous energy. It would've been beneficial if I could drink, or smoke, perhaps it would numb my emotions. But the car isn't equipped, and I don't want Winston telling my mother about my extracurriculars. So, instead, I try to focus on the scenery as we head for the private airstrip.

"Ms. Abadi," the gentle voice of the flight attendant jostles me awake, and I find that we're no longer in the air. The plane has already landed. I didn't expect to fall asleep, but my exhaustion must have gotten the better of me. "We're here," she tells me with a smile.

"Thank you." I push to my feet, before I stretch and allow my limbs to wake up. I grab my purse and sling it over my shoulder before disembarking onto the tarmac. A car waits for me, and it seems my luggage has already been loaded into the trunk. The driver holds the door open, waiting for me.

"Good afternoon, Ms. Abadi," he greets when I reach him.

"Hello," I say before slipping into the back seat. Once the door is shut and we're on our way, I finally flick on my cell phone. The moment it lights up, the notifications start flooding the screen. As much as I'd rather hide from the limelight, I should post about my arrival in Thorne Haven. A small smirk tilts my lips when I take a photo of the thick forest we're passing. I load the image and type out a caption that I know will capture Finn's attention. Even though I don't love him, it doesn't mean I can't have some fun.

The thought has butterflies awakening in my belly, but when my mother's words rush into my mind, it's like a heavy weight, sinking those same flurries. She's clearly got some plan that's playing out, one I want to know about, because it involves me and my future. But I know that no matter how many times I ask, she won't admit to it. She won't tell me the truth, and that stings.

A message comes through from her, asking if I've arrived safely. For a moment, I want to act like a petulant child and ignore her, but I don't. Instead, I respond with a curt, *yes, safely in Thorne Haven*, and leave it at that.

It doesn't take long before I realize we've turned down a private road. There are trees on either side as we weave amongst them. Even though it's sunny, there's a looming darkness that hovers over the vehicle. When we come to the end of the winding path, two enormous raven-hued metal gates greet us.

My driver pushes the buzzer and we're allowed

through. I can't see the house just yet, but from the gates that opened for us, I'm going to take a wild guess that it's more like a castle than a home.

I find I'm right when the building comes into view. My breath is stolen as the car makes it around the enormous fountain outside the front door. We come to a stop and I can't open the door quickly enough. The driver, I still don't know his name, rounds the vehicle to help me to my feet.

I tip my head back to take in my new home. The gothic architecture gives it a spooky, but ethereal feel. Windows overlook the front of the house, and the black balustrade that lines the second and third floors allows you to stand on the balconies from what I'm guessing are bedrooms.

There are four gigantic pillars on the ground floor, one on each corner of the house, and two on either side of the door. It slides open and I'm not expecting the older woman who steps out onto the porch. I was sure Finn would be waiting for me, but I can't ignore how my heart sinks when it isn't his face I see.

"You must be, Zaria," the older woman says, a large smile on her face. The gentle, maternal hold she envelops me in causes my heart to stutter in my chest. "I'm Joy," she tells me. "I'm the housekeeper who looks after the home. Also, more like an older mom to the boys. But don't tell them I call them that, they're all grown men, but I'll always see them as boys." She leans in as if she's telling me a secret, and I find myself smiling despite the reasons I'm here. When she steps back, she holds my shoulders, taking me in from head to toe.

"It's lovely to meet you," I tell her, a slight nervous feeling overtaking me as this woman peruses me. I wonder if she's trying to see if I'm a good match for Finn, who is like a son to her.

"You're beautiful." Her final assessment makes me smile. "And I have a feeling you're going to give him a run for his money." This she whispers conspiratorially.

"I'm not so sure about that, but I'm not someone who will take kindly to being told what to do, especially from a man I don't know." My honesty makes her laugh out loud, and her whole body shakes. The amusement written on her face is enough to make me smile.

"You're going to fit right in with the other Thorne girls," she says after she's wiped the tears from her eyes.

Confusion causes my brows to crease. "Thorne

girls?"

Joy nods. "Nesrin is Damien's wife, the eldest brother. And then there's Kalyn, who's Cassian's girl," she informs me. I knew the other brothers were taken, but I didn't realize I would be meeting their wives so soon.

"I didn't realize everyone lived here."

"Oh no, Damien and Nesrin live in London. Cassian and Kalyn sleep here at times, but they have their own house closer to town." It seems I'm learning so much more than I ever anticipated. I didn't even think about stalking the other brothers when I was researching Finn.

"Well, I'm looking forward to it," I tell Joy with my fake smile plastered in place. I can't tell this woman that I'm afraid of being here. She's welcomed me with affection, and I am sure she loves the Thorne family as her own. My negative comments will not be welcome. And I don't want to start off on the wrong foot.

"Let me show you to your room," Joy says as two of the male staff members appear with my suitcases. "Finn is out with a friend." The way she says the word *friend* has my gut churning. *Does he have someone already? If so, why am I here then?*

We make our way up the stairs before turning left. Joy leads me down a long hallway and stops short at a door. "This is Finn's bedroom," she tells me before continuing. "And this is yours."

I'm right next door to the man I'm supposed to marry.

"Oh," I gasp when she opens the door and allows me to enter. Everything is bright, with soft feminine colors that remind me of a summer's day. It's nothing like I expected. An enormous four-poster bed, draped in white bedding with light pink roses sits against one wall. While a window seat beckons me first, I take in the four windows that allow light to stream into the room.

The view is of the back yard, which looks like it's been made for royalty, including a maze that leads to the forest behind the house. Beyond that are peaks decked in a dusting of snow, giving the view a picture-postcard feel.

"Do you like it?"

I turn to regard Joy. "It's beautiful." I nod with a smile. "What is that?" I point at a closed door in the corner of the room, opposite the bed.

"It's the adjoined bathroom. Finn and you will be living quite closely." Her words hold a hint of amusement, but also a hint of something I can't quite put my finger on. Wariness? I'm not sure.

"Oh." It's all I can manage and I'm certain I must sound like an idiot, but I have nothing to add to that.

"I'll leave you to freshen up," she tells me. "If you need me, I'm in the kitchen. Down the stairs and to your left." With a quick wave, I'm left alone to get used to my new bedroom. It's nothing like the one from home, but at least it's comfortable.

I just don't know how I'm going to live with Finn's bedroom connected to mine.

Jarred

THE SUN IS SLOWLY SETTING AGAINST THE horizon as I stare out at the lake. I shouldn't be sitting out here because I should be working, but right now, all I can think about is Finn with *her*. I've never been a jealous person, but there's something about him getting married that's brought out a dark need inside me to fuck it up.

When Finn comes up from the silvery water, the water droplets trickling down his body, I can't stop my dick from hardening. He smirks as he nears me to grab a towel. I watch him dry off, but I don't say anything because if I do, it will only cause a fight.

I fell in love with Finn Thorne when I first saw him. It wasn't his perfectly-sculpted body, it wasn't his voice or his charm, it was his smile. The dimples in either cheek captured me, and I was fucked.

Since I was a teen, I knew I was bi, but one night after far too many drinks, I confessed to Finn. He shocked me by leaning in and kissing me. At first, I thought he was just fucking around because we were both drunk, but then he told me about his proclivities, and how they were a secret.

I didn't know why he would feel the need to hide himself from his family, but when I met his father, I realized the man would never accept his son as bisexual. When Finn flops beside me, I allow my eyes to trail over his skin.

"You're going to catch a cold if you lie naked in winter."

He laughs, those dark chocolate eyes landing on me. "Are you worried about me?"

"Yes," I admit easily. I know he's asking about more than just the cold. So, I tell him, "There's only so many years you can hide your true self. Especially from those who love you. And as much as you try to be the playboy, that's not who you are."

Finn is silent for a long moment. He ponders my

words. They're true because I've lived the life he's trying to. My family thought I was straight, and I allowed them to believe it. For years, I hid my feelings, until one night my mother found me with a guy, kissing, hands everywhere. And that's when my parents flipped out.

I've never told Finn what happened after that. He knows I left home, but he doesn't know the real reason I was no longer living with my parents. Deep down, I want so much to tell him, to admit my sordid past, but I'm not sure I can. Not yet.

My feelings for him are far stronger than his for me. At least for now. But if I keep pushing him, I'm certain I'll end up pushing him away, and that's the last thing I want or need. I was being truthful when I told him I wouldn't leave. There's no way in hell I can walk away from Finn Thorne.

"I know," he finally answers, before pulling on his T-shirt and then a hoodie. I watch as his sweats slip up his muscular thighs, and then, I'm left with nothing but his handsome face to look at. "Give me time."

"Time is all we have," I throw back. It might sound cliché, but it's true.

We sit in silence as the night steals the day. And

when it's dark out, and the moon hangs heavily like a beacon in the inky sky, we stand and make our way back to the house. Through the forest, with every step we take, we move nearer to Finn's fiancée, who's waiting back at the manor.

Suddenly, I'm shoved against a tree. The thick trunk digging into my back and Finn is on me. His mouth claiming mine in a heated kiss. Our tongues duel for dominance, and with both of us being so damn alpha male all the time, it's a fight we're both about to lose. My hands grip his ass, and I pull him closer, feeling his cock, thick and hard, as it presses against my thigh.

"It's the last kiss for a couple of days," Finn hisses against my mouth before tugging my lower lip between his teeth. He bites down hard, until a strong and tangy, metallic flavor bursts on our tongues. Finn laps at my mouth, and we share the crimson fluid between us in one last heated kiss.

The moment we break from our connection, I shiver. It's cold without him close to me. Finn is like a human heater, and I've always enjoyed nuzzling against him when we would sleep up on the roof to get away from his family.

"I can handle a couple of days," I tell him as we

breach the property. But before we go inside, I whisper, "just not forever." He doesn't hear it, but I know he can tell I'm tense. I don't know why I ever got involved with him, but the day his mother left, was the day I realized there was more to the beautiful, broken boy. When I first arrived at Thorne Manor all those years ago, I was convinced he was just another spoiled rich kid. He gave off the air of the playboy even in his teens. Girls used to fawn over him and he basked in the attention. But then, one night, I found him up on the roof of the manor. I had been exploring the house each night, and stumbled across the steps to the top.

Finn stood on the edge, and my heart had dropped to my feet when I saw him up there, balancing precariously, as if he would jump at any time. I shouted out to him, and in hindsight, it wasn't the best thing to do to someone standing on the edge. But I couldn't help myself.

He turned and regarded me as if I were insignificant, but he came down and flopped onto the mattress that had been placed there by his brothers. I later learned they would hide up there as kids. We laid side by side, watching the stars as Finn told me he was ready to end it all. I didn't understand how someone so perfect could seek death instead of life.

But he divulged his secrets to me and I never once uttered them to anyone else. I kept them locked up tight in a box, along with my heart. I knew from that day, I was falling for him. There wasn't anything I could do to stop it either. It was as if nature had taken its course and I had no control over my fate.

I don't believe in all that shit. But when I met Finn Thorne, I truly believed my broken parts, all those dark little demons that plagued me daily, had found their match. And they don't want anyone else.

The house is Illuminated when we reach the patio, and I wonder where the girl is. Finn told me his father wanted this union. And sure, we've shared girls before, but the idea of marriage seemed foreign to me. I believe it's an archaic demonstration of stupidity. It makes no sense to bind yourself to one person forever. Life is too short for such limits.

Finn turns to regard me from over his shoulder, the corner of his mouth quirking as those demons twinkle in his eyes. And I know that as much as I abhor the idea of saying, *I do*, to anyone, I would say it to Finn.

"Ready?" he asks, one dark brow arched.

I don't know if I am, but I nod anyway. "I guess so. It's not like I'm going to have to sleep with her." The words fall from my lips unbidden, and I want nothing more than to pull them back and hide them in that same little box I've named *heartbreak* because that's where this road is headed.

Finn reaches back, his fingertips brush along mine for a split second before he opens the door and we step inside. The delicious fragrance of Joy's cooking assaults our senses, and my stomach rumbles.

"There you are," Joy says as she notices Finn, but then her eyes land on me, and there's a small secret smile when she takes us in. "Were you two swimming again?"

"Yeah," Finn answers for us. "It wasn't too bad out there." The lie slips easily from his lips. It was freezing, but I've found that there are times he doesn't even notice the cold.

"Well sit down, the girl is here. Zaria." Joy tests the name slowly, and then nods as she turns back to the stove. "I'll get the table ready for dinner. Cassian and Kalyn aren't joining us," Joy continues talking.

"I'm going to change," Finn announces, before leaving me in the kitchen. My gaze darts to Joy. I've known her for years, and she knows most of my past.

There's something maternal about her and when she asks a question, you tend to answer truthfully.

"I know that you're in love with him," she says softly, but I hear her. Even though I'm standing at the table and she's feet away. "And I know he loves you."

My heart jolts against my ribs, making it difficult to breathe. "What?" The shock is clear in my voice. My feet carry me forward until I'm standing beside her.

She offers me a smile. "It's clear to me because I know you both so well." Her voice is tinged with sadness, and I wonder if she's rooting for Finn and me. "He does love you," she tells me earnestly, before looking into my eyes. "There's no doubt about it. And I know he'll never be able to walk away from you."

"What makes you say that?" Curiosity gets the better of me, even though I'm not sure I want to hop on this rollercoaster.

She closes the steaming pot and flicks off the gas before turning to me. "I've seen love and loss while living and working in this house. The way he looks at you, there's a yearning that's palpable. It may not be noticeable to everyone," she says, then continues, "but I can see it. He lights up when you're around.

Trust him, I know he'll find a way to make this work."

I shake my head. "No, he can't. There's no way his father would allow anything to happen between us."

"But things have happened between you," Joy insists, and I can't stop my cheeks from heating. It's like talking to a parent about the times you've had sex. I may be twenty-six, but it's still strange having this conversation with someone I regard as a mother figure.

"But he's supposed to marry the girl." I would never ask Finn to jeopardize his family or his responsibilities and that's why I told him I would leave. Even though it would break us both. Maybe I should just do it, sacrifice my happiness for him. That's what people who are in love do.

"Listen to me, Jarred," Joy says, gripping my shoulders as if I were a child. "You're both grown men, and love is going to be messy. No matter who you are. If Mr. Thorne could accept Damien and Nesrin, I don't see how he couldn't accept you, Finn, and Zaria."

"I don't even know if she's worthy of him." It may be my jealousy talking, but I feel more comfortable saying something like this to Joy than to Finn. Even though he's seen the darkest parts of me, the pained, shattered pieces, I have always tried to rein in my feelings. Partly because I knew we could never have a forever.

"You talk from a place of love," Joy says then. "But you also have to remember, you and he are both in this. It's not your choice to make. He needs to tell you what he's feeling. Don't force the decision on him."

"So, I just need to wait?" I question, frustration taking hold of me.

"Not necessarily, but don't write off the girl just yet. Who knows, you may find that the three of you can make this work." Joy smiles and releases me. Her advice slowly sinking in. "Now, go sit down. I need to finish up here and get dinner on the table."

With that, I start setting up the table. My mind replaying Joy's words as the scent of Finn's cologne which seems to follow me around wherever I turn. It's like he's with me all the time.

Both of us at almost six-feet, with broad, lean muscle, make us a match in a fight, and in bed. And I wonder how we'll fair with Zaria Abadi when she finally meets us both.

Finn

Seven Years ago

I MAKE MY WAY UP TO THE ROOF AND GET RIGHT to the edge. A bottle of bourbon dangles in my hand as I look down, taking in the enormous garden that lies behind the house. The tears haven't stopped. The pain is still fresh and raw in my mind. When people take their own lives, they don't realize just how it affects those left behind.

I'm angry.

I've been fucking angry for a year now and nothing has changed. It's the anniversary of her death and the hurt hasn't soothed itself in my chest. They said it gets easier, but it doesn't. It's just a fucking black hole of agony that's gripped my heart in its claws.

"Fuck you, Eloise," I shout to the darkness. She was both my best friend and the one girl who made me feel something other than emptiness. I told her I would always be there for her, but she still went and did it.

Creed took the fall because he didn't want her sister, Genevieve, to think badly of Ellie. But even then, we said it was an accident. There was no foul play, and Creed got off and the case was dropped. It was only Gen and Ellie; their folks had fucked off a long time ago.

I took Ellie under my wing, and then I laid her on my bed. She knew about me, the real me. I told her secrets I never told anyone, not even my brothers. She accepted the fact that I liked both sexes. It wasn't me being a confused teenager; I just enjoyed variety. It's the spice of life, or some shit.

"Fuck you, Ellie," I curse her ghost again. She haunts me day and night. And no matter how much I party or drink, it doesn't ease the agony of loss. The sting of tears as they trickle down my cheeks and the burn of the alcohol as I swallow back a mouthful can't diminish any of the feelings that overwhelm me. And my mind goes back to the night my heart broke and the misery began.

The woods are dark, the moon only a slice of white. And even though I didn't feel like playing this fucking game tonight, I couldn't stop myself from being here. Mainly because Eloise is convinced that she wanted to play cat and mouse. The difference with tonight is that there are a few girls here.

"Don't do this," I implore, when the rest of the guys aren't listening. I don't want them to think I'm an asshole for stopping the game. But she's mine, she always has been. And yet, she wants to play The Burning Roses. When Creed came up with it, we were bored and needed entertainment; I didn't realize it would still be going strong all this time.

"It's going to be fun." Her smile is bright as it always is and her eyes sparkle with mischief. Then, she shoves something in my pocket, and leans in. "Don't tell a soul. It's our secret. Lock it in a box forever." Her words don't make sense, but all I can do is nod. We always promised each other that we would keep our secrets safe. Anything I told her was hidden in the depths of her pretty eyes, and anything she told me was locked in my heart.

I haven't told her how much I love her. Not because I don't want to, but because she doesn't deserve the shit I come with. "Always," I tell her with a nod.

"You're my knight in shining armor, Finn Thorne," she whispers against my lips before stepping back. "Remember when the time comes, don't fight it. Allow yourself to fall for some pretty boy. Promise me." Her words are nothing more than a giggled murmur, and I can only nod. "Good." But before I can respond, she runs off into the night and the game begins.

Confusion wraps itself around me as I pull out the note she shoved in my pocket. When I open it, I find her perfect, girly scrawl and scan the words with the light of my phone.

Take care of yourself, handsome. My time has come. Remember, keep it locked up tight.

My brows furrow as I look up. There's nothing to see because the rest of the guys have all run off to find the girls who are deep in the woods. I look down once more, and then I turn the note over to find the words that make my blood run cold.

I've left you all my secrets in a letter in your bedroom. Goodbye my love.

And that's when my feet race through the darkness to find Ellie. But when I finally come across the beautiful girl, she's no longer breathing. Everyone stands around her body as if paying their final respects. I drop to my knees beside her, screaming for them to call for help. I know it's *too late. Eloise never did anything by half measure.*

This was purposefully done.

She knew.

She wanted this.

She came out tonight to seek her death.

"Don't fucking do that!" The shout comes from behind me. I spin around as annoyance wrangles me in its hold. There's someone on my roof. Even though Damien and Cass do come up here sometimes, I consider this my hiding spot. The boy standing there glaring at me looks like he's just walked off a goddamned emo music video. His black hair is long, covering one eye, as the piercing in his lip glints at me.

But it's his eyes the color of metal that look right through me. It's as if he can see all the agonizing pain, and he understands it. He's dressed in a black tee with sleeves of ink. I can't believe my father hired someone who looks like him, but he must be one of the new staff members. I recall in my fuzzy memories that Dad said he had five new staff coming in because of some party he wanted to throw.

"What the fuck are you doing up here?" I sneer, hoping the glare I pin on him is enough to scare him off. But he only chuckles. "I asked you a fucking question."

"I'm Jarred," he tells me, not answering me. "I'm one of the new gardeners, or well, handy men. Not sure you need that much around here, but I was brought here with a few of the others."

"I don't give a shit who you are, I don't want you in my space," I bite out. Nobody sees me like this. I don't show my pain to anyone else, only the goddamned mirror. And that's only because I deserve it. I let my best friend kill herself and I didn't even try to stop her. Granted, she didn't show the depression she suffered from daily, but I should have known.

"You should know I don't take kindly to being told what to do," Jarred informs me coolly as he flops onto the mattress. With his stare on the sky, I find myself curious at this stranger who's decided to invade my pity party.

"Well, I'm a Thorne, and since you work for my father, you work for me. So if I tell you to fuck off, you fuck off." I take another mouthful of bourbon as I step down from the ledge and make my way over to where he's lying.

He doesn't move. He doesn't even glance at me. Usually, I'd be willing to spar with someone, but there's something about him that intrigues me. Maybe it's his disregard for who I am. Most people in this town bend over backwards when they learn of my last name. And some people bend over forwards too. But not this guy.

"Where did you come from?" I ask then, allowing my curiosity to get the better of me.

This time, he flicks those silver eyes toward me. "Chicago, L.A., New York," he tells me. "All over the place. Hopped from foster home to foster home."

"And what? My father saved you?" The idea is laughable because Bradford Thorne is not a man who makes anyone happy. Not since my mother left. She left and took his heart with him, and since then, there wasn't a father in this house; there was a tyrant who wanted to run the house like a goddamned army.

"Nobody can save you if you don't want to be saved," Jarred informs me. I guess that's true. Nobody could save Ellie because she didn't want to be saved. My chest tightens at the thought. People think that by looking at someone you can see their depression, but you can't. I know that now.

I round the mattress and flop down next to Jarred. Lying back, I look up at the sky and wonder if Ellie is looking down at me right now. When I cast a quick glance to my side, I take in Jarred's profile. With the hair out of his face, I can't deny he's handsome. It doesn't mean shit though because I can't allow myself to fall down that rabbit hole.

"Do you think the dead sit up there and laugh at us trying to live our lives?" Jarred asks suddenly. The question jars me because it's as if he is reading my mind.

"Of course they are," I tell him. "They need to know that all those promises you made them are being kept." I'm talking about Ellie. I never once spilled the secret about what she did. Or why she did it. It's been a year, and each time someone mentions her name, I want to defend her, but I can't because she made me promise not to.

"And what if you break a promise?" Jarred asks, this time looking at me because I can feel his attention burning a hole right through me. It's as if he was brought here to dig into the deepest recesses of my pain and find the secrets I hold. The last time I ever felt such an instant and innate connection to someone, she killed herself.

"I don't break my promises," I say, turning my attention on him again. This time, we're face to face.

There's nothing between us just electric sparks. The air is charged thickly with need, desire warms me from head to toe as it zips through my veins.

I haven't been with anyone who I cared about since Ellie, and as I lean in to kiss Jarred, I wonder if this is going to be me keeping my promise to her. When my lips touch Jarred's, nothing else in this world exists for a second. His tongue darts out to tease my mouth, and I allow him to deepen the kiss. Our tongues tangle, tease, and taunt as they slide against each other. Warmth grows in my stomach, and pleasure tingles down my spine, my cock aches against my zipper as it throbs for more.

I reach for Jarred, my hand tangling in his long, dark hair as I tug his head back. And then I'm rolling us over. Him on his back, me straddling his hips. And then, I kiss him again. His touch trails down my back and up my T-shirt. The softness of his fingertips sparks my skin to life as goosebumps rise in the wake of his touch.

All my focus is on how hard we both are. I can feel his dick pressing against my thigh, and my mouth waters to taste him. His one hand grips my ass as he holds me closer, and we're both undulating as pleasure takes a hold of us. From heartbreak and pain to desire and bliss.

I'm so close. I'm right on the edge of coming in my fucking jeans like I used to do as teenager, making out with a hot guy or girl. And now, even at twenty, nothing has changed. But as I near the precipice, I pull away.

Out of breath, I push off this handsome stranger and sit up, trying to calm the fuck down. I can't find my words, not yet. All I can do is close my eyes and focus on taming my erection. There's no way I can go back into the house sporting a hard-on.

"It seems the boss has a thing for the help," Jarred remarks playfully as he pushes to sit up beside me. With my knees bent and my arms resting over them, I turn my head, side-eyeing the handsome bastard.

"Don't go telling everyone my secrets," I whisper, my eyes pleading with him to keep this to himself. I know for a fact this won't be the last time I kiss him because that felt far too good.

"I'm no narc," he informs me with a smile. "Your secret is my secret." And that's how I know I'm well and truly fucked. Because this boy has just made a deal with the devil.

Finn

Present Day

IN MY BEDROOM, I PUSH OPEN THE DOOR AND I hear the shower going next door. I needed time away from Jarred. Even though he's the one person I never want to be away from, I don't know what to do about my feelings any longer. My heart aches when I think about losing him, and the words he spewed in anger about him leaving only had me raging. I wanted to pin him down and make him see he can never walk away because he's mine.

I'd never claimed someone before. Not even Ellie. I loved her, I really did, but she wasn't mine. She was

a free spirit that came in and changed my life. She broke me down into the fucking bastard I am, and I'm proud of wearing those scars for her. I glance down at the silky white flesh that's never going to change. I can still feel the warmth of her blood as it drenched me. The broken glass bottle she'd used had sliced my arm open, and even though I managed to hide shit away, making sure nobody knew she'd taken her own life, the reminder is always there.

I shake off the ice that's gotten a hold of my veins and grab a pair of sweats and a tee before shoving my way into the bathroom. A shriek of surprise stops me in my tracks. Zaria is wrapped in a tiny towel that shows off smooth, tanned legs that go on for days. The towel hides just enough for me not to be able to see if she's shaven or not. But it doesn't diminish her ample tits.

"What the fuck are you doing?" Her voice is shrill, but all I can do is chuckle. "It's not funny. I need my privacy if I'm to live here."

I tip my head to the side as I lean against the doorframe. "Privacy?" I quirk a brow, waiting for her to say something more. "That's something you'll have to live without." There's no doubt this girl is going to be a challenge. Rage dances in her eyes, and for a split second, I wonder what she'd look like on her knees, choking on my dick.

"Get out!"

"No." I push in and shut the door to my bedroom before I leave my clean clothes on the counter. She doesn't move. Her defiance is sexy. It makes me want to see how far I can push. Would she ever break? I'm intrigued to find out.

I don't bother waiting for her to move. I tug off the tee I'm wearing and throw it int the hamper before I shove my jeans down my legs.

"Are you—?"

"If you want to see the Crown Jewels, you're welcome to stay," I tell her when I hook my thumbs into the waistband of my boxer briefs. Just before my cock flops out, she's in her bedroom and slamming her door in my face. A laugh rumbles in my chest as she curses me from the other side. Yes, this is most definitely going to be fun.

I hop in the shower, and I'm immediately engulfed in the gentle, yet spicy scent of cinnamon and warm berries. It smells like Christmas with a fire roaring on a cold evening. She's going to take over my space, which I'm not happy about, but if I get to see that fire in her eyes each time I invade her space, I'll get over sharing my bathroom with her.

Dad thought it was a good idea for us to have interconnected rooms. It's bullshit to be honest. She could just as well sleep in my bed since we'll be married soon. But then again, if she were in my private sanctuary, I couldn't have Jarred there.

The moment I step out of the shower, I stop and listen. Next door, a crash sounds and that has my feet moving so quickly, I don't think about it until I'm standing in Zaria's bedroom with only a towel wrapped around my waist. I'm dripping wet, and the only thing I can think of is Joy is going to kill me for messing up the carpet.

But the sight that captures my attention and steals all rational thought from my mind is Zaria sitting at the vanity with mascara streaked down her face. And she looks breathtakingly beautiful in her brokenness.

"What the fuck are you doing in my bedroom?" she sneers, but it doesn't escape my attention that she's taking in every exposed inch of my body.

I stalk toward her without a care that my towel could fall. I know she wants to see what's hidden under there, and I'll gladly offer her a show. But what I don't like is that filthy mouth of hers. The only time

I want her talking like that is when she's begging for my dick.

I tangle my fingers in her still wet hair and tug her head back so that those golden eyes can find mine. "If you continue talking to me like that, I'll have to show you exactly who's fucking room this is," I warn, my voice husky, but rigid as I lean in closer. The droplets from my wet hair drip onto her forehead and trickles down the side of her face. One lands on the apple of her cheek, mixing with the dark streak already there. "There will only be one instance that you will curse in this house and in front of me, it's when my dick is rammed so far inside your tight little cunt, you'll be screaming for mercy."

Her lip curls at my words, and I can't wait to hear her comeback. "Fuck. You." Her words are enunciated so beautifully, so perfectly, I throb against the soft fluffy material of my towel. "You may be a Thorne, but I don't take orders."

The corner of my mouth quirks. "Give it time, princess, you'll take orders, you'll obey orders, and you'll crave those same fucking orders from me when you're alone in bed touching your needy pussy, wishing it was my fingers." With that, I release her hair and step back. If I stay in here much longer,

I will bend her over and make her take me. "Wash your face, it's time for dinner."

I spin on my heel and stalk from her bedroom, slamming the door behind me. I stop for a short moment in the bathroom, and when she doesn't race after me to stab me with something, I chuckle and make my way into my bedroom after grabbing my clothes.

"Already asserting dominance," Jarred remarks from my bed. He's lying against the headboard, his feet bare of shoes with his ankles crossed while his arms are folded behind his head. He looks good enough to fuck, but there's no time.

"She needs to learn early on. I'm not taking that shit," I inform him as I tug on my sweats without underwear, then I shrug on my shirt. I can feel the heat of Jarred's stare on my body. He enjoys watching me, and I like when he looks at me. It's something I've become accustomed to. Even while fucking, I've had him hidden in the shadows, jerking off while I stuck my dick in some girl. Keeping up pretenses, I've managed to leave a string of broken hearts across the country, especially in Thorne Haven.

But there's one heart I could never break. I'd sooner die than hurt Jarred. But I have a feeling, someday soon, he'll shatter mine. Or what's left of it. He picked up the pieces when he came into my life and he managed to puzzle some together, but I told him, it would never work right. I would never be whole. Even if he wanted to keep me, there would always be fragile pieces of me to mend.

It was the truth then, and it's the truth now. "Joy said I should come and get you both for dinner," he tells me as he swings his legs over the edge of my bed. When he reaches me, he cups my face in his hands, and I do the same to him. "Don't let shit get to you. I'm here," he says. "Take it out on me." The darkness that I've come to love in his eyes glint with a reminder of how healing he's been for me. The need I've struggled with is easy with Jarred.

Lowering my head, I smile, keeping my eyes on him. "Let's go" is all I can manage because feelings and emotions are difficult for me. Jarred has understood and accepted that. Since the beginning, I told him how much I struggle.

We make our way down to the kitchen and find the princess seated at the table. Joy is regaling her with some story that I'm hoping isn't about me. "There they are." Joy is on her feet, rushing to get our dinner. There have been so many times I've told her I'm capable of getting my own plate, but she still sees us as her kids.

I slip into the seat across from Zaria and Jarred takes the seat beside me. Her gaze flicks between us, taking each of us in. Her shrewd glare narrows as she watches me. The smile on my face doesn't falter. I set a challenge, and I can't wait to see her fail. Perhaps I'll take her to the woods and get her to play a little game of chase. With that filthy mouth, I wonder how she'll fare when there's nothing between us but darkness.

Joy sets our plates in front of us and I quickly dig into my meal. I'm starving. I haven't eaten today, and I know Jarred hasn't either. We were busy out in the greenhouse, which I promised Mallory I'd look after for her. Since Cass no longer lives on the property, Kalyn hasn't been able to keep an eye on the plants. And with Nesrin in London, I'm the only one left. Maybe I can have the little princess get her hands dirty.

We eat in comfortable silence, well, Jarred and I do, but the tension radiating off of Zaria is palpable. Joy breaks the ice when she asks, "So tell us about your family?" The silver fork tumbles from Zaria's fingers, and she glances away from us.

"Her father just died," I say callously, not to hurt her, but more to get a reaction out of her. The tears that she shed earlier are an indication that she still hurts, and I know that pain. It never goes away.

Her gaze lands on me, the rage she's attempting to shoot my way is clear. I deserve it. Never once have I claimed to be a good person. There are only a handful of people I'm loyal to, and she's not earned my loyalty yet.

"I'm so sorry, dear," Joy says, taking Zaria's trembling hand before offering her a tissue. For a moment, I wonder if those are fake tears. I've watched girls online; I've seen what they do for the attention—filters and smiles—nothing is ever real.

Another reason I didn't want to go through with this. I recall Eloise, remembering how transparent she was at times. But then, when it came down to it, she faked her smiles to throw everyone off the path of her destruction. Even me.

Anger surges inside me as I shove a forkful of food into my mouth.

"My mother has taken over the company. She's trying to make sure my father's legacy lives on." Zaria's words are broken, tainted with pain. And when she looks at me with those golden eyes, I recognize the genuine heartbreak in them.

"I'm sorry to hear that," Jarred says then, shocking me silent. "I know what it's like to lose people you love." His voice cracks and it's the first time I've ever seen him show a stranger his emotions. But as soon as they appeared, he schools them once more and sits back. "Thank you for dinner, Joy." He pushes to his feet and offers me a look before he says his goodbyes. I watch him leave, and my chest tightens. My lungs struggle to pull in air as he disappears and I'm left with a girl I don't know, the same one I'm not sure I want to know.

"I think you can take Zaria around the property tomorrow, show her the lay of the land," Joy suggests. "And then maybe you all can go into town." Her words snap me back to the table, and I realize I'd been staring at the door for too long.

"Sure." It's a response I know she'd like to hear, but Joy doesn't realize this isn't the same as what Damien and Nesrin had. It's also not Kaly and Cass. I'm not my brothers. I can't have someone in my life, in my space, that doesn't understand it.

And I don't want to sit and explain it to a stranger.

"I'm going to bed," I announce before I push to my feet. "Dinner was lovely as always Joy." My words are muttered absentmindedly. I pray she doesn't notice, but I'm out of the kitchen before she can say anything.

I'm not sure where I'm heading, but I need fresh air.

I need to figure this out because I can't live in secret forever.

Zaria

THE MOMENT I STEP OUT INTO THE GARDEN, I inhale a deep breath. Dinner was a disaster. Finn saw me crying like a child in my bedroom. But at least his friend seems nice. With the sky pitch black now, the stars shimmer overhead. I take a step off the patio and make my way to the enormous glasshouse that sits in the garden. I didn't notice it from my bedroom window, but now that I'm here, I realize it's just out of sight from my room.

Inside, I'm assaulted by the beautiful scent of flowers. I move deeper into the space and take in the different colors. Even in the dimly lit space, I can

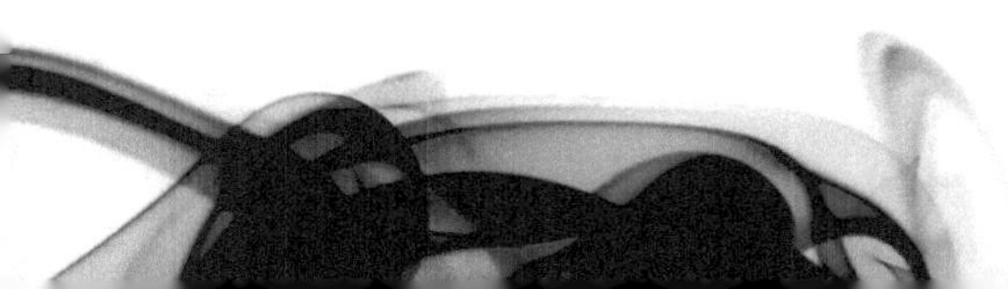

tell the colors of the roses. They've always been my favorite flower. Perhaps it's my mother's influence and that's why she named me Zaria, which originates in Arabic and means rose. A smile lifts the corners of my mouth when I think about being a child and having two loving parents. They did do their best, up until I reached my teen years.

I blink and a tear tumbles from my eye, landing on the petal of a deep purple rose. I lean in and inhale the fragrance. Suddenly, the back of my neck prickles with knowing. I'm not alone. I move slowly as I stand up to find the guy who was with Finn tonight standing in the doorway.

"Exploring your new home," he says with a smirk. He's handsome. Just like Finn. But the difference is, that this guy has tattoos running up his arms, and I spied a few on his neck when we sat at dinner. His eyes are the color of a crescent moon, and the piercings that glint in the light are the complete opposite to Finn.

"I love flowers," I tell him.

"Then you'll get along very well with your mother-in-law," he remarks as he steps deeper into the glass house. He doesn't come close though, there is quite a lot of distance between us and I'm thankful. After my altercation with Finn earlier, I don't need another hand in my hair and a threat of a stranger's cock in my mouth, or anywhere else for that matter.

"He's not a bad person, you know," the guy says. I want to call him a boy because he looks so young, but I'm almost certain he's Finn's age. He doesn't look at me when he speaks. "He's just a little bit broken."

"Aren't we all a little bit broken?" I offer, which causes those silver eyes to land on me. "I mean, life has broken everyone in one way or another. Nobody is perfect, even if their mask is firmly in place."

He ponders my words for a moment before he nods. "True. However, there are masks and then there are lies." As he says this, he offers me a pointed look as if he's talking about me. But then again, he can't be talking about me because he doesn't know me. Unless Finn has told him about my public persona. And like I told Finn last night, you cannot judge a book by its cover.

My brows furrow in confusion. "Judging someone before you know them is a form of a lie. You tell yourself the truths that you want to hear, but you don't actually know the whole story."

"And what is the whole story, princess?" Finn's voice cuts through the darkness like a blade slicing through skin and bone. Shadows dance across his angular jaw, making his appearance seem almost sinister. He's wearing a black hoodie, which covers his hair, and all I can see is his perfectly-sculpted face. "Jarred, do you think she's ready to live at Thorne Manor?" he questions his friend and now I know his name.

"Or are you too afraid to tell us both?" This comes from Jarred, who's regarding me with amusement. When I was in here alone, I felt calm; when he walked in, nerves set in, and now, I'm tense. Anxious energy zips through me as I take in both men.

"It may seem like my life is perfect," I whisper. "But it's far from it." I don't know why I'm about to spew my guts to them, but if I don't, they'll never accept me. Both men have been broken; Jarred admitted as much. Even if Finn may never tell me the reasons for his anger, I won't allow him to treat me like a liar.

"Oh?" This comes from Finn as he closes the distance between us. He's tall, and even though he's not huge, there's a menace to him that makes me shiver. Nothing gets past him, and when he realizes I'm afraid, the corner of his mouth quirks. "Then perhaps we should see how well you handle the dark," he says as he reaches for my hair. His finger tangles in the lock and he tugs it hard.

I didn't notice Jarred also making his way toward us, and for a moment, I wonder if there's more between them than just friendship. But I don't want to ask. I'll find out, one way or another, but right now, I can't deny I'm scared of them both.

"Just let me go back to the house," I whisper when Finn leans in. His mouth hovers over mine. I almost expect him to kiss me, but I'm a fool to even ponder that. He's not the type of guy to kiss someone; he'd most definitely fuck you into oblivion, but there's no tenderness in his demeanor.

"And why would I let my little princess do that?" he quips. There's a menacing, yet playful edge to his voice, and for a second, I almost think he's going to let me go. But then, he moves quickly and suddenly, and I'm sandwiched between him and Jarred. My front to Finn, my back to Jarred. Heat scores me from head to toe, and my spine tingles as fingertips gently dance their way from my neck to the base of my spine.

"What are you doing?" My question is a squeak, and I silently admonish myself for allowing him to get to me. I am stronger than this. I've handled far worse than Finn Thorne. He's just another guy trying to exert his dominance. "Is this meant to scare me?" Even though I feel no confidence at all, I tip my chin up, hoping I can fake it until he lets me out of here.

Finn regards me through narrowed eyes, his long lashes making those irises hard to see. There's a small smirk that curls his lips as he leans in closer to my face. We're inches apart. And my stomach flutters stupidly as I once again think about him kissing me.

"You're only here because your mother wants this," he informs me coolly. "There is no reason for you to ever think you'll be a Thorne. Not by blood, and most certainly not by name. We may be getting married," he says, before lifting his gaze to Jarred, then he lowers his glare on me. "But you're just another toy. Another little princess who's got money so you think you have sway in my town."

"I didn't ask for this," I spit, anger taking a hold of me, squashing the fear all the way down to my toes. "Don't you ever try to tell me I'm the one who walked in here and tried to become a Thorne. I'm proud of who I am, and I will happily keep my name than take anything from you."

Finn's laugh is dark, threatening, and for a moment, I expect him to hurt me. But he doesn't. Instead, he runs his knuckles over my cheek, the contact making my heart skip and flutters to come alive in my gut. Goosebumps awaken over my skin, and every inch of me is alight with need for more of his touch.

"I like that," he tells me. My brows furrow in confusion at his words. "I like that you fight back," he says then when he notices my confusion. "It will come in handy, little princess."

"I'm no princess," I bite out, only to earn myself a surround sound chuckle from both men. I'm out of my depth. I thought by coming here I would need to learn who Finn is, but now there's someone else, Jarred. Even though they've not given me any indication of their relationship, I have a feeling there's more to it than just platonic mates.

"No," Finn finally agrees. "You're not." He straightens, as if cold water had been sluiced over him. The moment is gone and he steps back. "Go to your room." The order is clear. I don't argue that he can't make me do something, because it's what I wanted. My feet carry me out of the greenhouse and into the living room within seconds. My breathing is ragged and my pulse is rioting.

I don't take in the rest of the house; I rush up the steps and to my bedroom, where I shut the door behind me and lean back against the wood. When I blink, tears fall, streaming down my cheeks as the salty emotion burns its way down.

I head for my bed and flop onto the soft mattress. I pull out my phone and find a message from my mother, telling me to behave and to not cause any problems. She would say something like that. When I open my social media apps, all I see are the ugly words that are spewed at me daily. With over two million followers, you'd think that I wouldn't see the negative, but they stand out more than the sweet, kind words.

The last picture I posted was of Thorne Haven. As the town came into view, I knew I needed to document it. Now that they know I'm about to be married to one of the wealthiest bachelors in the country, the abuse has only doubled, tripled. There are more vile words and comments than ever before.

I scroll through them and allow my sadness to take over once more. I wish I could forget. Numb the pain and stop the hate. One comment pops up and glares at me. It's a rumor. My father killed himself, but the press didn't report it as suicide. They spoke about how sad it was that such a prolific man could suffer a heart attack at such a young age. And it's true, at forty-eight, I suppose he was young.

But the comment in question has my heart halting all beats.

Do you think he killed himself to get away from you?

I'm not sure why someone would say that. Yes, they have been rather mean over the years, but this has taken it to a whole new level. There's also a message in my inbox, but I'm too afraid to open it.

When I tap on the Inbox, I notice it's not from Finn. My heart sinks. It's stupid, but even though he's acting like a world-class dick, I can't deny I'm attracted to him. Any woman with eyes would be. And I'm the lucky girl who's supposed to walk down the aisle and say I do.

My attention is brought back to the screen, and I hover my thumb over the message. But I can't bring myself to open it. The name is the same as the person who made the comment. I don't want to know what they do. I don't want to allow their accusations to hurt me. Even though I've already seen their comment, I'd rather not know what they said privately.

I shut down my phone without responding to my mother. I can't bring myself to want to speak to her just yet. There is no doubt that after a few days of silence, she'll call, but that is a chance I'm willing to take.

At this stage, all I want to do his curl into a ball and have the ground swallow me up. Maybe that's how my dad felt. Maybe life had become too much for him and he needed an escape. Perhaps, it was the only solution and he chose the quickest way out.

With that one thought in my mind, I settle in and hope that I can sleep tonight. A dreamless rest.

Zaria

The Past

LONELINESS.

The absence of love and happiness brings about the onset of pain, of heartbreak, and of anger. I didn't think I would ever feel so alone while being surrounded by so many people. The sound of the piano downstairs makes me smile because I know my father is in one of his moods. The soft tinkling filtering through the enormous house.

Every birthday, he's done this. Now that I'm sixteen, a teenager and slowly growing up before his very eyes, he told me that I will always be his little girl. Even though I'm already planning my future, where I'll be going to college, Dad says that no amount of plans will ever change how he sees me.

I think he's lying.

Mainly because when he does glance my way, I notice the proud smile that graces his lips. Over the years, it's changed somewhat. And now that I'm moving on in school, a year ahead of my peers, I've seen it morph into a shocked, yet happy grin that makes my chest full.

"Zaria." My mother's voice comes from my bedroom door. It's tight with annoyance, and I know that when I turn to look at her, I'll find the same pinched expression as she glares at me.

"Yes, Mom," I finally respond and glance her way.

Her arms are folded in front of her chest. "Why aren't you ready yet?" The clipped words cause me to wince. I look over at the dress she expects me to wear and I can't help but shiver.

"I think this outfit is a bit—"

"It's a designer gown," she tells me curtly. "You'll wear it and you'll sell it with your figure. I've asked Damiano to make sure that every nuance of the dress showcases your figure." My mother is the complete opposite of Dad. She's convinced that women should marry for money and learn to love their husbands. Also, she's of the mind that I'm ready to walk out into society and display my assets, so I can find a suitor who'll be worthy of her approval.

"I just don't—"

"I wish you'd listen to me for once and stop playing to your father's wishes. I'm a woman in this world that's filled with men who want to control every aspect of our lives. If you were to marry into the right family, you'll be able to offer some semblance of intelligence to your husband's fortune."

I want to fight and argue, but I know it's no use. When she's in this mood, my father ignores her and spends most of his time at the piano. It's how I learned to play.

"Sure." It's all I can say before she leaves me to get ready. I slowly slip into the soft pink dress that leaves my back completely bare. The skirts fall to the floor, covering my feet, while the front has two straps of material that cover my barely-there breasts. I'm uncomfortable. I don't like this, but I know if I were to try to push back, she'd find some way of guilting me into it.

Sighing, I slip on my shoes and make sure my hair is still falling in soft waves down my back. Thankfully,

Mom hasn't forced me to wear any makeup. So once I'm ready, I make my way down the stairs to find Dad in the music room. It's empty except for the enormous piano sitting against the one wall. From the small bench, you can look outside, taking in the manicured gardens beyond.

He stops playing as I enter and looks me over. I can tell from his furrowed brows he doesn't like the dress. But instead of saying something, he smiles. "You look a vision, darling," he says as he pushes to his feet and comes toward me. He presses a kiss to my forehead, his hands holding onto my shoulders.

"We're going to be late," Mother says from the doorway. There's a sense of anxiety that hangs in the air between my parents, and even though I'm not sure what it is, I know that it's not good. My father's grimace is enough to confirm this, and when I glance at Mom again, she's rolling her eyes and turning away.

"Is something wrong?" The words fly from my mouth quickly, as my gaze flicks back to the man who's been a rock to me. All my life, he's been there. When I skinned my knee, when I broke my arm, even when I first got my period, he was the one who got in the car and took me to choose tampons. My mother was far too involved in her social circles to worry about a daughter who needed advice.

"No, darling," Dad says as he wraps a strong arm around my shoulders. "She's just stressed." But even as he says it, there's a hint of pain lacing his words. It was in that moment, I knew if my mother were to ever walk away from my father, I would choose to live with him.

"Okay." Even as I say the word, it feels like a lie. It's not alright for him to be so tense on my birthday. And it's most certainly not okay for my mother to treat him, or me, like she does. But no matter how difficult it gets between them, my father doesn't walk out.

We make our way in silence to the venue, which my mother had organized. I'm sixteen. It's time for me to be introduced into society. With Los Angeles being so focused on social status, we're having one of the biggest parties in the city to celebrate.

The moment the car stops at the venue, my heart kicks against my ribs. It's a painful reminder that I'm here, I'm alive, and I'm about to walk into a party with fake friends and people who would rather see us burn than help us survive. My mother's friends aren't real. Their smiles are nothing more than masks they slide into place to ensure my father's business will partner with them.

Being one of the most influential information technology companies in the world, they hunger to be in a seat at his table. He has the money, the influence to buy and sell companies, and as he branches out of hospitality into retail, there are whispers about how he got his money. Nobody wants to believe it's hard work; they would prefer to ride along on the gossip train.

I follow my parents onto the red carpet. This isn't a birthday party for a sixteen-year-old girl. Not a normal one anyway. This looks more like a movie premiere. With celebrities, music stars, and politicians lining their way into the immaculate ballroom, it's as if I'm a second thought to everyone here, but my father. He reaches behind him, taking my hand as he pulls me beside him.

Inside, the decorations shimmer with crystal and gold. My soft pink dress matches perfectly to the silk drapes and tablecloths that adorn the room. My mother has always had a good eye for detail, and even her sleek gold dress that hugs every inch of her curvy figure is perfectly suited to catch attention.

Flashes go off as I move through the crowd.

Thankfully, my father holds my hand all the way through the room until we reach the bar. Even though I'm not old enough to drink, he orders a mimosa and hands it to me. He doesn't realize I've been sneaking his alcohol for almost two years. I found the numbness it brought a welcome distraction.

Eyes land on me as they watch me move through the ballroom. Mostly it's my peers. People my age, as my mother likes to point out. I've never been great with large crowds, and this group is worthy of the anxiety twisting in my gut.

"Don't pay attention to anyone," Dad whispers in my ear. "You're here to be celebrated, and every bastard in this room has agreed to attend because they know how special you are to me."

"What about Mom?" I ask as I gesture toward her, where she is already charming the guests with her perfectly-sculpted lips. My mother has been a fan of needles and surgery since I was thirteen. I recall the first time I saw her after a nose job; it was scary. I didn't recognize her for months. And when she finally healed from it, I still didn't see my mother. What came out of that hospital was a stranger, and since then, I've never felt further away from the woman who gave birth to me.

"She's mingling," my father murmurs, but he plasters on a smile and draws me with him as we make our way to the table that has been set specifically for my family and close friends. My name shimmers on the small, thick card that sits at the center of a long setting, and I slip into my seat.

It won't be long now. Once my father makes a speech, dinner will be served, and I'll be thrown to the wolves... so to speak.

My gaze drifts across the room, only to land on a man in the distance. He stands on the threshold of the room where he watches my mother. I know he is looking at her because his face is enthralled. She is beautiful, even though most of it is paid for.

When she turns her head, and she notices him, her body goes rigid and she moves so quickly, I'm not sure why he would spook her. And then, she nears him and stops, only inches from where he leans against the door frame. He looks like an actor. Dressed in a tailored black suit, crisp white shirt, and a dark tie, he gives off an aura of dominance, which sends ice racing down my spine.

I turn to look at my father, but he doesn't seem to notice. Once again, my stare lands on my mother and the stranger. Their conversation looks heated, but being so far away, I can't hear what they speak about.

It takes a long moment for my father to gather the crowd, but the moment his fork clinks against the crystal flute, silence falls across the vast space. Elegance shines from every earlobe and wrist. Jewels that cost more than most people make in a year blind me as guests move to get to their seats. Once everyone is seated, I find my mother making her way toward us. Her cheeks are flushed and her eyes are glistening when she settles beside me.

"Who was that?" I whisper before Dad can make his speech, but the moment my mother looks over at me, I swallow back the rest of my words.

"Listen to your father," she snips, then turns her attention to the crowd. When I look back at the tables, I find the stranger is gone and my mother has visibly relaxed. Confusion swirls like a hurricane in my gut. It doesn't make sense that she would act like that if it was just a guest that wasn't invited. We've had party crashers before, and none have had my mother in such a state.

An idea dances in my mind, taunting me, but I push it back down and focus on my father. He clears his throat and lifts his flute to his audience.

"I want to thank everyone for being here today," he starts. "My daughter has been the light of my life since the first moment I laid my eyes on her. And now, at sixteen, she's only burning brighter with each passing day."

My chest tightens, and my eyes burn as I look up at him. The man who always loves me, no matter what. He's the best father a girl could ask for.

"And as she celebrates her day with friends and family, I would like to take this moment to wish her a lifetime of love and happiness. My sweet, intelligent girl will do great things one day." The pride in his tone causes a lump to form in my throat. I can't respond. There are no words to ever explain how much I truly love my dad.

"And just remember," he says then as he leans in, "if you ever bring a boy home, he'll have to pass my tests before anyone else's." The joke rings through the room and people laugh. But even as I smile up at Dad, there's a dark, niggling in the back of my mind. My mother has done something. I don't know what it is, but there is something off about the man that came to see her and how she's been acting.

I don't want to admit it.

But I can't deny, the idea of her cheating on my

father is the only thing that burns bright in my mind
as the party continues late into the night.

Finn

BRADFORD THORNE IS HOME AND I'M NOT looking forward to talking to my father. As much as I hate being the youngest, I despise the fact that I'm being given a task of walking into an arranged marriage.

I zip up my hoodie and make my way into his office. I was summoned to the den this morning and I didn't get a chance to taunt my new toy. She was so deliciously fearful last night. I was hard as a rock just being close to her. Even Jarred couldn't deny that she's alluring. She doesn't yet know about our dynamic. I'm not sure I want her to know, but

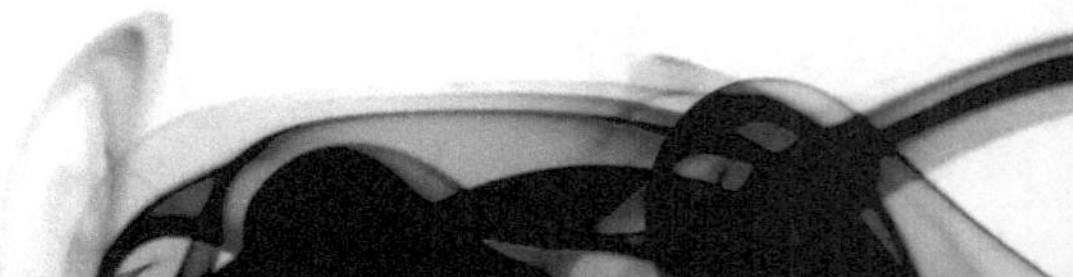

if I'm meant to be her husband, it's only fair for her to learn that she's not getting just one partner to please, she'll have two.

"Finn," my father says as I step into his office. "Nice to see you up so early." A chuckle vibrates through his chest. I don't react to his taunt, and I can tell it pisses him off because he scowls as I slip into the chair opposite his desk. I don't greet him, and I don't want to make small talk. "How is your bride?" The question I'd been waiting on comes quickly. Guess Dad isn't beating around the bush either.

"She's fine." I have no idea why he's even asking me about her when he can summon her himself. He knows I'm angry with him, but he continues to try making this better. He can't. There's nothing in this world he can say or do to fix the contract that confirms I'm to be married in a month's time.

"Finn," Dad sighs. "This is for the better of the company. You know that I can't do much to change it. Once that document was signed—"

"I don't care about the company," I bite out as I push forward. I lean my elbows on my thighs and meet his glare dead on. "I never wanted this in the first place. Yes, I'll work at Thorne Industries, but it never was my choice to do so." He knew this. All my life I'd wanted to travel. There wasn't anything that could keep me here—until Jarred. And now, I will have a wife to ensure I remain in Thorne Haven. My father will never allow me to leave. The legacy that remains in this house, in this town, it's ours. I should be proud of it, but I'm not.

"There's no choices here, Finn." He shakes his head, as if he's disappointed in me. As he always is. Damien being the eldest is the apple of my father's eye, then it is Cassian who obeyed without question. Me, on the other hand, I never listen to anything he tells me. I live my life the way I want to, and nobody can stop me. Even though he continues to try.

"I know that. You've made it abundantly clear," I say, and as much as I want to walk out, I know I can't because he needs to give me more information about the meeting I'm meant to be attending in a few hours. Thorne Industries will be branching out and I have to be the face of the company today. Usually Cassian goes, but since he's busy, I have to step up and be responsible.

"Here's the documents for today." He shoves a folder toward me, which I grab from his desk. "Damien will be calling in to attend," Dad informs me, and my gaze snaps up to meet his. "It's not because I don't trust you."

"Isn't it?" It's a challenge, one I know my father would hate. He doesn't like when I talk back, especially when I'm calling him out on not being as close to me as he is to Damien and Cass. "Because I'm sure you don't trust me."

"Finn, don't start this," he sighs, before shaking his head. "Damien signed the client, that's why he's sitting in. You'll be there in person. He just needs to finalize a few details, which you don't know about."

"And the fact that Damien was the one who could marry whomever he chose has nothing to do with the fact that he's the eldest? The favorite?" I push to my feet. "You should've named him Adam. The first man." The sneer in my tone is enough to have my father's fist banging on the desk. I don't flinch. I don't even react, which only annoys Bradford further.

"You're a Thorne," he tells me. It's the same speech I've heard since I was a kid. Being a Thorne means you have certain responsibilities, there are no liberties in this life. I have to do what is asked of me.

"And a Thorne never defies the legacy," I finish for him. Before Bradford could speak, I'd already mimicked his words.

There's a slight satisfaction in his face. The way

it creases with a small smile makes me feel as if I just made him proud. It isn't something I'm used to feeling. I'm not the son who makes him feel as if he raised us properly.

My father turns toward his safe. The clicking of the lock is loud, bouncing off the walls of his office before the door opens. He rummages around in the darkness, and when he pulls out an item, a large velvet pouch, he takes me in with a smile.

"You've finally learned the reasoning behind being a Thorne. We never defy legacy," he tells me before handing me the item. I'm not sure what it is, but when I take it, I feel the hard corners of whatever is hidden inside.

"What is this?" I ask, lifting my gaze from my hands to my father. Each time I've been in his office has brought about nothing but destruction to my life. There is no happiness that comes about in Thorne Haven, and within the manor, it's always ensured that either anger or fear is prevalent in my mind.

"Since you're going to be getting married, it's time you took the throne." His voice is nothing more than a whisper, but I hear every word. I'm not sure what he means, but when I drop my stare and unravel the bag, I'm met with a crown of silver. "There are two sovereigns within our society," Dad says as he rounds the desk to stop near me. "There is the Gilded Sovereign, from Tynewood, as well as the Silver Sovereign."

Shaking my head, I look to my father. "I don't understand. You've never mentioned this before. Not to Damien or Cassian. Unless they never told me about it, but all my life, I don't recall ever hearing about this."

My father nods. "There are two towns that run within families who have power over governments the world over," Dad explains. "Thorne Haven, run by us, and the Havens." This is something I know already. But when he continues, my father finally has my attention. "Then there is a town called Tynewood. It's run by four families. It's much larger than Thorne Haven, but it also has a myriad of secrets that hide within its walls."

"And the crown?" I lift the sparkling headdress, unsure of what to do with it. There are small engravings in the metal, and the stones that adorn it are the color of a deep purple sky when the sun is about to rise. As the light glints against the jewels, I can't help but wonder why I'm the one to receive this.

"You're the youngest son," Bradford says. "And

most times, it's the eldest son who has to take the reins, but since you never wanted to run Thorne Industries, and your passion was far more removed from Thorne Haven, I chose you to represent us in something as important as the family business."

Narrowing my gaze, I regard my father with as much trust as I would Zaria. I don't know her. I've only just met her, and yet, I may just trust her more than I do the man before me.

"And what could that be?"

"You've always wanted to travel," Dad says, as he gestures with his chin. "You'll be able to fly to the countries where you'll meet the Sovereign and represent our family in meetings. The men you'll meet aren't good people, and they will do anything to get ahead in life, that's what happens when you have money."

"And you want me to go to these meetings and what? Rub some shoulders so your name can be whispered about?" The incredulousness in my tone is enough to have my father chuckling. He shakes his head before he steps closer to me. His hand lands on my shoulders, and his fingers tighten with a grip so firm, I almost wince. But I've trained my features to never show weakness. There is only one person in this world who can now break me, and I've allowed him into my heart and mind.

"You'll take Zaria to Tynewood to meet with the Lancasters," Bradford tells me. "They're the ones we need to impress. I want their business, Finn. Once you sign them as clients," he murmurs, stopping to ensure he has my attention. He does have it. He's fucking claimed it because right now, all I can think about is leaving Thorne Manor. "I'll give you the option to decide your fate."

"What?" Shock laces my tone. My mouth falls open as I regard him staring back at me. He's never given me choices, not when I was younger, and certainly not after I'd turned eighteen. Growing up was difficult because all I wanted to do was please my father. I wanted to make him proud of me. I watched as he doted on Damien and Cassian, but he was harder on me than either of them. And now, I wonder if this is the reason for it. I'm meant to go sit in weird secret society meetings and hold my head up high.

I'm a Thorne.

And it seems like my father had been training me without me knowing about it.

The smile that curls my father's lips makes me take

pause. "If you can pull this off, I'll gift you the choice. You know, Finn," my father says, then pauses, and I know it's only for dramatic effect. "I'm an old man. I've been around the block a time or two, and I'm certainly not stupid." Something flicks inside my mind. My chest tightens as he speaks, and when those eyes that match my brother's look at me once more, I realize there's something that he knows and it's something I don't *want* him to know.

"I didn't think you were stupid, Dad," I tell him, but it's too late because he chuckles. It's a dark, foreboding sound that sends warning bells off in my head.

He knows.

I don't know how, but he knows about Jarred and me. It's the only thing I can think of because it's the only secret I've kept. Besides the fact that I knew my mother cheated on him. But that wouldn't cause him to change my destiny. My path was set out a long time ago.

"There are choices we all have to make when it comes to matters of the heart," Bradford continues slowly as he settles back in his chair. The fact that he's far away from where I'm standing eases my tension, but not by much. I don't speak, I simply wait for him to continue. "I'm not a prude," he tells me. "If you want to live your life one way, then I'm not going to stop you. But, if it becomes a hinderance on the family..."

The warning is clear. It hangs in the silence. In the words my father doesn't say. There's no longer a doubt in my mind that he knows about Jarred. I'm not going to deny it, and I'm not going to show any fear in my expression. I'll allow him to hold this over me for a moment.

"Just make sure you sign the contract." It's a dismissal, which forces my feet to move for the door. But before I can escape the lion's den, my father's voice halts me in my tracks. "And when you go to Tynewood, you can take him with you."

I want to turn around and see if he's joking. I want to laugh out loud and call his bluff, but I don't. When my father offers a mercy to me, I don't fuck with it. I take it and run.

In the hallway, I stop, breathing deeply as I shut the office door. I'm no longer a child, but my father continues to instill the fear of God in me.

I head for the meeting with my mind whirring at the possibilities of being able to be with Jarred. But I have a feeling as much as my father has laid out the terms, there'll be a lot more to this verbal agreement than he's letting on. He can't just let the Abadi family down. I can't walk away from a contract signed in blood.

And my father knows that as well as I do.

Questions remain.

But as I walk into the garage and slide into the driver's seat of my brand-new silver Maserati, I wonder just how Bradford Thorne is going to wrangle his way out of the shitstorm that's about to hit us.

Jarred

WHEN FINN RETURNS FROM HIS MEETING, I'm in the shed. I spend my time in here, hidden away from the prying eyes of the rest of the staff. Joy is the only person I really get on with.

When Finn saunters in, breaking into my thoughts, he glances at the smoke that hangs between my lips. He's dressed in his black slacks and white shirt. The tie he has wrapped around his hand catches my attention first.

He stops just inside the doorway, blocking the last remaining light. He looks like an avenging angel come to drag me to hell. And honestly, if he was, I

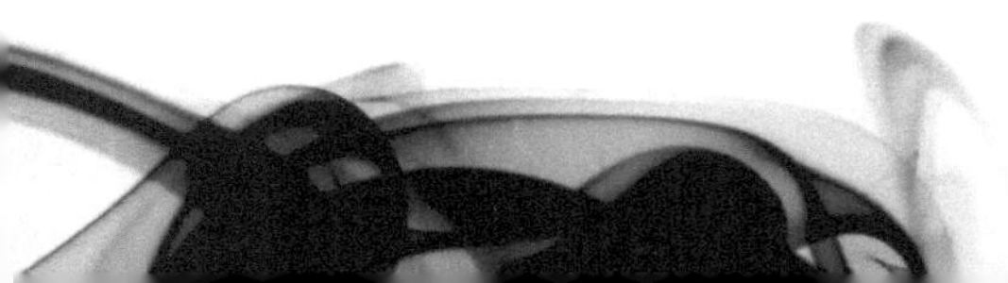

would go. Anything to escape the monotony of life on the manor. Granted, I'm lucky to have a roof over my head and a job, but knowing that Finn isn't truly mine doesn't ease the ache of an easy life.

"You look fucked," I remark as I pull deeply on the cigarette and allow the smoke to fill my lungs. The nicotine, however, doesn't quell my need to relax because of him being here. We've had words over the past few days, and even though Finn has assured me that he wants me, there's still a niggling in my gut that tells me he may not.

While his brothers lived at home, I would hide. They were larger-than-life characters, and not because they were mean, but they didn't really take notice of the staff who worked on the property. It was always only Finn. And the only reason he noticed me is because I made him look.

Of the three Thorne brothers, he was the one who caught my eye and I never looked at anyone else. And now that he's engaged to be married, my abandonment issues have sprung up like a volcano.

"I am." He moves closer, but doesn't come to me. "The meeting took far longer than I expected," he tells me, but his eyes don't meet mine. It's strange. He's always been honest with me, and right now, I have a feeling he's lying.

"Sorry to hear that," I say, but there's nothing more I can add because I don't know about the meetings he attends. He's told me about the family business, but because it doesn't involve me, I've only ever focused on the parts that involve him.

I watched him leave this morning, pulling out of the drive in his sleek new toy. And when his taillights disappeared in the distance, I got to work. The sun shone down on me all day, which tired me out. And now that the night has stolen the light, I'm exhausted.

"We leave in a couple of days. You need to pack a bag," Finn says suddenly, before he flops onto the makeshift chair made of hay. The horses are in their stables, but we keep the feed in the shed. He looks so out of place in here, I almost laugh, but his words sober me.

"What?" Confusion creases itself over my face as I regard him. He must be tired because he's not making any sense. I wouldn't leave Thorne Haven unless his father told me to. But also, I'd walk out if Finn confessed that he no longer wanted me around.

"My father has given me a job to complete, and you have to come with me," he says before running his fingers through his dark hair.

This time, I do laugh because I'm sure he's joking around. I work on the grounds. I don't do fancy meetings and shit like that. "Why would I go with you?"

"Well, you'll be with Zaria and me. But, my father knows," Finn admits, his eyes landing on mine for the first time since he walked into the shed. Even in the dim lighting, I can see every flicker of fear and anguish that's written on his face.

"Your father knows what?" This time, I push to my feet as I saunter over to where Finn is lounging. My eyes are glued to his movements as he unbuttons his shirt and settles back when I straddle his waist. "That I do this to his son?" I taunt as I run my finger along his angular jawline. The usually smooth flesh darkened with stubble. He's been growing out his beard, and I have to admit, the dark edge to his rigid face is attractive.

"Yes," Finn hisses when my thumb circles his nipple. He grinds his teeth when I twist it slightly, and I can't help but grin when I feel his cock pulse against me. "He told me he's not stupid and he wants me to take you with me on a trip to Tynewood."

All movement stops. I can't go with him. There's

no way I can walk back into that town and not allow Finn to learn about my past. That's why Bradford wants me to go with his son. If my secrets come out, he'll never forgive me for coming here and not telling him the truth.

"What's wrong?" Finn asks, and I realize I've been frozen in time for a few moments too long. Finn is perceptive. He can pick up on my moods, and the changes that occur when I'm down or frustrated so easily, it's like he's reading a book. He knows every page of my story, except for the one chapter I've kept hidden.

"Nothing," I say, hoping to seem calm and relaxed. Shrugging, I continue, "I Just don't know if it's worth me traipsing around the country with you doing something I don't understand." The lie burns on my tongue like acid.

I should have fucking told him when I arrived.

I should have told him before we kissed.

Before we fucked.

But my fear held me back, and now we're here.

"It's not that bad. You can chill out with Zaria while I finish up a few things. It won't take long, and maybe we can head down to the coast. My father didn't specify when we needed to be back."

He's serious. Dead. Fucking. Serious.

I open my mouth to respond, but I can't find words. I'm speechless for the first time in my whole damn life. When I ran away from Tynewood and found my way to an even smaller town, I thought I'd forever be safe from the past. At least, I'd hoped that nobody would ever come looking. I can't walk back into town and expect nobody to notice me. Because they will.

I lean in, my mouth inches from Finn's. "Why don't you and the little princess go," I say. "And I'll be waiting here for you when you get back." Even though I say it, I can already see the wheels turning in his head. Finn may be the only son who doesn't want to be a businessman, but he thinks like one. It's all those years of training his father put him through.

"I have to go, and so do you," he tells me with finality. "I have to go and find out about this fucking Sovereign shit," he muses with a grin.

My heart stutters in my chest, banging against my ribs. "The what?" I pray to the heavens above that I sound as confused as I hope my face looks. I know all about that fucking society, which is exactly why Bradford figured it would be a good idea for me to go.

Maybe he wants me to face my demons. Perhaps he wants Finn to see the real me. Whatever the reason, I'm fucked either way because the look on Finn's face tells me he's not letting me stay behind while he heads off with Zaria.

"The Gilded Sovereign," he tells me. "Some secret society that apparently I have to impress. My father gave me a crown today." This time, he smirks. I've known Finn for long enough to know that the bit of pride his old man showed him today is enough to keep him grinning like that for a few weeks.

For a moment, I recall my own need to impress. But then I ran. When I learned the truth about what lies behind those fucking town walls, I ran. And I ended up in a worse place than I ever thought possible. And then, something led me here. Or should I say, someone led me here.

I arch a brow as I regard my handsome man. "So, you're a prince now?" My words are light, teasing, playful, and I'm thankful I've learned to be such a proficient liar. If I didn't, he would see past my façade.

"I suppose so." Finn shrugs, his hands trailing down to my hips as he pulls me closer. "How about you kiss your prince?" He waggles his eyebrows suggestively. I find myself leaning into him before I have time to think through everything he's just said. Our lips fuse in a heated kiss.

Our tongues tangle and dance as I deepen the kiss. Finn's palms slide down to my ass and he grips me harshly. A groan rumbles in my chest as I press my cock against his crotch. Hardness against hardness.

My chest fills with warmth at the thought of him loving me, needing me, craving me as much as I do him. We kiss for a long while before I move down his body, pressing my lips to his chiseled torso. His chest has a slight spattering of hair, but his abs, which are tense when I trail my tongue along the peaks and valleys, are smooth and tanned.

When I reach his navel, I dip my tongue in before kissing my way lower. I glance up, asking for permission to continue, and when Finn nods, I unzip his slacks and fist his cock.

"No boxers?" I tease as I stroke his hard shaft in my hand. Then, I lap at the wet tip that has salty precum exploding on my tongue. Even though the scene before me is erotic and sensual, I wouldn't mind if Zaria were here watching. I take Finn into my mouth, his cock hard and throbbing as I slide my lips down the silky hardness of his erection.

The hooded stare that he pins me with has my own cock aching to be inside him. It's been a while, and I'm tempted to bend him over right here. But I don't. I savor the flavor of him as his arousal coats my tongue with every thrust of his hips.

He uses my mouth. He fucks my face. Fingers tangle in my hair as Finn loses control and tugs the strands until the bite of pain is enough to have me gagging on his cock. I love when he takes control, when he dominates the scene between us. And watching his usually playful demeanor change to something dark and sordid makes my cock weep.

He's close. I can tell because his grunts get louder, and his moans vibrate through his chest. My hands are palm down on his pectorals, and I can feel every movement of his sounds. It's the most erotic symphony I've ever heard. And I could listen to him over and over again.

I'm lost in the pleasure and the power I have over him, so I don't notice the audience we have until it's far too late. The moment Finn holds me down, and spurts of his hot arousal jets into my mouth, I hear a gasp, which shatters the passion that had been coiling inside both of us.

Finn and I move in sync. His dick pops out of

my mouth as we both meet the wide eyes of Finn's fiancée. Zaria is at the door, her mouth parted into a wide O shape as she takes in our lewd position.

Finn moves first, shoving his now softening cock back into his trousers before zipping up. I swipe my hand across my mouth, still savoring the taste of him when he glances at me.

"Go," is all I can manage. He races from the shed, making his way toward Zaria, who seems to have taken off running in the opposite direction. She knows. His father knows. And I'm certain Joy knows.

It seems our little secret is no longer so hidden anymore.

But that's the problem with secrets, they tend to be exposed at the worst possible times.

Zaria

I MAKE IT TO MY BEDROOM AND SHUT THE DOOR, but Finn knew I'd run for a safe haven, and he bursts through the interlocking bathroom like he's about to fight a war. His dark hair is a mess and as the shadows dance across his handsome face, I can't do anything but stare in awe. His shirt is still undone, the smooth defined muscles of his abs taunt me from where he stops in my bedroom. He doesn't near me, he doesn't come closer, but I find that I want him to do something.

After seeing him with Jarred, I don't think I've ever been more turned on. I didn't think I would, but now that their relationship is clear in my mind, I want to see them together again. I've only ever read about two men being together, never seen it before my very eyes.

"Are you gay?" I blurt, my voice a broken whisper of shock and desire. I stood watching them for a while before they both noticed. If he comes any closer, I'm sure he'd realize how turned on I am. My panties are soaked, my body is trembling, and I have to fist my hands to hide it from Finn.

"No," he growls, the sound low, gravely as it trickles over me like the icy drizzle on a warm summer's day. "I'm..." He doesn't complete his confession, but I want to know. He's meant to be my husband and yet, I have no clue who Finn Thorne is. "I'm bisexual," he tells me then, before running his fingers through his hair.

"Oh," is all I can muster because I've never met anyone who is, or at least, I never knew anyone who has those inclinations. I find it intriguing. I want to know more, how he found out, how it started with Jarred, but I don't ask even though my curiosity is at an all-time high.

"You cannot tell anyone about what you saw." Finn finally speaks again, breaking the silence with his harsh tone. He meets my eyes, and he must see something flicker in them because he moves closer. The slow crawl of a predator seeking out his prey. When he finally reaches me, he stops, inches away.

"I wouldn't tell anyone," I whisper as I take him in. His usually cocoa eyes are black, the pupils have hidden the irises, and he looks like a hunter who's caught his dinner for the night. "But why wouldn't you want to be with him?"

"What I want doesn't matter in this life," he tells me, and the sadness that drips from his voice makes my chest ache. "If I told my father I was bisexual, he would disown me."

"How do you know that?" I query as my brows furrow together. "You cannot know what someone else would do unless they do it."

The corner of his mouth tilts, the smirk salaciously mischievous, and his hand reaches for my face. He cups my cheek, his thumb swiping over my lips, tugging my lower lip to the side. His gaze burns with curiosity as he takes in my features.

"Such a wise little princess," he remarks. Then, he leans in even closer. "How long were you standing there watching us?" The question feels as if it's loaded with intent. He knows I was there for a while because if he didn't, he wouldn't be grinning manically at me.

"N-not t-that long," I stutter, but Finn chuckles, the sound vibrating through me.

Finn regards me, his head tipped to the side, his eyes narrowed. "Then why are your cheeks flushed?" He trails his hand lower, gripping the column of my neck, while his thumb rests on my pulse point. "And why is your heart racing?" Both questions are filled with answers already.

"Perhaps she liked the show." Another voice comes from behind Finn. Jarred. "Maybe the little princess is all wet and needy now that she's seen just what her husband has hidden behind his zipper. Or maybe, just maybe, she was standing there wanting to play with her pussy while she watched us enjoy ourselves." Each and every word Jarred utters is laced with amusement, and with every remark, he comes even closer. And now that both men are looming over me, I'm shaking.

It's not fear.

It's desire.

The emotion courses through me like a magnetic field. I picture it like sound waves, my mind awash with scenarios that could play out right now.

"Mmm, so if I were to touch you right now, I'd find

you wet," Finn says, it's not a question, because Finn doesn't need to ask permission. If he did touch me, I wouldn't deny him. My body would never say no because I am attracted to him. And he knows it.

"And if I were to press a kiss to your neck right now, your pulse would react in kind," Jarred remarks, and my gaze flicks to his. In those silver eyes, I find an electric storm so dangerous, it threatens to annihilate me right where I stand.

"Like I said, I wouldn't tell anybody," I repeat as I keep my eyes on Finn.

Finn doesn't release me. His hold only tightens. It's a warning. One that I won't ignore, and one that I'll never dismiss. "Pack a bag," he says then before his hand finally releases my neck. "We're going away in a few days."

"Going away?"

"Yes, I have some business to deal with and you're coming with me and Jarred." He turns on his heel and leaves me with Jarred. I glance at the man beside me, taking him in. He's beautiful. Like one of those princes in a Disney movie. Only, he has ink running over his skin, which makes him appear dangerous, like a rebel. And I can't help but smile.

"I know I'm right," he tells me as his mouth quirks.

"I know you enjoyed the show."

I want to deny it, but I don't. "I didn't think there was anything wrong with me exploring the grounds of my new home," I inform him before crossing my arms in front of my chest. "In the future, I'll stay away from the shed."

"I didn't say that, Princess." This time, he's the one who has my pulse racing when he leans in to whisper in my ear, "Next time, you should join us. Have you ever had two men worship your body?" His question is hot on my neck. The breath he releases has goosebumps dotting across my skin. A shiver wracks through me, filled with need and lust.

I don't tell him I've only been with one boy. When I turned eighteen, I allowed myself to fall into the trap of believing a guy actually liked me. But all he wanted was to tell everyone he slept with me. He wanted fame and recognition, which I gave to him on a silver platter. When we broke up, I knew I'd made a mistake.

"I think you should leave," I tell Jarred, "I need to pack."

He chuckles before he pulls away from me and moves to the door that leads to the bathroom. Once I'm alone, I can breathe again, but even as I inhale deeply, the scent of both men lingers in my bedroom. I'm not sure where we're going, but maybe getting out of the Thorne manor will change things. It will put both Finn and me on equal ground, so he doesn't have the home advantage.

Now that I know the truth about Finn and Jarred, perhaps I can finally find a way into his life where he doesn't hate me. I don't want to become a lonely wife where my husband doesn't love me. And I refuse to be a stranger to happiness.

I may have grown up listening to the bullies who tried to break me, but I'm stronger, and if I have both Finn and Jarred to stand beside me, perhaps I can find myself again. It's been a long time since I've seen the girl who lost her way. The one I hide deep down inside where nobody can find her, not even me.

In a few weeks' time, I'll be married, and I'll take on the Thorne name. I may not be their blood, but I can show them I'm loyal. I'll keep Finn's secret, but I still believe that he should be honest with those closest to him. He may not think they'd accept it, but people can surprise you when you least expect it. And I doubt the family has never noticed the magnetism between Jarred and Finn. I saw it the moment I met them.

I move to the closet, and I grab one of my now empty suitcases. I'm not sure how long we'll be away, but I make sure to pack for at least a week. Once I've zipped up my luggage, I pull it into the room and leave it at the door. The silence of the bedroom hangs heavily as I change into my sleep shorts and a tank top.

My mind is still replaying the scene I stumbled upon in the shed. The beauty of two handsome men finding pleasure causes my nipples to harden against the soft material covering my breasts. I want to watch them again. The thought comes quickly, stunning me before I pull open the bathroom door. I find Finn standing at the basin, his gray sweatpants hang low on his hips as he glances at me in the large mirror.

He's brushing his teeth, which seems like such a normal, mundane act, but his back muscles are like a piece of art as they tense and release with every movement. He finishes up before turning to me.

"Feeling better after some alone time?" he taunts with a mischievous smirk. I've come to realize that Finn hides behind his snarky comments. He doesn't let people in, just like I never allow anyone close enough to find my heartache.

"I've packed some clothes for our trip," I answer, but it's not what he wanted to hear. I grab my toothbrush and the minty toothpaste. Finn watches my every move. I've never had someone in my personal space before. Living at home, I had my own bathroom, where I could hide if I needed to. Now, I'm watched as if I were an animal in a cage.

I brush my teeth under the vigilant stare of Finn Thorne. Once I've dried my mouth, I grab my night cream and moisturize. "Are you just going to stand there and watch me?" I quip, looking at Finn's reflection.

The corner of his mouth quirks into a playful grin. "Was there something else you'd like me to do, princess?" His hand grips the waistband of his sweatpants, but he doesn't push them down or tug on them. His thumb hooks into the elastic and remains against the smooth, tanned skin.

I shake my head. "No, there isn't," I tell him firmly, but even though my words say one thing, my mind and body respond with something completely different.

"You know," Finn starts, "I thought you were this perfectly prim and proper princess." He takes a step closer, gripping my chin with his free hand, tipping my head back so I'm looking into those dark chocolate eyes. "But I think there's more under those layers of perfection."

He thinks I'm perfect.

At least, that's what it sounds like.

"And what do you think it is?" I whisper, my voice croaking out my query.

Finn's tongue darts out and licks along his lower lip. Then, slowly, he bares his teeth and trails his pink tongue over those pearly whites. It's almost as if he's about to devour me whole, and as the heat of his naked skin warms me, I find myself leaning in closer.

He dips his head to mine. The scent of his cologne—spicy and woodsy—envelops me in its darkness. I willingly go toward his shadows. "You're just as hungry to break free from the chains that have confined you for so long," Finn whispers along my lips.

A breath of shock leaves my lungs and whooshes out. The corner smile that curls his perfectly-shaped lips makes me shiver. And then, before he actually kisses me, he steps back and turns to leave. Before he shuts his bedroom door, he stops on the threshold of the room.

I wait for the click.

I watch for him to disappear.

But he doesn't.

The small space he leaves has a smile tilting my lips. He's left the door ajar. I'm not sure what he expects to happen, but the fact that he's seen past the veneer I've perfected is a reflection on just how perceptive he is.

I'm no longer alone.

I have him.

I just need to figure out how to break down his defenses.

I never expected to want to hold him. To want to make sure he is happy. Emotions weren't meant to come into this, but seeing Finn so vulnerable has twisted my perception of him. There was fear in his eyes, in those soulful dark eyes that made my chest tighten.

When we first met, I was convinced he was nothing more than a playboy, but that's what he wants people to see. I do the same. I show off a smile, a fake laugh, but deep down, the darkness that resides in my soul matches his.

Him and Jarred.

I'm still wrapping my head around it when there's a knock at my bedroom door. When I pull it open, I find Jarred, sheepishly grinning at me with that mischievous smile that's lured me in. I've connected with him easily, quickly, more so than I have with Finn. Until moments ago when I saw my fiancé for who he is—a scared boy, wanting the approval of his father, not wanting to disappoint anyone.

"Hey," Jarred says as he saunters into my bedroom when I step aside. "I wanted to talk about—"

"There's no need to, I won't tell anyone. I already let Finn know that your secret is safe with me."

He turns to me then. He's handsome. Breathtakingly so. Just like Finn. Both men are going to be the death of me. And with them, I think I'd go willingly.

"It's not that," he tells me then. "I..." Jarred runs his fingers through his hair, the nervous energy radiating off him is palpable. "I wanted... I mean... There are things..."

I move toward him, stopping inches from his tall, toned body. "You can tell me anything."

The corner of his mouth quirks. "We're both

enamored with you. Finn doesn't like admitting his feelings," he tells me. "He's... stubborn."

"I don't think he's interested in me." I'm shaking my head, but the look in Jarred's eyes tells me there's more to the story.

"He's scared, angry, and yeah, a little bit of a pain in the ass," he says on a chuckle. "But there is depth to him."

"I don't doubt there is." Our gazes lock for a moment. "But he will need to talk to me. Like you are."

"Do you see yourself with him?" The question stuns me. Not because he asked it, but because I don't have to consider my answer. I don't have to think about it. There's no doubt about it, I want Finn. And yes, I do see myself with him.

"I do."

He grins. "Then don't give up on him yet, he'll come around and he'll allow you in." The honesty in his words, and the affection he holds for Finn makes my heart ache. "And you, I know you'll fit into this family perfectly."

"Why?"

"Because you're strong," he whispers while reaching for my face. His thumb swipes along my lower lip, and for a long moment, I want him to lean in and kiss me. But he doesn't. "You'll be fine."

He doesn't say anything more, he steps back and leaves me wondering what just happened. Both men have come in here, leaving me breathless in their wake. They're both hurting because they have to hide their emotions, their feelings for each other, and their feelings for me.

I sit on the bed with my mind whirring with possibilities of how I feel. Seeing them together was a shock, but not as much as them both seeming to want me.

Can I do that?

I'm not sure, but I do know that I feel something for them. The emotions that are slowly stemming from my interactions with both men have left me wanting more.

I should hate this place.

I should want to leave and never return.

But the dark magic of Thorne Haven and Thorne manor is weaving itself around me, and I find myself wanting the complete opposite. I want to be with Finn. And subsequently, Jarred too.

Finn

THE PLANE WAITS FOR US ON THE TARMAC AS we pull up to the hangar. After my interaction with Zaria last night, she seems less afraid around me. I know it's partly because I figured her out and made it known that I see her; the parts that no one else seems to find. And now that she knows I've seen through her veneer and sussed out her pain, we understand each other more so than when we originally met. But even though she's slowly burrowing her way into my life, learning about who I really am, I have to make sure that she's not here to fuck with my family. My father may trust the Abadis, especially Zaria's mother, but I'm more wary of the woman because I don't know her at all.

With Jarred and Zaria behind me, I focus on the plane. The tension from the car follows us as we make our way to our seats in the private jet. Jarred sits opposite me, with Zaria beside me. He's watching me intently, knowing that, for the time being, we've got her to keep our secret. I have a feeling, though, that she's not going to sit quietly in the corner. Zaria Abadi is feisty, demanding, which if I had to be honest, I quite enjoy. But she could so easily burn everything I've built to the ground.

When I spoke about her hiding something, I saw the flicker in her eyes. This trip may actually be good for us. At least, I fucking hope it is. The moment the wheels leave the ground, I order a vodka neat, while Jarred has his usual beer. Zaria opts for a Coke, and I wonder if she's staying sober to keep a clear head around us.

My gaze flicks to Jarred, and I see him looking at her. I know he finds her attractive. You would have to be blind not to be enthralled by her beauty. I turn my attention back to her before I swallow back my drink and order another.

"Nervous?" Jarred smirks at me, his eyes flashing

with a challenge.

I can't help but return his smirk. "Why would I be nervous?" I ask, before leaning back in my seat. My arm brushes along Zaria's, causing and audible breath to whoosh from her lips. I place my hand on her thigh, my fingers wrapping around the smooth skin.

"Don't know," Jarred answers with a shrug. "Never seen you outside of Thorne Haven before." He chuckles playfully, his eyes burning into the connection I've made with Zaria. I want nothing more than to order her to spread her legs and have him watch as I pleasure her; the thoughts that are racing through my mind are downright filthy.

"I was just thinking about how much fun we could have on the four-hour flight," I whisper, then lean in to ask Zaria, "What do you think about joining the Mile High club?"

"Don't be crass," she bites out, causing Jarred to laugh out loud. I admire her fire. There's something alluring about it. The joy I get from taunting her makes my dick hard.

"So, have you ever traveled internationally?" Jarred quickly changes the subject, much to my little princess's relief.

"I have. We've been to most of Europe, as well as the United Kingdom and Australia," she informs us. "My father's company opened offices in most of the larger cities, which meant we had to be present when he cut the ribbon."

"And now you're stuck in little, old Thorne Haven," I say, the sneer on my face is apparent to Jarred, but I turn my eyes to the window. I don't need her to know I hate being home. As much as I used to enjoy the parties, the guests, and the town itself, my heart is always wandering.

"I think it's a beautiful town," she says, and even though my hand hasn't moved from her leg, she doesn't ask me to remove it.

"It is if you haven't spent your whole life there." Both sets of eyes land on me. There's no judgment, though, merely curiosity. "Being from a small town where everyone knows your life story isn't as magical as Hollywood may make it out to be."

"I didn't think it was. The same way being seen as someone popular on social media doesn't make it worthwhile. It's more of a hinderance to living a normal life than most think." Zaria's words slam right into my chest. There is pain, guilt, and heartache entwined in every word.

"It's the same way the past seems to linger, threatening to break down everything you've built. When you look into the future, when you hope for something better, whatever you think you've buried, will always come back to haunt you." This comes from Jarred which surprises me because he's usually silent about his history. Most times when we talk about his past, when I've asked him to tell me more about where he comes from, he's always been against it. But now, I wonder why he would speak up about it.

"Are you trying to tell me something?" I quirk a brow in question. A flicker of guilt in the silver of those endless orbs tells me I've hit the nail on the head. He is hiding something, but he's not confessing to it just yet which frustrates me. I don't like liars, and I don't like secrets.

"Not at all." He shrugs it off, as if it's nothing, but I know that's a lie. He wouldn't have said anything if he didn't feel guilt. He's keeping something from me, but I can't pinpoint why he would. "I just mean that sometimes, the past can suddenly fuck up everything you've worked so hard to build. And it usually happens when you least expect it."

Even though I know he's right, I don't respond.

I think back to when Nesrin came into our lives. Her father had left, walked out without so much as a goodbye. The secrets of her past came back and slammed right through our family, ensuring that everything hidden was made visible. It turns out her father was a lying, cheating bastard. He left his family for something better, or something worse. We don't know where he is, even though I know my father tried to find him. Not for anything other than to put Nesrin's mind at ease. But when every PI came back empty-handed, Dad gave up the search.

My stepsister, and sister-in-law, both in one, is no stranger to hidden truths. And she's doing okay. Better than that, she's happy now. And I hope that one day, Jarred will overcome whatever is bothering him. As much as I want to be there for him, annoyance has a hold of me. I've told him as much, time and again. But he's stubborn.

I guess keeping secrets runs through the people of Thorne Haven. We're not the easiest people to get along with.

"Why are you holding my leg?" Zaria whispers in my ear, the heat of her breath fanning over my neck and sending desire coursing through me. I glance over at the raven-haired beauty and smile.

"Because I feel like it, and you're mine, so I'll touch you whenever and wherever I please," I inform her. It's not a lie. She is mine. My future. It's the same with Jarred, but with him, it's mostly kept in private.

"I didn't consent to your hands on me," she responds easily.

I can't stop the tilt at the corners of my mouth. "And I didn't ask for permission."

"You're a bastard." Zaria throws me an insult I've heard a few times before. Most girls and women call me other names—asshole, playboy, joker. But I'll answer to any. I'm proud of who I am, even though I hide my relationship with Jarred, I only do it to keep him safe. That's what I tell myself anyway.

"I know." I release her leg and pick up my tumbler. I swallow back my drink and turn toward the window. "There's no need to tell me things I already know about myself."

"It seems you've accepted people's opinion of you." Her voice is low enough for only me to hear, but we're in a small space, and I know Jarred heard her as well. There's no doubt from the stifled chuckle that comes from the seat opposite me.

"I learned when I was young never to argue with fools," I tell her, turning my gaze back to lock on hers. Those golden eyes shimmer as they regard me.

"It's a good lesson to learn," Zaria comments, before offering me a smile. I've never been one to stare at women. I've looked, I've planned, and I've conquered, but when this woman gifts me with a perfectly genuine smile, I can't help but take notice. I flick my gaze between her and Jarred, and I note that he's seen it too.

Tipping my head toward her, I grip her chin and hold her stare before I speak. "It is. I'm guessing you've also come to that conclusion?"

She locks those glimmering orbs on me and says confidently, "I did. I've learned a few hard lessons while growing up. But it didn't stop me from pushing past those boundaries that had been set for me."

When she first walked into the manor, I thought she was nothing more than one of those fake plastic dolls, who love to show off their perfect smiles and perfect bodies. Her following is enormous, and her photos come across as plastic as the masks that most people slide in place. But Zaria is different. I noticed it before, and now that we're here, alone in close proximity, I once again see right through her social façade.

"I'm sorry to hear that," I say. "Jarred and I have

found a connection through the difficult times we've both gotten through."

"You've been through difficult times?" she teases with an amused smile.

I can't help but lean in, bringing my lips to hers, but I don't kiss her. Instead, I say, "Don't judge a book by its cover." It's the same words she gave me a few days ago when I spoke to her via her private messages. She responded and then went offline, leaving me hanging in the darkness. I recall that night with clarity, lying in bed, wearing nothing but a pair of boxers, and glaring at the screen.

Zaria's lips curve up at the corners. "Touché."

I release her and sit back. My eyes turn to Jarred, who's sitting quietly. The silence that follows our conversation is heavy with something I can't quite put my finger on, and it's coming from Jarred.

The pilot announces that we'll be landing soon, and I note how his shoulders tense and his jaw ticks. I run through the possibilities in my mind, wondering what could be bothering him, but nothing makes sense. Jarred didn't say anything when I mentioned Tynewood, so it can't be the fact that we're going there. He's never said anything about a fear of flying, not even when we boarded, so I rule that out too.

But when those silver eyes lock on mine, I see it—fear. I want to ask him what the problem is, but I don't because, seconds later, we're descending toward the small town of Tynewood.

It doesn't take long to land and disembark. Waiting for us is a black Rolls Royce Cullinan, which has the windows darkened. It's quite a car. Not exactly my style, but it will do the job to get us from here to the Lancaster estate.

Once we're in the back of the vehicle, the driver pulls away and we're on our way. The roads aren't busy at all, and I'm thankful for that. Exhaustion has taken a hold of me, and even though I know sleep won't come until tonight, I hope we have a relaxed afternoon.

My father explained that I'd be meeting Ares Lancaster, one of the four crowns of the Society. He heads up the Gilded Sovereign with his brother and two of his best friends. It reminds me of the Thorne and Haven men, all six of us taking on the roles of our fathers. I know that if anything were to happen to Bradford or Octavius, we would need to keep the legacy of Thorne Haven alive.

Even if we don't want to, we don't have a choice because it's in our blood. And there is no running away from it, even if I would love to. As much as I tell myself I'd walk out the first chance I got, I know it's a lie. And my father knows it too. Perhaps that's why he's always been so hard on me.

With Damien in London and Cassian no longer living in our childhood home, I'm the only son who is still lives at Thorne Manor. Even though that may seem like I'm not independent, our family is nothing like what one would assume a *normal* family is like.

When we come to a stop at intricately designed jet-black metal gates, my shoulders tighten with tension. I don't know these people. I'm not sure what this meeting will entail, but I need to fight the anxiety and focus.

It's part of being a Thorne.

You roll with the punches, and you hit back even harder.

Jarred

Thankfully, we're staying with Ares. The car takes us through town, past my old home with the Birchwoods stopping outside the one home that used to be party central when I was growing up. I'm not sure who would be working for the Lancasters at the moment, but I pray it's someone new to town, someone who doesn't know me. The staff are usually brought in from out of town, so maybe over the years, Ares and Philipe have hired new butlers and housemaids.

As soon as we exit the vehicle, my muscles tense up, but I calm down again when the front door opens

and I don't recognize the woman who steps out. She doesn't even cast a glance my way, but I know it won't be long until Finn finds out who I am. Or at least, that I'm from the society his father wants him to join.

Even though I walked away from it, I still have an obligation to them. It makes life hell, but I've gotten so used to living with my demons, they've become friends.

"Welcome," the woman greets us. "It's so lovely to have you here. I'm Ramona, and I'll be your host for the next few days when Mr. Lancaster is out. I know you don't have a time limit on your stay, so please, feel free to let me know if you need the rooms for extra nights."

"Thank you," Finn says before I can respond. "We'll only need the three nights." It seems he's just as ready to leave here as I am. Don't get me wrong, Tynewood is a beautiful town, but I don't think I can bring myself to live here indefinitely. Not with my past haunting me.

"Not a problem," she says with a smile. "Follow me and I'll have Luther bring your luggage up." We make our way up the staircase to the first landing, where we turn right. Before us, there are three rooms, and

I'm almost certain we won't need all three, but we don't tell Ramona that small detail.

"This is the first one," she announces before pushing open the door. I take it, since I know Finn will want Zaria between us. We've come to a place we don't know, and the threats are real when it comes to the two factions of the Sovereign.

Ramona tuns and leaves as I shut the door, before leaning against the wooden surface. I can relax for a few moments, before I have to decide how I'm going to come clean.

I'd rather it be me telling Finn the truth.

It's best if he hears it from my mouth.

But, deep down, I know that, that might not be the case. He's stubborn. And, at times, he can be cold as ice when it comes to learning he's been kept in the dark.

I pull out my phone and tap out a message to Ares. He'll keep my secret for as long as I need him to. If I can get past the initial meeting, I can take Finn out to the churchyard, where I used to hang out with Ares, Etienne, and Tarian, and talk to him in private.

I can't do it here.

I need to be in a place I feel at ease. I've always enjoyed sitting in the yard, where there was nobody but me and the tombstones. Maybe I can ask Finn to go with me now. But I know if I were to tell him to come with me, he'd refuse. Right now, Finn is all-business because his father needs this contract signed.

Sighing, I exit the room to go find him. But the moment I reach his door, a voice from down the hallway calls out to me. "Jarred?" Finn's door opens right at that moment. I glance over my shoulder to find Tarian Calvert. One of the four. He, Ares, and Etienne are the three men who stepped up to sit in the Elder's chairs four years ago.

He hasn't changed. His pitch-black hair still falls across his eyes. The glint of his piercings, one in his eyebrow and the other in his lip shine in the light streaming in from the window.

As he nears us, I can tell his bright blue eyes hold shock and confusion. At twenty-seven, Tarian looks all man now. But there is still a boyish charm to him. He reminds me so much of Finn, it's disconcerting. Perhaps I did hold a flame for him when I was younger. But not now. Because the man I love is standing in front of me, more confused that someone here knows me.

"Tar," I greet, using the nickname he's had since I

can remember. It started as a joke, when one of the girls he'd been fucking said his hair was as black as tar. But also, it is a play on his name.

"What are you doing here?"

"You two know each other?" Finn asks, looking between Tarian and me. Tynewood shouldn't be familiar to me, and people here shouldn't know who I am, at least in Finn's mind. But unfortunately, there are. I'm too late to stop it now. I can feel my house of cards tumbling down.

"Yeah," Tarian says, "this bastard grew up around here." The confusion in his expression makes me edgy. I doubt Tarian understands why I wouldn't have told Finn about my past. I left so long ago, and I've tried to bury a lot of my memories. I wanted a new life. The thought of having to live under the rule of the Society wasn't something I wanted, so I walked away.

"He did?" Even more tension emanates from Finn as the truth slowly comes to the surface. I should have known that it would. There has always been a threat of it happening, I just didn't realize it would happen before I could tell Finn myself.

"It was a long time ago," I try to soothe the shock.

"It was," Tarian agrees. "But when you upped and

left, we missed you, man. You didn't even tell us where you were going. Your dad didn't even know." His mention of the man who left me in Tynewood has anger racing through my veins.

"I know." I nod, turning to Finn to find questions dancing in his dark eyes. I flick my gaze to Tarian. "Can you give us a minute? We'll be down in a bit." He watches us for a long moment before nodding and heading down the hall.

"Finn," I start slowly, as he shakes his head. Zaria steps out of the doorway to her bedroom before making her way over to us. She's overheard the whole conversation, and I expect her to scream and shout, but she merely sets a hand on my arm.

"Don't," Finn says, the anger is clear in his voice as he walks back into the bedroom, leaving me on the threshold with Zaria. I've seen him angry before, but right now, he's beyond it. All I see is a broken man.

"Finn, please listen to me."

He spins around, fire blazing in his stare. "Listen to you? Why? So you can tell me more lies? Or hide the fact that you're not who you say you are?"

"No," I bite out. "I never hid who I am. With you, I was always me, you saw me for who I really was. When I left Tynewood, I needed to find out who

Jarred was. And I found him with you."

"And you didn't think to ever tell me the truth?"

"I did, so many times."

Finn scoffs. "Yeah, I'm sure you did. Was that before or after you fucked me?" He throws out the question, which makes me wince. I expected the backlash. I fucking deserve it. I hid a part of me from him even when I wanted all of him. I know he won't believe anything I tell him now.

That's the problem with hiding the truth, once you finally admit to it, nobody believes you. I've brought this on myself.

"Jarred," Zaria says, stepping up beside me. "Maybe you should give him time. It's difficult to find out someone has been holding back."

I know she's right. I'm sure that if I were to walk away now, give him a few hours and come back to it, he'd hear me out. He may be stubborn, but I know Finn better than I know myself. But I can't bring myself to turn around and walk out of the room.

Not yet.

"Finn, I love you, I always have," I plead, hoping he'll see past the frustration, past the anger. Those dark eyes land on mine. I wish he would lash out, hit me, something. Perhaps the act of violence will calm him down once he's gotten it out of his system.

But he does the complete opposite.

He stands silently watching me.

"It's not going to be easy," Zaria says, loud enough for him to hear. "But you both love each other. This road is littered with bumps, but you can get over it."

"I'm over it," Finn sneers angrily. His hands fist at his sides. I know he's holding back the need to punch me, but I'd rather he just do it.

"Hit me." The words are out of my mouth before I have time to think about them.

"No!" Zaria's voice echoes in the room. She steps between us, her back to my front. As she faces Finn, I wonder if she's silently pleading with him. I can't see those golden eyes, but they're latched on the man I love. "Finn, look at me." Her voice is calm, and I wonder how this young woman can be the voice of reason between two volatile men.

"Get out of the way, Zaria," I tell her, wanting her to move, so Finn can come at me. I won't fight back. I'll allow him the shots because I deserve them. But she flashes a glare over her shoulder at me.

When she looks at Finn, she says, "You're angry, and that's understandable. Nothing can ever make it okay. Jarred is wrong for not telling you everything, but also, you can't hold something in his past against him."

"I was with him for years, and he couldn't once tell me the truth?" The pain that flickers in his eyes cracks my heart. My chest is tight, my lungs struggling to work. I've hurt one of the only people who ever gave me a chance.

I wanted a new life.

I craved it with every essence of my being.

When I got to Thorne Haven, all I wanted was to be anonymous, and I was for a long time, but then Finn sauntered into my life and all my carefully laid plans were shot to hell. I was going to stay in Thorne Haven for a couple of years and then come back to Tynewood and take my place in the Society, that was what I told myself over and over again.

But then, I fell in love with a man and I knew I couldn't leave him. No matter how difficult our road had become, I wanted to ride it with him. And for a long time, I thought it would be okay. There was no way he'd ever know more about me.

"I held you at arm's length," I admit slowly. "I just didn't want to lose you." My confession has his hands fisting once more before he releases the tension. At first, I'm convinced he's listening to me, that he's seeing the fear that kept me from telling him everything.

But then he shakes his head. "That's not the truth," he says. "You didn't tell me because you were far too happy playing house without facing your past."

"And you found it easy to face yours?" I throw back in his face. He knows what I'm talking about. He hasn't yet told Zaria about it, but he will have to. Finn is a broken man; he's held onto his wounds for so long, they've become part of him. But there comes a time when we all need to heal, when we have to realize that the scars may remain, but the hurt needs to go away.

"Don't you dare throw that in my face."

Nodding, I say, "Fine. But you have to realize that I didn't do this on purpose. I love you, Finn." The words are the truth.

The only question now is if he can forgive me.

Finn

NOTHING IN LIFE PREPARES YOU FOR HEARTBREAK. There is no getting ready for listening to someone tell you they spent years with you, but lied to you all that time. I didn't think it was possible to be this angry, this on the verge of hate, while loving someone. But right now, as I stare at Jarred, I find it completely plausible. I doubt though I could ever hate him completely. But my anger has certainly taken a hold of me.

"You're not really some random runaway." It's not a question, so Jarred doesn't need to answer, and he doesn't. The realization of what I've just found out

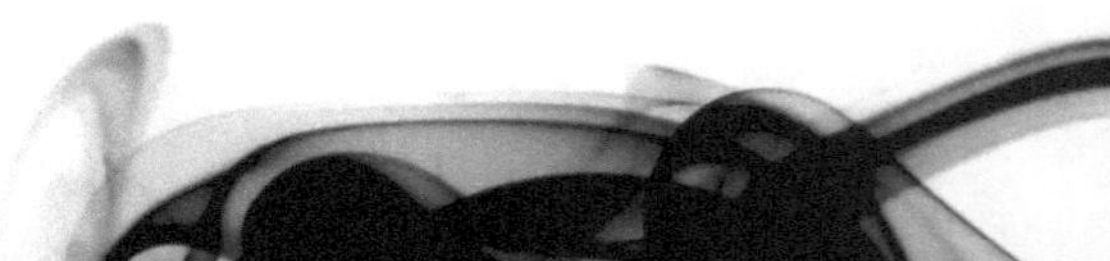

has clearly slammed into us both. "You knew that coming here would expose the fact that you lied, and yet, you came anyway."

"Finn," Zaria chastises me, but I can't find it in my heart to care. The fact that I gave seven years to my relationship with Jarred, and he couldn't tell me the truth leaves a me angry and heartbroken.

I thought we were more than that. I told him everything about my past, about how much I hated my mother for walking out, for not even saying goodbye to us.

"No," Jarred says, looking at Zaria, "he's right. I did come here knowing it, but his father wanted Finn to find out about my lies. I don't know how, but he learned about my past and that's why he allowed me to tag along on this trip."

I don't deny that my father would have done that. He must have known. How he found out, I doubt we'll ever learn, but the fact remains that the man before me is still a liar.

"I don't want to see you," I tell him. "I need to think." My words cause him to wince, and even though in the past, I would've gone to him, to comfort him, I can't bring myself to do it right now.

With a nod, Jarred leaves, shutting the door to

his room. Zaria turns to me, her gaze shimmering with tears. I don't know why she's sad; she's only just come into this relationship with us.

"You can be a real bastard," she bites out as anger drips from her words. "Can't you see that he's hurting. Coming back to a past you would rather put behind you isn't easy."

"And you know all about hiding things. Don't you?" I throw back. When I'm angry, I'm a dick, and I don't apologize for it.

The slap comes before I have time to stop her hand from making contact. I deserved that. "Love is not an easy road to follow," she tells me. "You have to listen to someone else, understand that the fear of losing what they've found is real." The plea in her tone makes my chest ache.

I've never allowed fear to take hold of me. It's one emotion that I fought for years. My frustration and pain are directed at Jarred, but my anger is focused solely on me. I allowed myself to believe in honesty and love. Even though I never told him how I felt, I know deep down that I do love him.

"When someone lies to me, I don't take kindly to it."

"And when you act like an asshole, you deserve to be

held accountable," Zaria throws back easily. "When I first arrived at Thorne Haven, I was shattered. I didn't know if I would be able to feel anything for anybody. I wanted the approval of my mother for so long, that I figured I would substitute it for the affection from you and Jarred."

I turn away, needing to breathe without Zaria in my face, in my mind. But when I step away from her, she reaches for me, her hand gripping my arm gently. Her touch electrifies me. It's done it since the first time I came into contact with her. It's the same feeling I get when Jarred touches me.

She's slowly burrowing herself in my life, and with every moment I spend with her, I know that she is learning who I am. She knows more about me than my family does.

I perfected my armor to the point where not even my brothers could see past it. It may not have been ideal, but it was the only way I knew how to survive.

As I young child, I was doted on by my mother. Being the baby, her baby, I was showered with her love. And then, she left.

"Are you really angry at him for lying or are you feeling that rage because you know that he only did it because he loves you."

"Everyone leaves," I tell her, staring at her hand wrapped around my arm. She doesn't release me. I didn't think she would. "It's not uncommon for those I care for to pack up and walk away."

"Because you push them away?"

"Are you trying to say I made my mother leave?" I sneer, my blood turning hot as it races through my veins, boiling through me from head to toe.

Zaria's mouth falls open, and I realize she didn't know about it. I never confessed anything about me to her. Jarred knew about my mother walking out, but that's only because he has lived in Thorne Manor for so long.

"What?"

Those glimmering golden eyes stare into mine. Zaria has a way about her, when she looks at me, it's as if she's trying to find a chink in my armor. I wonder if she'll ever find a way to dig into my goddamned soul even when I try to push her out.

"My mother walked out on us," I admit softly. "I was always her favorite, she told me so. It might sound overconfident, but it was the only time I ever felt seen. And then, one night I overheard her and my dad fighting, they were arguing. It was so loud, it woke me up. I followed them to the staircase and watched her tell him she's leaving."

Zaria steps up to me then, her body flush with mine, and her arms wrap around my middle. When I told Jarred, he had the same reaction. But as she looks up at me, I don't see pity in her eyes. I never wanted anyone to feel pity for me because my mother left me. And that's the reason I never told anyone how it made me feel to see her walk out.

"I loved her," I tell Zaria. "She was the only person who ever knew me." My words are soft, a gentle confession that seems out of place because, only moments ago, anger fueled me. "And I love Jarred. He was the other person I allowed into my heart."

"So all that anger you held toward me for my posts and fakes smiles on my social media wasn't only because of me." Her lips tilt as she realizes how much I've hated myself for years. I wanted my brothers to know I was hurt, but I could never bring myself to tell them. I was scared of being weak in their eyes. Instead of showing my pain, I covered it with jokes and fake smiles. So, instead of breaking down, I stood tall and hid behind the playboy exterior.

"It's sometimes easier to fake something than to allow anyone to see your pain," I tell her gently.

"But you let Jarred see it." She guesses, and I nod.

"He didn't do this to hurt you though. And I'm sure your mother was hurting just as much when she left." I can't know that for sure, but I can't deny that in my mind, Mom was heartbroken to leave her kids. All three boys meant a lot to her, we knew we did, but there are times I think back to the night she left and wonder why she didn't say goodbye.

"I don't know for sure what she felt, but she never made any effort to reach out to us, even years after." I shrug it off, but I can't conceal the pain that must be painted across my face. "Jarred was the first person, besides Eloise, that brought out some form of emotion in me. But even Ellie had no clue about my past."

"But you loved her too." Zaria whispers slowly.

For a long, silent moment, I think about it. I cared about her a lot. She was the one person I vowed to protect and I couldn't do that. "I spent years feeling guilt for what happened to her. I thought I loved her, but perhaps it was more the protective obsession I had. I didn't want her to leave."

"Like your mother did," Zaria says.

I nod.

"I'm sorry, Finn," she whispers as she leans up on her tiptoes. Her lips find mine in a gentle kiss. "But you can't push Jarred away. This time, he needs you to be strong, the same way he was strong for you in the past." I know she's right, but I don't like admitting to being wrong.

"I need time." It's all I can manage right now because if I did say anything more, I'd probably get angry all over again. I can't afford to do that. "I need to go talk to Ares," I tell her. "Stay here."

"Okay."

I leave Zaria, with my focus solely on speaking to Ares about business. I find him in the office, where he told me he'd be. For the moment, he's alone, so I venture into the room.

"I'd like to get this contract done and signed as soon as possible."

"What's the rush?" he asks. Knowing that he heard everything that went down between Jarred and me, he's either trying not to encroach on my business, or he finds it amusing. They are, after all, the Gilded Sovereign.

"I need to get back to Thorne Haven. I have a wedding to plan," I inform him as I settle in the chair opposite his desk. It's true. I do have an event coming up, and Zaria and I need to sit down and make a few decisions.

"I understand," he says. "Since my brother is only on his way to Tynewood now, I'll go through the contract."

"It's the same one my father sent through to you." I slide it over the desk to him. Ares picks it up, flicking through the pages slowly. His gaze scans the information. The most important is the cut we take for installation of our systems in all their venues. The Lancasters have taken over the clubbing scene after Philipe, the eldest Lancaster brother, started his nightclub in New York.

"Twenty-five percent?"

"We have to ensure we're running at a profit," I tell him. Even though they'll pay full price for installation, it's the running of the systems that need constant monitoring. When it comes to criminal organizations, you can't leave anything to chance.

"Understandable," he responds, before turning the page and screening what's written there. I did read through it; it's a standard agreement, which shouldn't be an issue. "What are your thoughts on joining the Sovereign?"

"It depends on a few things," I tell him. "My father and I still need to discuss it. I only learned about it yesterday." The fact that my dad didn't think it would be advisable to talk me through the Society beforehand frustrates me. But, there must be benefits or it would have been shut down years ago.

"It's a good place to be," Ares says. "I've wanted to be one of the Elders since I was a kid. My father, however, used the society for his own perverse intentions. I run it differently."

"Why the hate between the Gilded Sovereign and Silver faction?" I ask. It's something that's been bothering me since I heard about the two factions.

A small smile dances on Ares's lips. "All men are prideful bastards," he tells me. "It's nothing more and nothing less than that." With a shrug, he chuckles then picks up the shimmering gold pen and signs the last page of the contract before initialing each one separately.

"Perhaps I'll join then," I tell him. "Pride may be a sin, but I've never been afraid of breaking the rules." We smile, a knowing one that confirms we both have similar ideals.

"We will welcome you," he says. "I think both factions need new blood and that will ensure we bring down the old mindsets of our fathers and forefathers. They ran the society like a goddamned criminal organization. I like to keep my nose clean, to a certain extent."

"Once I get back, I'll sit down with my father and talk to him about it. We can confirm in forty-eight hours."

Ares nods before pushing to his feet. "I'm sorry you couldn't stay longer. Perhaps in the future you can visit with your new wife and Jarred."

"I don't know about him, but thank you for the offer."

Ares laughs. "Trust me when I say Jarred is stubborn. He won't give up easily."

I leave it at that because I'm just as stubborn. This will be an interesting few days.

Jarred

THE MOMENT OF HEARTACHE THAT SLAMS INTO his chest is obvious. I see it shimmering in his perfectly dark eyes. I never thought this secret would come out. But there comes a time in everyone's life when they need to face their demons. This is mine.

Finn stands silently as the chill in the air hits us. Zaria stands just behind him, watching, waiting, confusion creasing her brows. The ghosts of the past join us as we stare at each other.

"You're from here," Finn says again. His words are carried on the wind toward me. He doesn't come near me, but as I hold onto the ice-cold tombstone, I

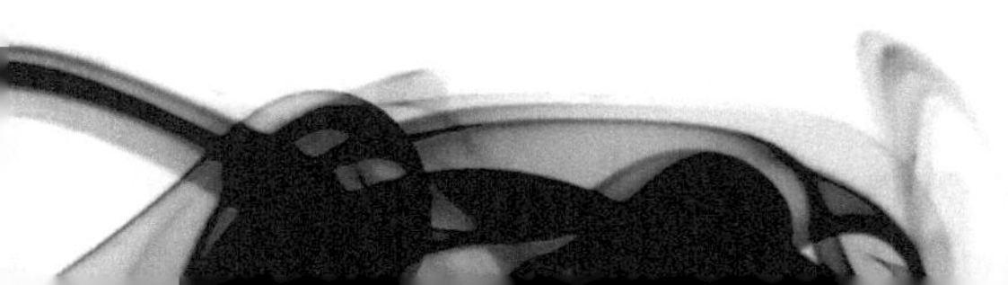

nod. "And my father knew, which is why you're here in the first place."

The guilt that weighed heavily on me for months, for years, finally comes to a head and I don't know how else to tell Finn that I lied to keep him with me.

I don't have words. I can't bring myself to say anything to him because I know he'll walk away and there is nothing I can do now, but to let him go.

"I never deserved you," I tell him honestly. "All these years, I knew that. But I took you anyway." My throat closes with heartbreak and pain. "I needed to keep part of myself from you to safeguard our hearts."

"This was never about that. You know I accepted you for all that you were," Finn insists. And that may be true, but I don't know how to fix this.

"I was scared," I whisper. It's a quite admission, but I know he hears it. I want to go to him, to bend him over a tombstone and fuck him into submission. To make sure he knows that he's mine. I glance at Zaria, her eyes shimmer. Even at this distance, I can tell she's just as hurt as Finn.

The past few days we've grown closer, there were some things I told them that I've never told anyone else. But the one thing I didn't admit to was what I had done. The wealth I was born into didn't fix my mistake. I had to suffer alone, and I did, for a long time.

Until him.

Until I found solace in Thorne Haven.

"You're just like her," Finn finally spits, his words hitting me right in the chest. I know who he's talking about, and since he told us the story, Zaria knows who he's talking about as well.

"I never left you," I tell him. "I didn't give up on us, on life." My words cause him to wince. It's the truth though. They say the truth hurts, and I've seen it so many times before. The destruction a few words can bring is nothing like a fist to the face. Perhaps that's why there are so many broken people out there. They're all searching for happiness. But just one simple phrase could shatter everything they built.

"Don't you dare—"

"Leave Finn," I tell him, my anger and pain taking a hold of me. Like I always do, I push those who care about me away. But this time, his father forced the situation on us. "It's what everyone does." My words may come across as confident, but my hurt forces them from my lips. I don't mean it, not with him. And he should know it. At least I hope he does.

"Why did you lie?" He steps closer now, and all

I want to do is pull him even closer. "Why did you not tell me that you're part of the same society my family is? Did you think I would send you away? Did you think my feelings for you were so fucking fleeting that I'd just change my mind and tell you to fuck off?" With every question, Finn shoves at my chest until my back hits a trunk of the large oak tree behind me. He's inches from me, I can feel the heat radiating off him.

"Finn, stop," Zaria pleads with him, her hand on his arm, and it's only then that rage clears from those dark eyes. I don't blame him for being angry. I would be too. And I wouldn't blame him if he wanted to walk away.

"Why? Just tell me the fuck why, Jarred?" His voice cracks with the betrayal of what I did. Even though I never initiated into the Gilded Sovereign, I am still one of the sons born to the legacy. And it's a well-known fact that the two societies may work in sync, but we're rivals at the best of times. "Why, Jarred?" Finn asks again, this time through clenched teeth.

"Because I didn't want to lose you," I shout to the darkness, to the ghosts that listen as we fight. The truth spilling from my lips as easily as a damn volcano erupting in its anger.

Finn doesn't respond. He just looks at me as if I were a stranger and that hurts more than seeing him walk away. Over the years, we've come to know each other, we've had our arguments, our debates, and challenges, but this, the cold look in his eye, it's new. And it slices a hole right through my gut.

"We're going to head back to Thorne Haven," he says, gesturing to Zaria. "I think it's best if you stayed here, perhaps thought about what it is you need and want in your life. If it's not us, then I'm not sure what else I can say to you."

He turns and walks away. The movement is slow, controlled, but Zaria remains. Her golden eyes shine as she regards me with both confusion and hurt.

When she steps up to me, she smiles. "He'll come around," she says. "I know he loves you and I care about you, more than I thought I would or could." Her voice is a salve to my broken soul. I pray that she's right. I throw up all my prayers to the sky, to a deity I'm not sure I believe is listening.

"I don't know," I tell her. "I've never seen him so angry."

"Anger is not forever. Love is stronger than any emotion, even hate. And once you've given your heart, no matter how much it hurts, you cannot dig someone out.”

“I don't know if he felt as strongly about me as I did him. Even when I told him I love him, he never once said it back to me.” The admission pains me to say, but she needs to know where I stand.

“He does love you,” Zaria whispers. “He just doesn't know how to show the emotion because he's never witnessed it between his parents. His brothers may love him, and may have been there for him, but that's a different kind of relationship.”

She may be right. Perhaps Finn does feel something and that's why he's so hurt by my lies. But even so, he's walking away, and I can't stop him. Even if I tried, the bastard is stubborn.

“Give him some time,” Zaria says, cupping my face in her delicate hand. The contact is like electricity. I knew from the moment I saw her I would be attracted to her. She's an exotic beauty.

“I will be back in Thorne Haven,” I inform her. “I'm not giving up on him, but I'll allow him a few days to calm down.” It's the truth. As much as Finn wants to walk away, I won't let him. “Take care of him.” It's a whispered plea, but she hears and nods with a smile. Zaria leans up on her tiptoes and presses her lips to mine. The warmth of her feels like coming home.

It's the same feeling I get when I'm with Finn. And I know that no matter what happens, she'll love him just like I do.

Once they're gone, I stay in the graveyard. It's quiet. The silence of the dead is far more calming than that of the living. I take in my mother's tombstone. She should have been buried in the family crypt, but because my father walked out of Tynewood, leaving me with the Birchwoods, she's been put with the rest of the townsfolk—the commoners—as the Elders would refer to them.

Perhaps I should head down to see Grecia, to talk to her. Grecia Birchwood is one of the only daughters of the Gilded Sovereign. There are times when I wondered if she would be accepted into the society that was so adamant about only allowing men to join.

I haven't seen her in so long. I grew up beside her, as if we were siblings, and I miss seeing her. Knowing that her father is out of town has me moving to my car without another word to my mother's grave.

My heart was broken the moment my dad told me he was leaving Tynewood. I was alone here, having to make a new life, with no family. He thought the Society would offer me what I needed, but what he didn't know, is that all I ever wanted was him.

I haven't spoken to him since that day. And I have no desire to do so. I forgave him for walking out. I will move on; I have moved on.

I turn my focus to the car and slide into the driver's seat. Once the engine purrs to life, I pull out of the lot and head straight up the main road that leads to the east end of Tynewood.

It doesn't take me long to find the house I spent three years in. When I turned eighteen, I walked out and vowed never to return. It's strange how life throws you obstacles that bring you back to places you never thought you'd see again. I didn't think being part of Finn Thorne's life would force me to come back to a place I know I don't belong. I knew it then, and I most definitely am convinced of it now.

I pull up to the entrance and press the buzzer. Without acknowledgement of who's at the drive, the metal gates slide open and I'm welcomed without so much as a hello. By the time I pull into the circular drive that stops right outside the front door, it's open and Grecia is standing on the porch.

"Never thought I'd see your face in town again," she tells me. A smile curls on her full lips. The girl is a stunner, but she's always been like a sister to me.

And even if I wanted to go there, I know her heart lies with Tarian Calvert. One of the four who now sit at the Elders' table of the Gilded Sovereign. Only, he's never allowed her in. Come to think of it, he has never let anyone get too close.

"I came to you for advice," I tell her as I pull her into my arms. "I need your thoughts on a situation I've gotten myself into." We enter the house, which seems as if things haven't changed.

"So," Grecia says, when we settle with a drink in hand, in the familiar living room where we used to sit as teenagers. "Tell me all about what you need help with." Her eyes shine as she regards me.

"I'm in love," I blurt out quickly. I don't have to think about it because I know I am. There is no question in my mind that Finn is mine, and now, Zaria too.

"Who's the lucky bastard?" she asks with a glittering smile. Grecia has known about my inclinations since we lived in the same house.

"Finn Thorne," I tell her easily. Her eyes widen in shock. She knows all about our link to the societies, to the Thorne Haven faction. Even though I hadn't met or seen the Thorne brothers before I got to Thorne Haven, I knew of them.

"Jesus fucking Christ," Grecia curses, "It's like a

blast from the past walking in here, Jarred."

"Hey, you know me, why take the easy route when you can dive right into the deep end." I shrug it off, but my stomach twists as I recall the memories of meeting Finn, falling for him, kissing him the first time. All of it culminates and hits me right in the heart. "I fucked up," I tell her, admitting to my mistakes. "I should have told him who I was when I arrived in Thorne Haven. But I was scared he knew about the societies and wouldn't want anything to do with someone from the Gilded Sovereign."

"And he's angry because you hid the truth from him," she finishes for me, and I nod. "Well, you shouldn't have hidden who you are and where you come from," she tells me nonchalantly. She's always had a level head dealing with our party-animal ways. Even being around all the males of the Sovereign, Grecia being the only female for so long, she's become something of a therapist to us.

"I know. I knew it the moment I looked into his eyes the first time and realized I loved him."

"Loved or love?" She challenges in that way she has. It's why I came here tonight. I needed someone to hit me across the head with something fierce. A bucket load of common sense.

"Love. I'll always love him," I tell her. There is no lie in my words, and she won't find any in my eyes either.

For a long moment, she watches me. Her stare penetrating those walls I'd built when I left. I never wanted to see them again because I knew my darkest secret could never be forgiven, but sitting here with her, I realize that they love me unconditionally. She does. Ares, Etienne, Philipe, and Tarian. All of them are my brethren and I ran from them, instead of stepping up to take my place in the Society.

"You need a big gesture," she tells me, as if I should've figured it out on my own. "You can't just apologize and hope this will work out."

I sip the sharp whiskey that burns on its way down my throat. "And what exactly would you propose I do?" I ask, meeting her stare.

Grecia sits back and ponders my query for a long while. Even though I try to come up with something, I just can't figure out what I can do other than asking him to fucking marry me. But he's already engaged, so that wouldn't work. I could buy something for him, but that's not feasible because the bastard can get anything he wants with his own money.

And then Grecia says, "Give him something he can't get for himself." And I know exactly what it is I'll give him.

Finn

EVERY DAY THAT HAS PASSED SINCE WE GOT back to Thorne Haven, I've gotten more and more anxious. It's almost been a week, and I haven't heard from Jarred. Thankfully, Zaria has been here to distract me, but I can tell she's getting more depressed not knowing where her mother is.

My father has kept me busy with work, so I haven't seen Zaria all day. The only thing I want right now is to get lost in her, to forget about everything. But when I walk into the room, I'm stopped dead in my tracks as what I find.

"What are you doing?" My voice is rough, anger

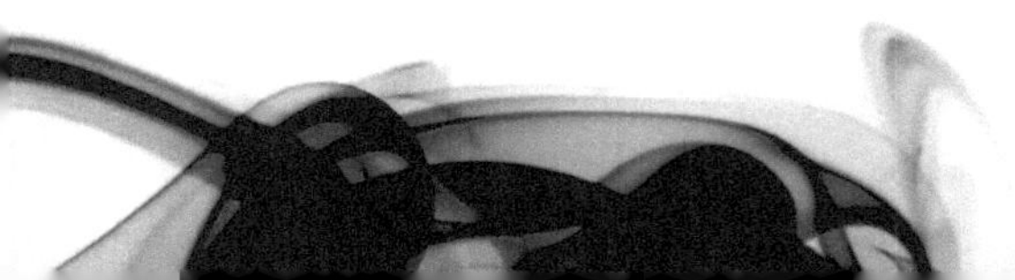

surges through me like a violent storm raging against anything that's standing in its way. My nerves are shot. I don't know how I'm going to get through the next few days, let alone the rest of my life. Everything I thought about Jarred was a lie. He knew exactly what he was doing when he came to Thorne Haven. Leaving him in Tynewood was the least of my worries, though, because now, Zaria is sitting in the dark and I can tell she's been crying.

"Nothing," she mumbles, but as she pushes to her feet, she stumbles. My hand shoots out quickly to catch her, and her body molds against mine. This isn't the first time we've been close, her curves against my solid frame, but the way her head tilts back and her dilated pupils find mine, I realize she's drunk.

"Tell me what the fuck is going on?" I bite out, frustration and anger, once again, taking hold of me. Emotions aren't new to me; I tend to have them consume me at times. When I found out about Jarred's lie, I saw red, my blood burned with the deceit of what the unfaithful bastard did.

Zaria doesn't respond, she shoves her phone at my chest. The device hitting me right at my heart, and I grab it with my free hand while I lead her to her bed. With a flop, she falls to the mattress, and then curls up as if she's been punched in the gut. I use her hand to unlock the damn thing and see the article that's been splashed across her screen.

"He's been around all my life," she tells me in a whisper. "He was at my sixteenth birthday party." The man photographed with her mother looks familiar, but I can't quite put my finger on why. The headline states that her mother has moved on from her father's untimely death. The *happy couple* are walking out of the courthouse, and it's clear that the large diamond on her mother's left hand is a wedding ring.

I'm pulling my phone out and tapping dial on a number to our PI. We have a few who work for us, and I know that Harris will be able to find out who this bastard is. There's something so familiar about him, but I can't quite put my finger on it. The dark hair and tanned features aren't all that I recognize though, it's his eyes. They look so much like Nesrin's, it's startling.

"Hello, Mr. Thorne," Harris answers before I have time to let my brain wander too far down a path I may not like.

"I've told you before, I'm Finn." Even as I say this, the chuckle comes through because he knows it annoys the fuck out of me. "I need you to do something for me."

"Anything," is his response, because he would do anything for us. He's been like family and knows us far too well.

"There's someone I need information on. And I mean everything you can dig up. There may be some hidden files," I tack on because my gut tells me there's more to this stranger than meets the eye. He's now married Zaria's mother, which means he knows about the Thornes, and he must know that I'm about to marry Zaria.

"Send me the info and I'll get to it. Is there a deadline?"

I grin. "I'll give you a couple of hours," I throw back, because I know that Harris will have it to me in less than that. I hang up and send him what he needs before I turn my attention back to my little princess. "Get up," I tell her, the order is cold, swift, and commanding.

Her eyes lock on mine, but she doesn't move. She doesn't respond to me. I'm not sure what the fuck she drank, but she's out of it. I didn't expect to see the well put-together woman like this. But I can't deny if that were me, I'd be a mess too. Granted, when my father remarried, I didn't blame him. He was alone for years before Marcia came along.

I know I'm going to regret this, but I stalk to the bed and scoop Zaria up, throwing her over my shoulder. Now that she's hanging upside down, and she's drunk, I'm expecting her to throw up before I reach the bathroom. But I'm impressed when she doesn't. I flick on the shower after setting her on her feet.

"Take your clothes off," I tell her as I wave a hand at her outfit. When I first saw her in the dress earlier, my cock responded and wanted to know what she had underneath. And even now, as the possibility of her getting naked is presented to me, I can't deny I'm hungry to see her curves.

"What?" Her brows furrow as she regards me. "No."

"You're my wife, take your fucking clothes off, or I'll take them off for you." My voice has turned to ice, and I see her shiver at my tone. When she doesn't comply, I take a step toward her. The steam has filled the room and it billows around us as I near her. Once I'm inches from her, she dips her head back to regard me.

"What are you doing?" she whispers as she watches me. She's still wobbly, but I quickly grip the dress she's wearing and tear the material from her body. There was no other way to get it off her, because I did ask her to undress, and she refused me. "Finn!"

Ignoring her, I point to the shower. "Get in." I half expect her to refuse. She's fire where I'm ice. But with those sad eyes on mine, melting me slowly, she complies and steps under the spray. The fact that she's not wearing underwear doesn't go unnoticed, but I'll talk to her about that when she's sober. As much as I do enjoy alcohol, I'm not one to stick my dick anywhere near a girl who's inebriated so much that she can hardly stand.

When she leans against the tiles, frustration gets the better of me and I pull off my T-shirt and I step under the spray. My sweatpants are soaked through, but my arms wrap around her and I hold her up. Gritting my teeth, I turn on the cold tap, before shutting off the hot one. The moment those icy prickles stab at us, a scream is wrenched from Zaria's lips.

I recall seeing my father do this to my mother when I was little. She struggled the same way. I didn't know what was happening, only that mom was screaming and dad was holding her. Everything was blurry at the time, but now that I'm in the exact same position, I realize my father isn't the bastard I always thought he was.

My mother was ill.

The love he had for her had overtaken all the shit they went through, and even as kids, he hid the fact that she wasn't well. We didn't know anything about her mental health. It was only when she left, when I was older, did I look into it. Most of the files were hidden. My father is good at keeping secrets.

Zaria moves in my arms, bringing me back to the present. Those pretty fucking gold eyes that look like honey. They pierce me right through the heart and I find myself leaning in to steal her whimpers of being ice cold. I turn off the tap the moment my mouth finds hers.

She's shaking, but she's sobered up. Thankfully, as I pull her from the shower and wrap her up, she stops trembling. The towel that's covering her wet skin hides her from my gaze, but I can't deny I did look when she was in there, under the spray. I never claimed to be a gentleman.

"Y-you s-s-should forgive him," Zaria mumbles, her words slowly sinking into the anger that has held me captive since I found out about Jarred's secret. Confusion settles in my chest, my mind trying to figure out what she's talking about, but then she smiles and says, "Jarred, he loves you."

I can't think about him right now. I can't bring myself to ponder what the fuck happened between us that he hid the truth of why he was here in the first place. He always told me that honesty was the best policy. And then he lied.

"That doesn't concern you," I bite out as I grip Zaria's arm and drag her into her bedroom. I'm about to take her to the bed, but she pulls out of my grip and has me stalling all movement. I spin around to take her in, and it seems like the little princess is sober and feels like arguing with me.

"I'm not bringing him back here. He lied." There's one thing I will never tolerate, and that is secrets. I've seen how it breaks down relationships, love and happiness, how it rips through a household like a goddamned storm and it leaves destruction in its wake.

"But you can't push someone away because they were afraid of losing you, Finn," she insists, the tears that had fallen earlier linger on her lashes as she regards me. "That's not how this works."

"And you're the expert on relationships?" I throw back. My defenses already making their way up, needing to hide what I feel. I do this all the time. I've done it with Jarred so many times over the past few years, I am surprised he didn't leave. But he was here because he wanted all the secrets of Thorne Haven, so he could take them back to Tynewood. At least, that's what it seems like.

"No," Zaria says, "I'm not an expert, but I know human emotion. And I can see that he loves you." Her voice is small, but firm. There's confidence that glows in her. She wobbles slightly, causing me to step closer and pull her into my arms. The softness of her curves makes me hard. I know she can feel it because the gasp that tumbles from those soft lips is audible in the silence of her bedroom.

"And what about you, little princess?" I whisper my question against her mouth. "Do you want a man in your life who wants you and someone else? Can you handle it?" I didn't think I would ever want someone my father chose for me. But as the days have passed, I've found myself more and more enthralled by her. My need to lay her down and finally have her is an idea that has become more and more enticing.

"I can handle anything you throw at me, Finn," Zaria informs me confidently. "I'm not a weak little girl," she says in a stronger tone. Her lips moving against mine. She doesn't lean in to kiss me, and I don't inch closer either. We're standing in her room, she's still naked, my cock is hard as fucking steel, and yet, we're both frozen. "Would you like to feel us both against you?" She utters the question in a low tone that is a breathed whisper.

I ponder the thought for a moment. I've been with Jarred and multiple girls over the years, but not a woman that I'm meant to marry. "Yes," I finally answer her. "I want you on my dick while watching his mouth on your tits. I want to see you bent over, taking my dick in your tight little pussy while you suck him off."

Zaria's moan is like a shot straight through my chest. She likes it. She wants us both. "I... I..."

"I've thought about it a lot," I confess. And it's true. Since I realized she enjoyed watching us in the shed that night, my mind has been awash with situations where it was the three of us, naked, writhing in pleasure, spent and satiated. That was before I walked away from Jarred and left him in Tynewood.

"I'm sure you have," Zaria says, a small smile dancing on her lips as they curl against mine. Her eyes are fire, burning like liquid gold as she regards me. Her long, black lashes flutter when I dart my tongue out to lick her lips. The flavors of sweetness that hit my tastebuds zing through my veins.

"Have you been fantasizing about us late at night, princess?" I ask as the thought of her lying back, spread on the mattress, while those delicate fingers taunting her sweet cunt, invade my mind.

Zaria doesn't answer, so I press my lips to hers. I claim her lips, the softness of her molding against me as if she was always meant to be there. My chest tightens, my pulse spikes into a racing fucking time bomb, and I know that I can't ever *not* taste her lips. She whimpers against my mouth. My hands trap her hips against mine, and I grind my hardness against her.

"You feel that, princess?" I murmur before pulling her lower lip between my teeth and biting down on the plump flesh until she moans. I'm shocked when she deepens the kiss by tasting me, and I can't stop myself from tangling my tongue with hers.

We do a dance of desire, as it courses through my veins, and when Zaria twines her arms around my neck, I lower my hands to that bubble butt and lift her against me. We move effortlessly as I slam her back against the wall. Her heat right at my cock, sending more zaps of pure lust racing through my body.

Our lips mold to each other, as if we were always meant to fit together. "Finn," she mumbles when I pull away for a second to take her in. Those eyes focus on me, her pupils dilated, and her lips now swollen from my kiss.

I'm ready to finally have my fiancée, but as she trails her nails down my back, my phone buzzes wildly in my pocket. I ignore it for a long moment, but the incessant ringing doesn't stop, and when it does, it only starts back up.

"Fuck."

Zaria laughs. "Maybe next time." Her taunt doesn't go unnoticed.

I meet those pretty eyes and grin. "There is no maybe about it," I inform her before letting her to her feet. "Get into bed and sleep. I'll see you in the morning." With that, I leave her in the bedroom and make my way to my own.

Jarred's name flashes across my screen. But I can't talk to him. Not yet. I need more time; if I spoke to him right now, I'll only hurt us both with thoughtless words. So, instead of answering, I change for bed. Perhaps tomorrow will be a different day, and maybe my mind will change, but for tonight, I'll miss him and sleep alone. Because the moment I claim Zaria, everything in our dynamic will change. And I know I need to talk to Jarred before that happens.

Jarred

I SPENT MOST OF MY LIFE RUNNING AWAY. I DON'T recall a time I stood up for myself, for what I wanted. Instead of fighting, I always turn my back and leave. It's easier that way. But it's been five days without Finn and Zaria, and I miss the connection I felt. I have to go back.

I try calling Finn one more time, but he doesn't answer. Since he and I started our affair, we haven't been apart for longer than a week. The last time was when he had to go to London to see Damien. Other than that, we spend every day together. And because I have the ruse of working at Thorne Manor, I'm able

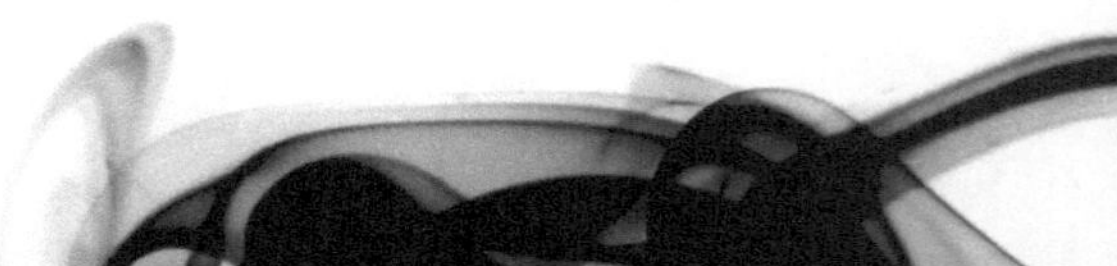

to see him whenever I want. But this distance that's between us, the emotional separation is difficult.

But with Finn leaving me in Tynewood, I have time to think. Too much time. And I have finally figured out what it is I want. I know he will never take me back. That is, if I never do anything about it, he will accept the fact and move on.

I can't accept it.

I won't let what I have with Finn die, just like everything else in my past.

Stalking down the hallway, I make my way to the office, where I know I'll find Ares. The Lancasters have been good friends with my father for years. And even though I didn't want the life that I was born into, Ares was still a good man, and one that I know will help me.

I knock twice before pushing open the door to find him and Philipe, his older brother, sitting on the sofas near the fire. I shut the door and move deeper into the antique-filled room.

"It's good to see you," Philipe says, pushing to his feet and offering his hand, which I accept with a smile. We shake once in greeting. "I didn't think you'd ever return to Tynewood." He's right, not even I thought I would ever come back. But I didn't have a choice. It was taken from me. But I don't tell him that.

"Same. How's the Big Apple treating you?" He is the eldest of the four who run the Gilded Sovereign. Being the first born, he was to step into his father's shoes. But I get the impression that Ares has been holding it together while his brother runs a club in New York.

"It's busy," he admits. "I'm opening three more venues over the next few months, so I'll be away. I thought I should come and see how my little brother is doing before I disappear into the club scene for six months."

"And he wanted to make sure I haven't killed anyone," Ares throws in as he leans back and settles his ankle on the opposite knee. He looks like a king. He has the air of a ruler, and I wonder why Philipe doesn't just walk away from the Sovereign. It's something I would do. Which is what I'm doing in his office.

"I need your help with something," I say, glancing at one of my oldest friends. Even though I left Tynewood, I know I can always come back here, and the Sovereign have to help. My father walked out, leaving this life, and living in the next town over.

When he left me with the Birchwoods, I thought my life was over, but I realized he only wanted me to become part of a society that could propel me forward in life.

"Anything for you, Jarred," Ares says. "Sit. Let's talk and I'll see how the Sovereign can help you." With connections all over the world, in every city on every continent, they have grown substantially since I last heard about them. Growing up, we were to learn about the traditions, the rules, and all we can achieve as part of the Society. But I didn't go through with it. Instead, I focused on the *normal* life I believed I wanted.

"I need to get back to Thorne Haven, but I want to go back with an offer," I tell Ares. Philipe settles on the opposite sofa, in his hand a tumbler with bourbon. The scent is strong, and I want to smile at the fact that he's drinking at midday. I suppose when you're used to the lifestyle of partying non-stop, you pick up certain habits.

"And what offer would you like to give the Thornes?" Ares seems interested, so all I can do is pray he'll allow me to take my place in the Sovereign and do what is required of me. Whatever that may be.

If I can become one of them, I can impress

Bradford, but I can also put myself on Finn's level. I can show him that I did lie, but I changed who I am to be with him. And being part of the society will give me the option to offer Finn the chance to live a life he wants.

I take a deep breath and dive right into my favor. "I'd like to go to the Elders of the Silver Sovereign and offer myself to them in place of Finn Thorne."

Silence.

Ares watches me for a long moment before glancing over at his brother. I know they will have to talk about it. This isn't a decision they can take lightly. Being born as part of the Gilded, I should become one of them. But with me asking to leave them and join another society, it's against all the rules. They may work together to run the world, but they don't like each other. It's all part of the business. Agreements set in place thousands of years ago.

The reason I'm asking this is because if I become one of them, Finn can just be him. He doesn't need to do anything that is requested of him. And as I pray that they will accept my choice, I hope it's not too late.

Finn will have to get his tattoo soon. Each one of them branded to the society. They no longer belong to themselves. Every decision they make is bound by the law that doesn't follow rules. It's all bullshit.

"I'm concerned," Ares says as he turns to me again. "I've spoken with Bradford, and it seems that the girl, Zaria, is to marry Finn. Now, I didn't tell Finn this because his father requested it of me and I cannot go against a promise I've made."

Concern rattles me. I thought Zaria was honest, that she was real. I've seen her talk about her life, about her family, and none of it seemed *off*, but I wait for Ares to continue.

"Her mother wants this wedding to go through because of his connection to the society," Ares tells me and my chest tightens. "The agreement was that the moment Finn takes on his role within the Silver Sovereign, his position would ensure their security for the family company."

"I don't understand. Zaria's father had a lucrative business that is doing well, even after his death." Nothing makes sense. My confusion has taken on a whole new high now. I know the Abadi chain was making more money than ever before. Her mother is at the helm, running it so they don't lose anything. Even if Zaria didn't marry Finn.

Ares pushes to his feet and heads for his desk. He

picks up a folder and brings it over to me. "This is what I was given. There has to be a decision from my side before Finn completes his initiation. Perhaps you can take this to him, talk to him and see what his choice is. I don't want him to be integrated into a society he doesn't want. I was born for this; I've always wanted it. But I'm not my father, I will not force anyone to join if they don't want to."

"I don't understand how you could sway the Elders. What could you say that would change their minds? And why is it Finn and not Damien that takes the seat?" I know the rules of the Gilded, the eldest son will always step up into the role the father played.

"Bradford, like Abner, was an Elder. He chose to put Finn in his position when he stepped down. Because he was an Elder, he made sure that Damien and Cassian would not be called on," Ares explains, then he shakes his head. "It's not an easy decision for any parent, I know it broke my family up. My mother was angry with my father for even considering having both me and Philipe step up into his seat, the only difference is, it didn't end well for my parents."

As Ares explains the situation that occurred within his own family, I wonder if Finn's mother left because of the society. Perhaps she knew about it and wasn't happy that Bradford chose his youngest son to become a part of a group of men who thought they could rule the law, the government, and the country, with violence and destruction.

"We'll have the plane ready for you." Philipe speaks this time. "It will take you straight to Thorne Haven. From there, you'll need to talk to Finn. You'll have twenty-four hours before my brother has to make the call," he tells me.

I'm sure that will be enough time to get Finn to read what I hold in my hands. If I have to tie him up and shove this in his face, I'll do it. Anything to save him from making an uninformed decision.

"Thank you," I say to them both. With every moment that passes, I know I'm running out of time. I have to get there and do this as quickly as possible. "I don't know what to say." I'm grateful they're offering me a second chance, it's not something that comes with the Society.

"You know we will always have your back," Ares tells me as we all stand. We walk out to the front door, where my suitcases are waiting. Thankfully the butler brought them down. "The car will take you to the airstrip."

"I'll be in touch," I tell Ares before we say our

goodbyes. In the car, my stomach tightens with anxiety as I try calling Finn again. The call is dropped within the first two rings. He's been ignoring me since he left. Even when I leave voicemails, he doesn't listen to them. But I try once more. "Finn, I need you to talk to me. I have information that you need to hear about the wedding." When I hang up, I pray that he stops being angry long enough to listen to the message.

I sit back and watch the town pass by. It's just as gothic and disturbing as Thorne Haven. With an enormous woodland surrounding it, the little oasis in the center is nothing more than a blip on a map, but it holds more secrets than anywhere else.

In a few hours, I'll be home. I still consider Thorne Haven and the manor my home. Even though I didn't grow up there, it's kept me safe, it's given me a second chance, and it's given me a love I can't lose.

I check my phone again, but there's no reply from Finn. When I check Zaria's social media, I notice she's not posted in a few days. The last image on her profile is her arriving in Tynewood.

I open my news app to see what's been happening in the world. At times, when I'm lost in my mind, I forget there's a world out there. The first story that pops up is of Zaria's mother. But it's most certainly not what I'm expecting to read because this is going to break her heart.

"Shit," I mumble. The woman has already remarried. It's only been a short while since her husband passed away and she's moved on. It makes no sense. But when I see the photo of the man beside her, the world stops and my breath is stuck in my lungs.

There is no doubt about who he is because his daughter looks just like him.

Finn

I DIDN'T EXPECT TO SEE JARRED AGAIN FOR AT least a few weeks. When I left him in Tynewood, I told him I needed space. But as I pull open the office door, I find him sitting opposite my desk. He turns to regard me when I step into the room.

He's dressed in a pair of jeans and a T-shirt that shows off his inked arms. All the time we've been together, I've always loved how he was like a walking canvas. When I make it to my desk, I stop and turn to him.

"What are you doing here?" I ask him as I slip into my chair. Even though I'm trying to keep my tone

calm, there's a hint of frustration at seeing him. I'm still angry he kept a whole part of who he is from me.

"Did you not listen to my voice message?" Jarred asks, his eyes glowing with frustration. The silver turning to ice as he regards me. I've learned to read him like a book, and I know that most times, I drive him up the wall because I can be overly stubborn.

"No." I open my laptop, ignoring him for a moment before I glance his way. "If you need to tell me something, do so now. I'm busy."

"Don't be a dick."

"Don't be a dick?" Incredulity drips from my words. "I'm the one you lied to for all the time we've known each other. Fuck you," I bite out. "I am allowed to be fucking angry at you because I trusted you. I told you things I haven't even told my brothers and you sat there, hiding shit from me."

"I deserve that," Jarred agrees with a nod. "But if you grew up in that bullshit secret society, rules and regulations, you'd understand why it's part of my life I wanted to put behind me."

People think growing up wealthy is easy. They believe that everything falls into your lap without consequence, but it's the complete opposite. All the opportunities that come from a family name or legacy, all those perks that appear without you having to lift a finger, they come with terms and conditions.

"Fine. You're forgiven," I tell him with a nonchalant shrug.

"Don't bullshit me," Jarred responds as he pushes to his feet. "You're angry, I can see it written all over your face. You need to listen to me, to really understand," he insists, so I wave a hand for him to continue. "When I was growing up, there was only one path for my future, one I didn't want. And even though I told my father I wasn't interested in the society, he told me that if I didn't want in, I could leave."

"So you left," I finish for him. "I'm not angry about anything other than you lying to me. My father found out and sent you along on the trip, so I could find out, and trust me, I'm going to talk to him about that," I say, before leaning my elbows on the desk. "I'm angry because someone I loved, someone that I gave my fucking heart to lied to me." I'd never told Jarred I loved him. Ever. He knew, I was sure of it, but I never once brought myself to utter the words. They weren't who I was. And even now, it's foreign to talk about my feelings.

Jarred's mouth pops open, shock painting his handsome face. The glint of his piercing shimmering in the sunlight that streams through the windows.

I can't draw my attention away, but the office door opens, and I glance Zaria leaning on the door frame. "Come in," I call to her, so she can shut us in for privacy. I don't like the staff being able to listen in on my conversations. They're usually pretty good and will close the door if I'm in here, but right now, there's a lot to discuss.

Zaria smiles at Jarred who seems perturbed that she's here. "I think you need to see this," Jarred says, without greeting her, and sets a folder on my desk. It's thick. When I pick it up, I glance at him, but there's not a hint of what's in there for me to find.

Sighing, I flick open the cover and find police reports, agreements, and photos, profiling the newlywed couple. The images I find are different to those that were on the website. But it's clear that it's Zaria's mother and her new husband.

I turn a few pages to find an agreement between the society and my father, as well as Zaria's mother. She was the one who came to Bradford and asked for me to marry her daughter. It goes on to state that I will soon take my father's seat with the Elders of the

Silver Society. All of this is foreign to me because I only learned about them a few days ago.

"Where did you get this?" I look at Jarred who's back in his chair, watching me intently with those stormy eyes. "I don't understand."

"I went to Ares and asked him to help me make an offer to Bradford to get you out of your responsibilities. I told Ares that I will take your place at the table, so you can live your life freely, without recourse." When he explains slowly, the words sink in, burrowing their way right down into the marrow of my bones.

"You did what?" This has me pushing to my feet. He should never have done that. I have to take my father's place because it was my destiny. Even though I don't want it, I will not forsake what was given to me. I may have been a bastard who fought my father tooth and nail, but I knew that the legacy of the Thornes goes way back, and I knew I had to do something about it. I couldn't allow our name to disappear and be forgotten.

"It would be the same as if you were there, I would represent the Thorne name, but you get to live a life of your choosing," Jarred continues, and that's when I realize what he's doing.

"You can't sacrifice yourself for me," I tell him.

"I don't understand what is going on, guys," Zaria says suddenly, dragging both our attentions back to her. I am still shocked at the news about her mother. She looks at us confused; her brows furrowed. I mentioned the Society to her on our trip to meet the Lancasters, but I never went into too much detail. She isn't my wife yet. It makes me weary. Until she's a Thorne, I am not sure I can trust her fully.

"Did you know your mother was the one who set up the arranged marriage with my father?" I ask, turning my full attention on her. If she did know, she would tell me because if she lies, I'll torture the fucking truth out of her.

"No." She shakes her head. "It was my father, he spoke to me about it before he..." Her words falter, but she doesn't break eye contact with me. She's been trained to be poised around people, especially when being questioned. I've watched her on red carpets, at events her parents attended, I've studied her, and I know that she has tells. But right now, none of them are present.

"It's in black and white," I tell her as I pull the contract from the folder on my desk and hand it to her. "Your mother thinks that my link to the

Silver Sovereign will ensure the Abadi name will be connected to the Elders, who can bring her more money than fucking God." The woman is nothing more than a gold-digging wench. I didn't see that in her at the funeral, but then again, when you've spent your life pretending, it's easy to lie with a poker face.

"I don't understand," Zaria mimics her previous words. "She had never spoken to me before about any of this." Golden eyes scan the pages, before lifting to me. "I really had no clue about any of this."

"I believe you," I tell her. "What I don't get is why my father decided to agree to it." Honestly, there's nothing in the documentation that says anything about the Thornes. It doesn't even mention the Havens: the other family who owns this town. When I think of them, I wonder briefly if they will also become a part of the Society. I doubt Creed would ever set foot in one of those meetings. Or Keirin. Or Brody. They're too independent and prefer doing their own thing.

"Another thing," Jarred says, bringing my gaze back to his. "Have you looked at the photos in the folder? I mean really looked." He moves around me, to the desk where he lifts the polaroid and hands it to me. It's the man who married Zaria's mother. He looks familiar, but if I had to take a guess, I would say he's some celebrity or something.

"I've seen him, but can't place the name," I tell Jarred.

"Really?" he challenges me, and I know I'm missing something. I bring the image closer, focusing on his features, trying to figure out why he looks so familiar to me. It's as if I've seen him somewhere before, but never met, so I can't quite put my finger on his identity.

Jarred picks up the frame on my desk and hands it to me. The image inside is of the three Thorne brothers on the day of Damien's wedding. Beside my eldest brother is the beauty that stole his heart. The moment I look at her, my heart sinks down to my gut.

"Fuck," is all I can manage. Last night when I first saw the article, I knew I'd seen this man before. There was just something too striking about him, but as I look at her right now, I realize I've just found Nesrin's long-lost father. "How did I miss this?"

Jarred steps up beside me, with Zaria joining us. The two photos side by side are living proof the Nesrin's father is in fact alive and well. I need to talk to Marcia. Nesrin's mother, my stepmother, needs to know that her ex-husband is back.

"Is that your sister-in-law?" Zaria takes the photo from me as she makes the connection, staring at her mother's new husband. She's just as shocked as we are as she stares at the image.

"Yes," I finally answer as I pull my phone from my pocket. I hit dial on my stepmother's number and hold the ringing speaker to my ear. When she answers, I don't greet her, instead, I say, "Nesrin's father has just married Zaria's mother." She knows my fiancée, so there is no need for introductions. Silence answers me, and for a second, I wonder if the line went dead, but then I hear her.

"Where is he?" Her voice croaks, and I can imagine the look of shock on her face. When he walked out on them, leaving Marcia alone with Nesrin, after cheating with her sister, Mallory, the bastard never made contact again. He never spoke to his daughter, never even tried to be a good father. It's not like he didn't know she existed; he watched her early years while keeping the sordid secret of what he did.

"Currently in Los Angeles, but I have a feeling he'll be coming to Thorne Haven pretty fucking soon," I tell her. "I'm calling Nesrin because she needs to know this piece of shit is back."

"I'll do it," Marcia says in a rush. I don't trust that she'll tell her daughter; she's kept so much from Nesrin while growing up. But, I'll give her twenty four hours.

"You have a day to do it, or I'll call her myself," I inform Marcia. She doesn't argue with me because she knows I'll do it.

"I'll call her right now." I hang up without a goodbye. As much as my father loves the woman, I can't stand her. But I don't need to spend too much time around her, so I can deal with the odd greeting while we pass each other in the hallway.

"This is definitely the man I saw the night of my sixteenth birthday," Zaria whispers. She looks up at me, questions dancing in her eyes. I wish I had the answers, but right now, we're all in the dark.

"I fucking hate secrets," I mumble as I move around my desk and settle in my chair. Jarred sits down while he holds out a hand to Zaria. For a second, she glances my way, and I nod. As much as I want to be angry at him, I know I don't blame him. He'll have a lot to make up for with me, but Jarred knows I'll never leave him. And I can never allow him to leave me.

"Now what do we do with this?" Jarred asks as

he pulls Zaria into his lap with a squeak. They're beautiful together; it's fucking distracting. I have so much work to do, but all I can think of is to finally have them both in my bed, while I devour each one slowly.

"I'm going to get Harris on Nesrin's dad," I tell Jarred. "Then, I'm going to have him bring them here. I want that man in my office, so he can finally admit to what he did."

"And what about the Society?" Jarred looks more concerned than I've ever seen him. I know there are a lot of rules that come with this role, but I don't want him to sacrifice his life for mine. "I have to tell Ares what you decided because he needs to give them the green light."

"Let me sit with my father, I'll call Ares and tell him to hold off as long as he can," I finally say. "I'll see what my father recommends. I know he wants me on that committee, and if it can help us, I'm going to do it, Jarred."

"But you'll never be free," he insists.

"But he'll be able to keep us both close," Zaria suggests, which is correct. After I spoke with Ares about my little situation, he gave me a few ideas on how to get the Elders off my back about the wedding.

This is why I'd rather talk to Dad first, and then, once I've explained everything to him, I pray he'll come around. He has to, I fulfilled his request for meeting with the Lancasters.

"She's right," I tell Jarred. "I am not losing either of you. And you have a lot to make up for." I point at him, making sure he understands I'm not just letting this go. We will sit down and get all those ugly little secrets out in the open, and when we do, we'll be able to move on.

He nods as if he had already planned on making it up to me in ways I couldn't even think of yet. And I look forward to it. Then he asks, "Are you sure?"

"Always," I tell him.

Zaria

When Finn walks into my room from the adjoining bathroom, I know he's going to want to talk about the night we almost had sex. He found me drunk, crying, in pain, and I couldn't voice it, so I took a few pills to calm myself and ended up downing half a bottle of whiskey I'd found downstairs. It was my go-to when I was hurting. I would numb myself. But there is still something that Finn doesn't know, and if he probes, he'll find out. He said he didn't want secrets between the three of us, so I should admit to what I did.

He settles on my bed, his dark eyes holding mine

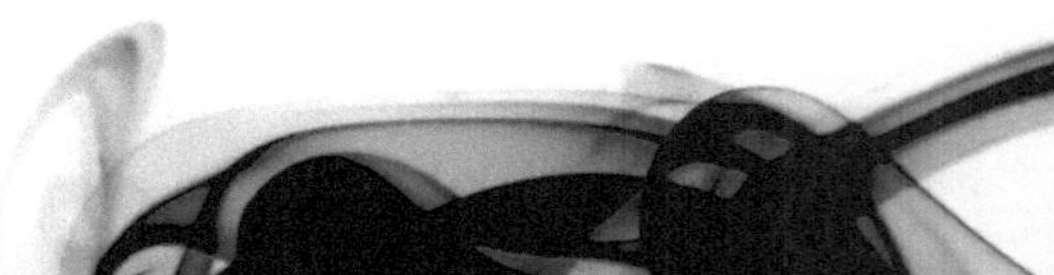

hostage. But I don't want to look away. *Can someone be a willing victim?* If it could be with Finn and Jarred, I'd do it. He watches me for a long, silent moment. It's uncomfortable, as if he's trying to dig for answers with just his stare.

"You need to talk to me," he finally says in a firm tone that holds no debate. I knew it would eventually come to this. With our connection growing slowly, and our relationship forming more deeply, I realize that I wanted a good man to marry, and he is that. He's everything and more. I've watched him during the time we spent together and his light shines brighter than I could ever have expected.

"I know." I nod. I hear Jarred's soft footfalls before I see him. When he appears from the bathroom, I offer a small smile. Both men are here to listen to my story. And I know that if I don't come clean now, I'm going to jeopardize what I've built with them so far. We've come a long way since the night I arrived.

Jarred settles on the other side of the bed, his focus on me as he cocoons me. The heat from him, and the warmth from Finn calms my nerves. They're both strong, beautiful men. Both have their own quirks and talents. Both of them, however, are staring at me as if I were a painting hanging in a gallery.

It's almost as if they expect me to run, from their focused gazes and those clenched jaws.

"When you found me, I'd been having a rough day." My voice is croaky as I start, my eyes on Finn's. "It's not the first time I've chosen alcohol to numb the pain, the frustration inside me."

"We're here," Jarred offers, taking my hand in his, he presses a kiss to it before releasing me. "You can trust us."

Nodding, I continue, "The drinking started when I was fifteen. My mother had forced me into this circle of friends. They were all daughters of her social group, and even though I would have been happier to stay at home, working on my studies or even just reading a book, she said I had to get out. To meet friends."

Both men are silent as I find myself back there. It was the most stressful visit I'd ever had at the country club. My mother was the butterfly, fluttering around with her bright colors and her intoxicating smile. Everyone loved her, at least, that's what I thought.

"I sat with the girls for a while, talking about music and movies, and nothing seemed amiss. At first, I thought perhaps I was being a snob because I was convinced that they weren't my friends. But when I went to the restroom, I wasn't gone for too long. When I returned, they didn't see me at first." I struggle to find the words. It's like the first time I had to talk to a therapist. Reliving something that hurt you tends to bring you down; it takes you to that moment when you are crushed. And there is nothing you can do to stop it. All that happens is there's a black spiral that drags you in further.

"I overheard them talking about my mother, and then me. Specifically, about how I was a freak because I didn't look like them. They laughed at my nerdy clothes, how I wore braces, they tore apart every aspect of who I was, right down to how my mother must be sleeping with all their fathers just to be a part of the elite group of ladies who attended the country club."

When I finally take a breath again, Finn scoots closer, his arms wrapping around me. He pulls me against his solid chest. I can feel every peak and valley of his abs and his pectorals. Jarred moves behind me, leaning back against my pillows, allowing me to rest on his chest. My focus, however, is on Finn.

"It's okay, you can continue," Finn says, gesturing with his chin for me to talk. There's something calming about them, having their strength surrounding me is like a fortress built to withstand anything. They're my protection, my knights.

"I thought I could handle it, but then one of them said I was nothing more than a bastard child, that my mother had me before my parents met." The moment had shattered my entire being. Confusion and heartbreak had taken hold, and when I went to Dad to ask him about it, he denied it.

"And were they right?" Finn asks as his brows furrow.

"I still don't know. My father said it's a lie, that he was my real dad." Even as I say it, I can hear the doubt in my tone. I wanted so much to trust my father. He was everything to me, but where there is rumor, there is usually some form of truth. "I stewed on it over and over again, and when I brought it up with my mother, she scoffed at me. It was on my sixteenth birthday that I... I was so hurt, that I did something stupid, and I will always be ashamed of myself."

Finn scoots even closer while Jarred's arms tighten around me. They hold me as if I'm fragile. Both men waiting for my admission. The one thing I haven't told anyone outside of my parents. Not even our staff found out about it.

"I tried to commit suicide because I just couldn't handle the nasty words that kept coming from those girls. They didn't stop there. My phone and computer were bombarded with emails and messages. In the end, I felt like I was drowning." It's only when I blink, do I realize I'm crying. The weight that had been sitting on my shoulders for so long, has finally lifted after I admitted to Jarred and Finn about what I had done.

"Princess," Finn murmurs the nickname he's given me as he moves beside me, his arms tangling with Jarred's as they cocoon me in their warmth.

"Fucking hell, Rosebud," Jarred grumbles as he presses his lips to my head. The other nickname I've been gifted coming from him. With both men here, I finally let go and allow my pain to fall from my lashes. It trickles down my cheeks in rivulets of salty heartbreak. I have held onto it for so long, it feels as if I'm finally free. It's strange how a few words can change your mindset, sometimes good, and sometimes bad.

"I'm so sorry you had to go through that," Finn says softly, his lips moving over my cheek. "It's not easy. No fucking pain is, but to make that choice is scary. I can't imagine not having you here right now." The genuine emotion in his voice makes my chest expand and my heart fill with affection.

"My father found me in the bathroom. He managed to get me to wake up, even though I was delirious. And ever since, he doted on me more than usual. I just…"

"You survived," Finn tells me. "And that's what's important. I want us to do something," he announces. "It's been on my mind for a while, and I think it would be something we can share."

I arch a brow. "Oh?"

"Tattoos. Matching infinity symbols, which will show our love, our connection, and our future." Finn isn't smiling, but there is a gentle affection burning in his gaze.

"We should," Jarred agrees.

"I'd like that," I tell them both. "I think my dad would like that too." The tears in my eyes blur my vision, and they continue to slowly tumble down my cheeks.

"Did you ever find out about your dad?" This comes from Jarred, and I shake my head *no* in response. "Surely your mother would have told you now that your father has passed," Jarred ponders, and I want to nod, but I remember the strange conversation we had when I left. When I asked her why she was allowing this, she told me she had a plan. And I realized then, that I had to tell them both.

"Before I arrived in Thorne Haven, I was saying goodbye to my mother," I start as my brain starts clicking into place. "I tried to get her to tell me why she signed the contract for the marriage, but she didn't give me a reason," I inform them. "But she did say something strange,"

Finn tenses beside me, and I know he's worried after seeing the folder Jarred brought for him from Tynewood. He asks, "What was it?"

The memory slams into me and I recall her words with clarity as if she were here in the room with us right now. "...learn about the Thornes, enjoy your time there, and when everything falls into place, it will all make sense."

"Did she say anything else?" Finn asks, his words gritted through clenched teeth. For a second, I wonder if it was a good idea to tell him, but when I turn to look at him, I realize he's not angry, there's a small glint of fear in his eyes, which has me even more curious as to what my mother could have meant.

"She just said something about me being queen

or something similar to the IT world, which I don't understand because I'm not even interested in—"

"Fuck." Finn is on his feet, his phone in hand before he presses the screen and holds the device to his ear. Jarred's hold on me tightens, his calm demeanor easing my tension, but not by much. "Harris, I need you to look into Thorne Industries. I have a feeling my father might have done something utterly fucking reckless."

He listens for a long moment, and I wonder what his private investigator will find when he does his research.

"Yes," Finn says. "And then as you're busy running those, get into the Abadi records," he tells Harris as his eyes find mine. It's almost as if he's asking permission, so I offer him a small smile because I don't know what he's going to do, but we all need answers. If my mother is attempting to steal his family's company from them, they should know.

I know for a fact my father would not have known about this because he was a good man. Even though he must have had offers to cut corners, and get involved in underhanded dealings, I'd never seen or heard anything untoward about him. But my mother, there has always been secrets that she's kept from me and Dad. It's time her lies come to light.

When Finn finally hangs up, he looks over at Jarred and me. "You two look too fucking good like that," he growls while running his fingers through his hair. The dark shadow of his beard is slowly forming on his angular jaw, making him look rough, yet elegant in his button-up shirt and black slacks.

"Why don't you join us?" Jarred coaxes, pulling me closer, so there's space for Finn to slide onto the mattress. I've never been with two men, hell, my first and second times were with one fumbling college boy. It was over in a couple of minutes and I was left to my own devices once he passed out.

Over the years, I've become accustomed to finding pleasure with my fingers. But Finn and Jarred are men. They're mature, experienced. And for a long moment, as Finn stares down at me with dark eyes, I feel as if it's my first time.

Finn slowly moves those deft fingers to the buttons of his shirt, and with each one he flicks open, I see more of the smooth, tanned skin below. There's a dark smattering of hair on his chest, which only makes him seem more mature. Then, his toned torso comes into view, and my breath is stolen from my lungs.

"Beautiful. Isn't he?" Jarred whispers in my ear, his hot breath at my neck as he kisses the sensitive skin under my ear. His teeth graze my flesh, tugging on the lobe and sending heat jolting through me.

"For now, we're focused on this," Finn tells me, his eyes boring a hole right through me, right down to my soul, which is on fire for him and the man beside me. "Tomorrow," he says, "is war." And then he prowls over to the mattress where I'm nestled against Jarred.

Finn's lips find mine, just like they did last night when I was practically climbing him like a goddamned tree. His tongue licks against mine, his flavor bursting on my tongue. The sweet, minty taste of Finn. Jarred doesn't let up as his mouth continues its trail of hot wet kisses over my shoulder as he tugs at the tee I'm wearing.

Both men help me out of the item of clothing, which finds a home on the floor. Finn kisses me once more, and Jarred joins in, our tongues tangling, sweetness, mingled with spice and coffee. Jarred is fire burning me from his passion, while Finn is like a storm raging against me, breaking me down.

They're the complete opposite of each other, but they fit together perfectly. I lean back with a smile dancing on my lips as I leave them to kiss. The sight is so erotic, I'm squirming as I watch their lips mold together. Tongues dual for more. My nipples harden against my bra, and my panties are slowly soaking through with arousal at the sight before me.

When they break their kiss, it's Jarred who now tugs at his clothes and, soon enough, Finn and I are awarded with the erotically inked, tanned skin of the chiseled man who looks like a walking canvas.

"Sexy. Isn't he?" This time it's Finn who admires Jarred, and I have to agree. They both move quickly, tugging at my sweatpants, which are pulled down my legs, leaving me in only my underwear. I feel exposed, but I haven't been more turned on than I am right now.

"Spread those pretty legs, Princess," Finn commands, his voice low, gravelly, skating across my bare flesh. I lie back and obey, giving them what they want. The power that courses through my veins at watching both men freeze, their gazes hooded with desire, is intoxicating.

"Now let's see how you play with that pretty cunt," Jarred murmurs, coaxing, taunting his filthy words, and my hand has a mind of its own as it doesn't fight what's happening. Both men reach for the other, as they watch my fingers dance along the silky material. I tease them for only a couple of seconds before I shift the underwear to the side and dip my fingers inside my pussy.

I'm wet.

I'm dripping wet.

"Fuck," Finn hisses, and Jarred growls. Each man takes either of my legs, and they spread me wider, before they settle between my thighs. Watching them from where I am, each mouth taking turns to lick and lave at my wetness has my toes curling into the mattress. Their faces glisten as they share my arousal, kissing and licking at me, before they tangle their tongues together.

The scent of sex hangs in the air, like a perfume clouding my mind, taking me out of all the darkness that I've lived in for so long. I'm so close to finding my release, to leaping over the edge, and then, Finn and Jarred each insert a finger inside me, pumping deep, before crooking their digits, which sends me soaring high above the clouds. White sparks behind my eyelids as I scream my orgasm.

My palm tingles as I run my fingers over Jarred's short and spiky hair, while Finn's is longer and tangled between the fingers of my other hand. I cry out again and again as they don't relent, sending me over the edge a second time before I finally feel the emptiness of their missing fingers.

"Time to play, Princess." Finn grunts as he shoves his slacks and boxers down his legs, and I'm met with the sight of his thick, silky cock, which has a silver ring through the underside. When Jarred's clothes disappear, I'm shocked that he's got a full Jacob's Ladder piercing. Six silver bars from base to tip glint in the low light of the room.

"Think you can handle us both, Rosebud?" Jarred smirks.

Jarred

PLEASURE.

I've become accustomed to finding it with both men and women. And having two people I care about so deeply right here, it's pure bliss. The fire dancing in Zaria's eyes makes me smile. I know she's a strong woman, but seeing her shift onto her knees, before gripping both Finn and me in those delicate hands is more than I can take. My hips move toward her instinctively.

A hiss of pleasure is expelled from Finn's lips, and then, I watch in awe as her plump lips wrap around his cock. I throb at the sight, seeing her take the man

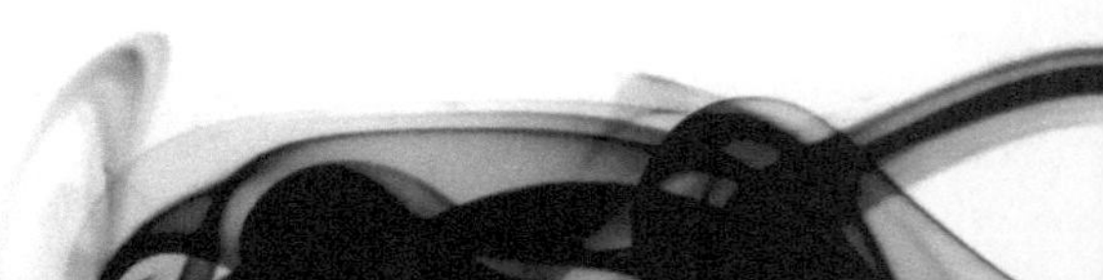

I love into her mouth, and gift him the euphoria I know he enjoys.

Finn's head drops back, his eyes closed, and he tangles the fingers of his left hand with mine, while the right hand fists Zaria's dark hair as the soft choking sounds echo in the room.

He tips his head toward me, his lips finding mine as our tongues dance alongside each other. Erotic, sensual, and utterly delicious. His flavor is one I enjoy, and I can still taste Zaria as we deepen our connection. Then, I feel warmth on my dick, which has a groan rumbling in my chest. Her warm touch, stroking us both to the point of agonizing need.

"Princess," Finn murmurs as he pulls her up to her knees. "You're going to finish us before we've even started," he whispers along her lips before saying, "I think you need me inside you."

I release Finn and grip my dick, which is pulsing for more of both of them as Finn lies back and tugs Zaria to straddle his hips. Her wet heat right at his crotch as I watch in awe. The sight making my arousal leak from my cock as Zaria slides her pussy down Finn's thickness.

The soft moans of the beauty that's taking Finn inside her is like music to my ears. I glance at Finn, who's staring at me and Zaria as I move closer, my lips finding her neck and I bite down on that supple flesh as he drives his dick deep inside her body.

"Fuck," Finn grunts when I reach for his balls, squeezing tightly. I know it makes his cock throb, and when Zaria whimpers, I realize she can feel every pulse. I undo her bra, freeing her perfectly full breasts, and I cup them in my hands. The soft flesh warm against my touch as I tweak her nipples between my thumb and forefinger.

"Jarred," Zaria whimpers, her hand reaching behind her, and she grips my shaft as she strokes me right to the edge and I almost fly off, into the darkness that's slowly consuming me. Bliss takes hold of my muscles, but she eases her fingers from my cock, edging me into oblivion. I shift on the mattress, positioning myself to the side of my two lovers.

Finn's arm snakes around my waist and his hand reaches for my ass, and he tugs at me, needing me closer, while Zaria leans over his body, and for a moment, I'm uncertain as to what they'd doing. My mouth falls open on a groan of euphoria as Finn and Zaria take my cock and on either side of the hard shaft, run their wet, warm lips over me. From base to tip and back again. My balls are tight with the need to come, but I bite my cheek, holding off until the last moment.

I meet Finn's burning gaze before he offers a grin and takes my cock down his throat until the soft gagging sounds echo in the room. Zaria's mouth captures my balls as she twists her body to accommodate me. My hand fists in her hair, holding her steady as she moans against me while Finn's groan vibrates through my dick.

"Fuck, I can't hold off," I grit, leaning over to trail my finger over Zaria's ass, teasing the tight ring of muscle, which has her moaning once more, and I fill Finn's mouth with jet after jet of my release.

It doesn't take long for him to groan, as he swallows me. Zaria's mouth pops off my balls when she cries out her own orgasm from those plump, swollen lips that are wet with saliva. Finn pulls her down and kisses her deeply, teasing the drops of my cum from his tongue to hers.

I don't know how long we settle on the bed, sweaty and sated. With me nestled into Finn's one side and Zaria in the other, we're nothing more than a tangle of limbs.

"Are you okay?" Finn asks, his gaze locked on Zaria.

We both watch her intently. If she didn't want this again, it would make things difficult. And I would walk away, as long as Finn is happy. My love for him knows no bounds, and I would sacrifice my own happiness for his.

"That was amazing," Zaria whispers, her cheeks darkening with a soft red that makes her skin glow. She's such a beautiful woman, strong and sensual. Her curves are luscious, and her tits are perfect. Every part of her should be admired.

"Good," I tell her, pulling her closer as I press my lips to hers. "Next time, I'll be the one making you scream."

"And when you're ready," Finn adds softly as he strokes her hair affectionately. "We'll both take you at the same time." The promise he makes is one that will happen. And the spark in Zaria's eyes makes me think she's looking forward to it.

"I haven't ever…" Her voice trickles from a whisper to nothing. The silence informs us that she may not have been a virgin, but her experience is limited.

"We'll look after you," Finn assures gently. He's not as commanding as I am, and even though I would love to have taken her tonight, I know we have to give her time. Coming to terms with marrying one man is a lot in and of itself, but learning that you'll have two men who want you, it must be overwhelming.

"You did good tonight," I murmur as I rub my thumb along her lip. The naughty little flower sucks my thumb into her mouth, and it has my cock stirring to life once more. I'm almost certain this woman was sent here to kill us both.

I move silently, crawling over Finn to reach the beauty. I tug her legs toward me, and they splay open. Finn shuffles to the side, giving us room. His fingers dart between her thighs, and a whimper tumbles from her lips. He brings both digits up to my mouth, and I suck them clean of her juices. The sharp, sweet and salty flavor bursting on my tongue. It causes me to moan, needing so much more of their arousal. I lean down between Zaria's thighs and I lap at her pussy. The glistening lips are smooth, but her mound has a trimmed triangle of hair. Her legs press against my head as I part her cunt and suck her clit into my mouth. My tongue darts out to dip into her warmth, and the sticky, sweet cum drips onto my lips.

"Fuck," Zaria moans as her hips lift, rising up to ride my face like she is about to explode once more. I don't let up my ministrations, and when I glance up, I find Finn's captured her nipple with his mouth. Her body is merely a plaything for us to enjoy. And fuck, I'm enjoying myself more than ever.

Zaria's one hand pulls at me for more, and I don't deny her anything she craves. I thrust two fingers inside her, crooking them to rub against her sweet spot, which has her crying out my name over and over again. I can't help but smile against her pussy as I feel her pulse around the digits, and I pump them faster and faster. My hand a blur as I bring her right to the edge. I watch her face contort in pleasure, but the moment she's about to leap over the edge, I pull my fingers out and hear a "what the fuck?"

"Just playing with you, Rosebud," I tell her, a smirk curling my lips. I count to ten, watching her narrow her eyes on me. Her frustration is evident, but she'll thank me later. I start again, dipping into her tight heat, finger fucking her until she's about to come then stop again.

"Jarred, you're a bastard," she bites out through clenched teeth, causing Finn to chuckle. "I'm serious." The need is thick in her voice, her nipples are tiny little peaks of want while Finn taunts them slowly, methodically. He knows what he's doing. The man is a fucking expert when it comes to pleasure.

I would know. He's done it to me far too many times in the past. And I know there'll be many more in the future as well.

I drop my head and get back to work on Zaria's tight pussy as I move my hand back and forth. Her walls are tightening around my fingers, sucking them in deeper. I give her another digit, stretching her open, and laving at the wetness that's coating my hand. The scent of her is like a drug, and I inhale her like I'm a dying man in need of sustenance.

This time, as I bring her to the precipice of pleasure, I don't stop. I move my fingers against her G-spot, my tongue flicking over the hardened bundle of nerves, and the moment I feel her flutters of an orgasm, I move faster, thrusting my fingers so deep, taunting that spot inside her. It doesn't take long for her to fly free as her body shudders, her legs tremble, and my name is screamed out like a prayer sent up to heaven. Her juices flow from the sweet spot, and I lap it up happily.

Finn moves toward me, and he brings my mouth to his, our tongues enjoying her release as we mold together like we always do. We were meant to fit together, and Zaria seems to be the glue that will keep all our pieces intact.

Slowly, I pull out of her pussy before I bring my fingers up to Finn's lips and run them along the plump flesh, which has him licking and sucking my digits clean. I'm hard again, but I know we need a moment to relax. But Finn's hand finds my erection, and he strokes me slowly. We glance over at our girl, who's lying against the pillows, satiated, a smile on her face as she watches us.

"Can you…?" she says, but doesn't finish her question. The shy innocence of her smile is obvious, and I have a feeling I know what she wants.

"Can we?" Finn urges. It would be nice to give her another show, but we need her to say the words. She needs to initiate it because this will be the first time, we do anything with her right here, wanting it.

"I'd like to watch you both," she finally whispers. The red on her cheeks darkening with her admission, and I smile. This woman is burrowing her way into my heart. And I can no longer deny I want her.

Finn looks at me, and I offer a nod. He hops off the bed and heads for the bathroom; when he returns, I know he's gotten the lubricant. I move to Zaria once more, this time, I'm kneeling while facing her. I watch as her eyes lock on Finn's movements behind me. The snap of the cap echoes in the room and the cool liquid on my skin sends goosebumps rising in its wake. Finn grips my ass cheeks, before his finger dips between them, and he teases the liquid against my opening.

The pleasure that zings through me when he nudges two fingers inside has my eyes rolling back. I'm lost to the pleasure when he removes both digits and then I feel the blunt head of his cock. With ease, and a gentle push, he inches into me slowly. As I stretch, I can't stop the groan of bliss that rumbles through me.

Zaria leans up on her elbows, and our lips meet in a soft, sensual kiss. Her tongue dances along my mouth, from left to right. She teases me as Finn fucks me. His cock thrusting deeper and deeper with every roll of his hips.

I want to say something, but before I can, Zaria reaches for my hard cock and strokes me with a tight fist. I'd been fucked while jerking off before, but this is so much more. My body zings with electricity, my nerves are sparking with euphoria as Finn grips my hips and fucks me in earnest. We're both close. He thickens inside me, his cock throbbing, ready to blow.

"I'm close," I mumble, as Zaria's hand starts

moving quicker. Everything feels like too much. But it also feels like enough. "Oh fuck," I bite out.

"Jarred, fuck, I'm going to come," Finn tells me seconds later, and then he slams into me, as Zaria's hand brings me to completion and I shoot jet after jet of my release all over her smooth, tanned skin.

I can't find words.

I know I'm falling.

And I know there's no longer a way to stop it.

And I wouldn't want it any other way.

Finn

MY FATHER'S OFFICE IS NOTHING LIKE MINE. His resembles what I would imagine Hell to look like. Dark, dreary, filled with the pain of the souls he's stolen. When I step into the room the next day, I find him behind his desk. When I spoke with Harris earlier, he confirmed that the man who married Mrs. Abadi is, in fact, Nesrin's father.

I'm not sure how my father will react to this, but Marcia is definitely in a tailspin after I told her about finding her ex-husband. But my sister-in-law needs to know that her father is alive, that he's back, and there is no telling what he's up to.

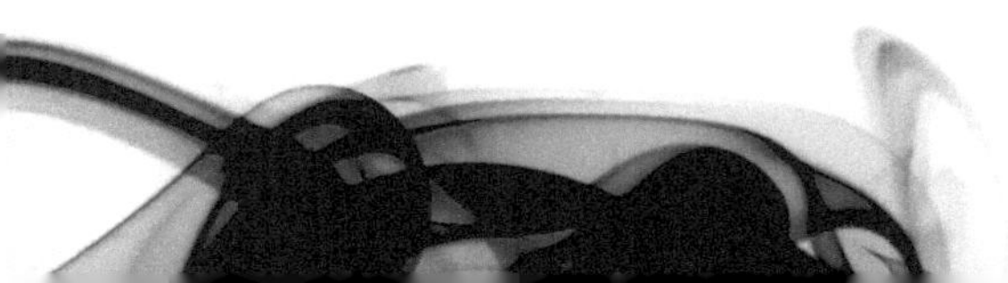

"Finn," my father greets me, as if I'm a member of the staff rather than his son. "I spoke with Marcia last night," he tells me. "She told me your concerns about Isaac," he says, leaning back in his chair and watching me with those deep blue eyes. I'm the only Thorne who has brown eyes, just like my mother. Sometimes I wonder if I'm even Bradford's son.

"Yes," I answer as I take a seat opposite his desk. "He's weaseling his way into this family using the Abadis." I'm almost certain he knows exactly where his ex-wife is. There's no denying my father and his new wife live a public life, which means that Isaac would have seen them either in the press, or on television. Perhaps even at events. But Marcia has never mentioned him before, and my father definitely doesn't seem perturbed by this turn of events.

"We have a lot to discuss," Dad says, his fingers a steeple under his chin, his elbows now leaning on his desk as he moves closer to the large wooden furnishing. "Firstly, your trip to Tynewood was successful," he tells me, something I already know. "I'm proud of you." The four words I have never heard from my father hit me right in the chest.

I'm speechless for a moment as I swallow the praise

like a starving child. "Thank you," is all I manage a short time later. "But there's more—"

"Your boy toy has returned as well," Bradford remarks, the snide comment rankles me, but I don't bite. He's fishing for information about Jarred, but I refuse to play this game with him. My father is intelligent. He's been in the business game for a long while, and he knows how to get people to talk. There's no doubt he sent us to Tynewood, insisted Jarred accompany me so I could find out about his past. But what Dad didn't plan on is the fact that my feelings for Jarred are far stronger than his games.

"Nesrin needs to know," I say, instead of responding to my father's taunt.

He sighs as he tips his head to the side. "Yes," he says, "I agree. And you have a choice to make. I have to let the Elders know what you want to do. Ideally, you'll continue the legacy and take a seat at the table."

It's now or never. I have to negotiate with my father. I'm not new to this, not by a long shot. But when I come up against an expert who knows everything about me like Bradford does, it makes this trickier. "If I do," I start slowly, knowing that I'm going to have to get him on my side. And since I managed to secure the Lancasters as our new client, I don't see why he will refuse me. Unless his promise was a lie. "I need a couple of things in return," I tell him while I keep my eyes on his.

It's never been easy talking to him. Being his son came with limitations, with rules so strict, it was as if we were being raised by an army sergeant.

"And what is it that you'd like, son?" Bradford questions as he narrows his eyes on me. There are wheels turning in his head. He knows what I'm about to ask for. It's clear that my feelings for Jarred have been exposed. Perhaps I was too relaxed about the time I spent with him.

I may be wary of my father knowing. But I'm not at all ashamed. I've always been proud of who I am. Even though I didn't admit it to my family, what held me back was fear of rejection. No kid wants their parents to tell them they're disowned because of who they love.

I've heard the horror stories about that happening. I've seen those tales being recounted, and it set me on a path of hiding my feelings for so long, I don't know how to release them from the cage they're locked in.

After last night with Zaria, seeing just how well she accepted Jarred and me, I realized that I can do this on my own if my father decides to send me away. I'm an adult, and my choices are now my own. But the legacy of the Thorne name comes with shackles.

If he wants to release me from those, I will walk away.

The realization hit me last night as I watched Jarred and Zaria sleep beside me—I'm no longer just a Thorne; I'm someone who is loved unconditionally. Granted, my brothers do love me, but they don't know my secret. Deep down, I don't doubt their affection for me, it's what comes after. The retaliation of our father.

"I want to move out," I tell him finally. "I want Jarred and Zaria with me." The words fall from my lips easily. "I'm in love with Jarred, I have been for a long time, and Zaria is mine. I'm not letting her go."

"So you want to live a life of treachery, hiding this boy—"

"I won't be hiding anything. We will live as three. People do it and I intend to as well. There's nothing wrong with who I want in my life, or who I love. But if you cannot accept this, I will walk away from the Thorne legacy forever." I don't know where my confidence comes from, but I can't live in the shadows anymore.

Listening to Zaria's story last night, knowing what she went through, has given me a new outlook on life. The strength of both Jarred and Zaria has made me want to fight for us. They've gone through so much in their lives and come out on the other side. I want to have that as well.

"You've always been a party animal. You don't think about the consequences of your actions until it's too late," Dad says on a breath. "And that's why I've always been hard on you. But," he says, holding up a finger when I open my mouth to say something. "I see how much you've grown. You mother didn't believe you could sit at the table," he whispers.

"What?" This has my attention. My brows shoot up in surprise that he's talking about her. He's never mentioned our mother before. Not even when we asked about her. When we were kids, he would wave us off as if she meant nothing to him.

"Your mother and I never saw eye to eye when it came to you boys," he tells me. The emotion thick in his voice. I've always seen my father as a cold, hard businessman. But right now, all I see is a father, who wanted to do what was best for his sons. "I wanted her to understand that the company was for you boys. I started it with nothing, and I built it into an empire. Each of you would have a piece of it once I was gone."

"But why did she leave? Why not just sit down and talk it out with you?" I ask, hoping he doesn't shut down. All I ever remember were their fights. The night my mother left, I remember sitting on the stairs that lead out to the entrance hall. Her bags were packed. She didn't have anything more than two suitcases and the clothes on her back. My father offered her money, and she told him she'd rather die on the streets.

Deep down, I knew she was lying because my mother had connections. I recall her friends who lived in houses just as big as ours. She had people she could go to; I was sure of it.

"That night, I told her I chose you for the Silver Sovereign," Dad says, his words dragging me back to the present day. "She didn't want you to be the one because she knew that the society was filled with men who did immoral things to get ahead. They were people she didn't want her sons associating with. But I had to decide who would be my successor."

His words finally sink in as he speaks them slowly. "I grew up thinking you hated me," I tell him honestly. "I was convinced that you thought of me as a mistake. I could never make you see *me*. All these years, you never once told me you loved me, you never said you were proud of me." My throat clogs with the pain and agony of the truth finally hitting me right in my soul. It bypasses my heart, and it slams into me like a wrecking ball.

"That's not at all the reason I did that." Dad shakes his head slowly. The guilt of what I just confessed dances in his eyes. "I needed you to be hard-hearted, to be commanding and dominating. The society will eat you alive if they think you're weak."

"I'm not weak. I never was."

Bradford shakes his head. "No, you weren't. But you are a lot like your mother," he says. "She had a good heart, and I made it ugly with my darkness." I'm not sure what to say so I stay silent. I can't find words to explain the emotions rushing through me. "You are a good person, Finn," he tells me. "And that's why you're able to love two people."

"So, what happens now? There are so many loose ends to tie up." Even though my father has just changed my mindset on my mother completely, there are things we still need to sort out.

He nods. "I'll talk to Marcia. I think we should get Damien and Nesrin out here, so she can decide what she would like to do. And as for the society—"

"I'll do it as long as they accept my lifestyle," I tell my father. "I'm no longer hiding who I am. I can't live like that."

"And what about the girl?"

"Zaria knows." I sigh as I think about last night again. It was perfect. Jarred and I have had a girl together before, a few times in fact. But never like this. Something clicked. It was as if we were meant to all three fit together.

"And she's happy with this arrangement?" My father arches a brow at me. It's rather strange explaining this situation to him, but he needs to know where I stand.

I nod. "Yes. She is and she's happy to go ahead with the wedding once we sort out the reasoning behind the marriage." I recall the paperwork Ares gave Jarred. It's still on my desk where I left it. "I have information from the Lancasters about Mrs. Abadi and why she wanted the union to take place. I want that agreement torn up, nullified and a new one drawn up. She has no legal claim on anything that came before the marriage."

"I want all the paperwork."

"No," I tell my father as I push to my feet. "I want

the original destroyed and I want proof of it. I will not take a vow until that happens. And if there's a problem, she can come to me."

"What if we cancel the wedding completely?" My father suggests. "You can then stay with Jarred, and—"

"No. You wanted us to break up because you knew sending him to Tynewood with me would send us into a tailspin. It worked for a short time, but he was willing to give up his freedom for me. I won't allow that. I'm the Thorne, and I will do what is necessary to ensure the two people I care for are safe."

For a long moment, all I can hear is the thundering of my heart. It rings in my ears as I wait for my father to deny me. He's never given me anything I wanted, and I don't expect this to be any different. The only change is that I am happy to walk out of this house and never look back. And from the look on his face, I can tell he sees it.

"Fine," he murmurs. "A new contract. And you start your initiation to the society, while I make sure that Mrs. Abadi knows we're no longer going through with her original request."

"And you'll talk to the Elders and ensure there are no qualms about Jarred. He was meant to be part of the Gilded Sovereign, but since walking out, there can't be any friction."

A smile dances on my father's lips as he looks me over. "You've grown into a man, Finn," he tells me. "I'm so fucking proud of what you've become." I don't expect anyone to understand what it's like to have your father be proud of you. Some kids don't even have a father figure to speak of, but when Bradford Thorne murmured those words, a strange, calming feeling washed over me. I spent my life rebelling against him. I hated everything he stood for. But now, I'm convinced that he made me this way so I could step into his shoes and those of my grandfather and the ancestors that came before us.

Thorne Haven has always been a fountain of secrets and mysteries. And even though I never believed in the hearsay, I don't doubt my father would have made up things that he saw as a child.

I push into the library and make my way to the safe that's hidden behind a Picasso painting my mother hung there years ago. As a child, I knew it was a cover for something more mysterious, and when I figured out there was a little hidden door behind it, I became obsessed with finding more secrets.

He pushes to his feet and rounds his desk. He

comes to me and for a second, I wonder if he's going to kill me, perhaps stab me in the back for talking back to him, for demanding my own life.

But he doesn't.

He pulls me into his arms and hugs me.

Finn

I CAN'T DESCRIBE THE FEELING THAT BURNS through my veins. I've never been speechless before, but right now, I can't fathom explaining the need to fuck Zaria so deep that she never forgets who owns her. It's more possession than lust. It's more than just a physical need; it's visceral. It's as if she's dug deep into my soul, to the marrow of my bones, and she never wants to leave. And I don't want her to.

Her curves are deliciously shimmery with sweat as she looks down at me. Her pussy tasted like a drug I'll forever crave. I'm addicted, and there is no cure for this woman. At first, I was convinced she

was nothing more than an empty shell, but since learning her pain, I've come to want to devour it.

I guide her down my body, the flavor of her arousal still thick on my tongue, and I never want to taste anything else again but her and Jarred. I glance at him as he settles beside her, and I can't help but smile.

With his help, Zaria takes me in that tight little pussy, which has me hissing approval. The warmth and wetness of her sliding down my shaft forces a groan from my lips. I pull her down over me, the soft curves of her tits against my chest sends hunger racing down my spine.

Jarred moves behind her with the bottle of lube, and I know he's getting her ready for us to both enjoy her body. Zaria looks at me as if I hang the goddamned moon in the sky. Her lips part on a soft whimper as I know Jarred's fingers must have entered her.

"Look at me, Princess," I coo against her lips. My breath fanning over her mouth as she mewls her soft, erotic sounds. "Focus on the pleasure," I coax in a whisper as I lift my hips against her. The way her walls pulse around my dick has me edging closer to release. The tightness of her cunt grips me as I slide in deep, hitting that spot inside her that earns me a yowl of bliss from those plump, wet lips. I'm so close, I could come, but I bite the inside of my cheek to keep from losing all control. "He's getting you ready for me."

"What?" Her mouth is a sexy pout when her eyes roll back, and her focus is on the pleasure and pain that's slowly climbing its way through her. I hold her close, casting a glance over her shoulder to Jarred, who's grinning like the horny bastard he is. We decided it would be easier for her to take me in her ass for the first time. With all his piercings, it would have been a bit of a struggle for Zaria.

"You ready, Rosebud?" he asks as he leans over her back. Zaria nods and whimpers when I thrust into her pussy. We need to move. Jarred helps her up and off my cock, which has my girl mewling. Gently, we have her turn around, her back to me as I scoot against the pillows. And that's when I have to hold onto my shaft as she slowly, inches down with Jarred's help.

The tightness of her ass sucks me in like a fucking vacuum and I shut my eyes so tight to focus on not coming too soon. "Jesus, fuck, that feels like heaven on my dick," I bite out as Zaria groans. It was the same words I ground out when I took Jarred the first time. But Zaria is so fucking tight, I'm lost to the sensations of her body accepting me and gripping me.

I move slowly, not wanting to hurt her. Even though Jarred prepped her tight entrance, it's not something I can do quickly. Once she's taken me all the way in, and I'm fully seated in her ass, I allow her to lean against me, her back to my front. And then I spread her legs on either side of mine. She's open to Jarred, who gazes at her like she's a porcelain doll.

"Are you ready for us both?" I whisper in her ear. "I want to hear your words."

"Yes," Zaria hisses through clenched teeth. Jarred shifts closer, kneeling between our legs with his cock in his grasp. And when he nudges Zaria's pussy, her ass clenches around my dick, sending me into a frenzy of need.

"Fuck, Princess, you have to stop doing that or you're going to make me come," I grit, focused on Jarred as he eases into her slick pussy. The slide of his cock is apparent. I can feel every movement he makes as he inches into her.

"Oh fuck," Zaria cries out. "Fuck, fuck, fuck," she chants, as her head drops back against my shoulder. My hands move to her tits, teasing and taunting her nipples as she takes Jarred's cock, while mine is still balls deep inside her. The tightness of her body is like a vise around me. And I know that Jarred feels the same.

"Fuck is right," Jarred grunts as he finally stills all movement. His hands grip Zaria's hips, while mine cup her tits. His mouth captures a nipple as I hold them up to him. He sucks each bud, causing her body to pulse and tighten. It's as if a flutter of wings are trailing their way up and down my shaft. My body is nothing more than a coiled rope, ready to snap.

"You have to move," Zaria whispers, her body shaking between us. "Please, just move." Her voice is a moan as I lift my hips and Jarred moves back then thrusts toward her. Every minute movement of our bodies sends pleasure radiating through me, my blood runs hot. Desire courses through my veins as a reminder that I'm with two people I love.

The realization hits me right in the chest, and as Jarred's movements hasten, Zaria's body clenches around me, and I can't hold back any longer. I'm lost to the need and the lust, as the physical pleasure tingles its way down my spine.

"I'm so fucking close," I manage to murmur as my

teeth sink into Zaria's shoulder, the softness of her flesh warm against my tongue. Jarred captures her mouth with his as we move faster. Her body pliable between us. "Ours."

"Ours." Jarred mimics my word as we race to the finish. My cock thickens, my release shooting down my spine, my balls emptying into Zaria's tight little ass. I drop one of my hands to tease Zaria's clit, the little hardened nub twisted between my thumb and forefinger. Her muffled scream is a beautiful sound as she comes, tightening around my cock, and Jarred's grunt of his orgasm rumbles through his chest.

We don't move for a long while.

I press a kiss to Zaria's shoulder as Jarred makes the first move as he slips from her body. Zaria is next, and soon enough, I'm cold because their heat is no longer against my flesh. I shift off the bed to help our girl to the bathroom, where both Jarred and I take her to the shower. Once the spray is warm, I step under it, offering my hand to the princess and she gratefully accepts. The fact that she enjoyed what we did is another confirmation that she is ours. She was brought here under the force of her mother's contract, but now, she's here because she wants to be.

"Are you okay?" I ask her as I brush the hair from her face. Jarred joins us, the warm water cascading over us as she nods.

"Yes," Zaria whispers. "That was intense." Her eyes lock on mine for a long moment before she smiles. "You were... I mean..."

"You felt amazing," I tell her because I know she's trying to tell me she's never had a man inside that sexy ass. I feel pride that I own that part of her. I know Jarred will have his turn, but being her future husband, know that she's taken me first.

I've never been in a triad relationship. Fucking a few girls with my best friend isn't the same as loving two people at the same time. I've never been great with emotions. I hide them behind my cocky personality. At least, that's what Damien used to tell me. Cassian agreed. But now, I feel changed.

"Hey," Jarred says, grabbing the back of my neck, capturing Zaria between our naked bodies. "Get out of that head of yours." He's seen me at my worst. When I was convinced that nobody could love me, he walked in and forced me to recognize that I'm worthy of love and a lot more. He made me see that I can be happy.

"I'm right here," I assure him, but Jarred knows me. He can see through my fears. Zaria leans up and presses a kiss to my lips. It's a gentle touch of her mouth against mine as she allows me to savor the moment before breaking the connection.

"I am happy," she tells me, before turning to Jarred and mimicking the kiss with him. "I'm very happy." Her assurance calms me, it quiets my mind. There are so many things we still need to talk through. Tomorrow I go to the Silver Sovereign to complete my initiation. But I have a plan in mind for the three of us once I'm done. I haven't told either of them yet, but once the ceremony is complete, I want Jarred and Zaria to join me in a ritual of our own.

I grab the body wash and squirt some onto the cloth. The foam building as I rub it along Zaria's soft skin. The glistening droplets on her body has me smiling as I think about taking her out into the forest and showing her the game that Creed and Damien came up with all those years ago. I haven't told her about Eloise yet. But I know I need to. Now that she's in my life forever, she needs to know how broken I am. She needs to learn how destructive my thoughts have become over the years.

"Perhaps we should play a little game." My gaze

flicks to Jarred. The glint in his eyes tells me he knows what I'm about to say. "A little game of cat and mouse," I whisper while I lean into Zaria. My lips brush along her ear. "Would you like that, little princess?" I coo the nickname, causing her to shiver.

"What do I have to do?" she whispers, but there's no doubt about what the game would entail. A mouse runs while the cat catches it.

"All you have to do is run," I tell her, my voice low and gravely at the thought of her fear racing through my veins. Even though I lost Eloise to the game, I do it anyway. I run through the woods, and I lose myself in the darkness. It's as if I'm out there looking for a ghost I'll never find.

"Are you sure?" Jarred asks, concern clear in his tone.

I shouldn't do it. But Zaria needs to know what she's getting into. "Yes." My answer is confident. I keep my eyes on Jarred, and after a long moment, he nods. I drop my gaze to Zaria. "Would you like to play?"

"Okay," she responds, but I'm sure it's more to please me than it is to enjoy herself. But I'll make sure she does. Perhaps the Haven guys would like to join. The idea of them catching her before I do has jealousy coursing through my veins like a goddamn poison.

"Then we'll do so tomorrow night," I tell her. When we make it back to the bedroom, I pull Zaria onto the mattress to my left. Jarred slides under the covers on my right. It feels as if I'm a king with two hearts to love. And tomorrow, with the crown in hand, I'll become one of the Sovereign.

As we fall asleep, I realize that it won't be long before I'm married. And before, it would have scared me, but now, I smile as sleep steals me.

Zaria

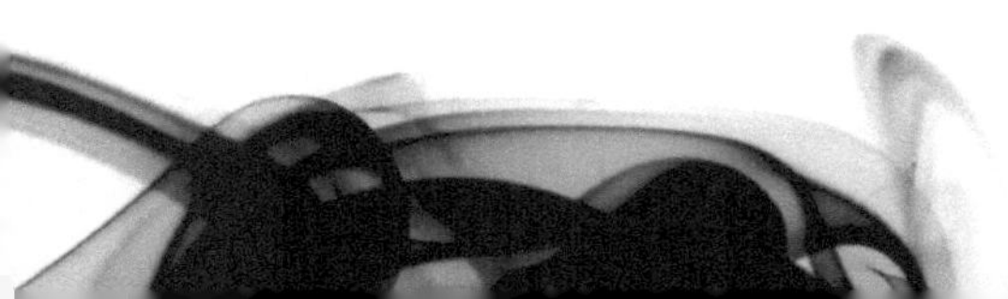

THE FULL MOON IS THE ONLY LIGHT OFFERED TO me to guide me through the thick expanse of trees. I wanted to do this. When Finn told me about the game, I was confident I could race through the darkness and hide from him. The only thing is, he grew up here. He knows every inch of this forest. He's the lion, a hungry hunter, and I'm nothing more than a deer about to be devoured.

Thankfully, the black clothes I chose to wear offer some camouflage in and amongst the trees, which look like black shadows, watching over my demise. My light footsteps don't make a sound as they carry me through the dense forest. I can't hear him or Jarred behind me. My heart thunders against my ribs, reminding me of the life that flows through my veins.

It wasn't too long ago that I wanted to stop that thrumming. I wanted to let go. And as I move through the darkness, I recall that night with clarity.

"Dad," I whisper when I walk into his office. I know it's late. There are times my father will tell me to leave, when he's busy, but he doesn't this time. "Can I talk to you?"

"Of course, Zaria," he says with a smile as he gestures for me to sit. The chair opposite his desk has been something of a haven to me for most of my life. I would come in here when I needed to talk, or just for him to be a presence in his space. Dad had a calming way about him that put me at ease when I was worried. And growing up, that was a lot. "What's on your mind?"

"I was with Mom at the country club today," I start, still unsure of how to bring up what I overheard. I shouldn't have listened to them talking about me. I should have stood up for myself, but I know that anytime I cause a scene, my mother is there, admonishing me. So, instead of telling them they're liars, I listened to them laugh about my father.

"And?" When he urges me on, it's with a smile, but

when he sees the look in my eyes, the grin falters and his expression turns serious. "Zaria, what's wrong?"

"There were a few girls talking about us," I tell him. "I went off to the restroom and when I got back, I overheard them laughing about us. About you." I twist my hands in my lap, my nerves taking over. Perhaps I shouldn't tell him this. Maybe he knows and he'll get angry. But it's bothering me too much for me to let this go.

"Zaria, what happened?" Dad asks again. I'm not sure what emotion is in his voice, but it makes my chest ache. He watches me for a long moment, and my fear that he's going to shout at me for eavesdropping twists in my stomach.

"They said you're not my real father," I finally blurt out, without thinking too much about it.

The silence that follows my revelation is heavy. It makes me feel as if I'm drowning. I used to do that when I was younger. I would be in the bath and slowly sink into the nothingness the water offered. It was always so silent. It confirmed that there are places where quiet exists.

I would seek out the silence because it was the only time that I could truly focus on something other than the noise of press, of social media, of the constant barrage of people wanting my attention. And even those forcing me to look at who I was, a liar. A fake. They called me these things because it's true, I wasn't truly happy. I was only showing them a shiny version of myself.

I became addicted to the feeling of my lungs not being able to pull in air. Just like now. I watch my father's face contort in pain, then guilt flickers in his eyes, and I want to take it back.

But I can't.

I can never swallow those words again.

"I don't want you listening to them," he says to me. "They're just trying to cause trouble in our family," he continues adamantly. "Are you listening to me, Zaria?"

"Yes, Dad," I tell him with a nod. But I can see it in his eyes, he's lying. He's blinking too quickly, and his hands are twisting on the desk. And when he picks up the pen, he swivels it round and round and round. It's hypnotic, watching my father panic. The movements are slow, but they're there. If I were a stranger, I would never know, but I'm his daughter.

"These rumors are nothing more than that." His voice is firmer now, but he's already given it away. The truth was there, in his eyes. My father just lied straight to my face. There are no take backs.

It feels as if my chest cavity has been knocked in. As if the breath from my lungs have been stolen, and I doubt I'll ever be the same again. He's just like everyone else in this world—a liar. Fake.

"I have to finish my homework," I tell him as I push to my feet. I don't wait for him to say anything more before I rush from his office. The pain of the lie slices right through me. It's worse than the taunts I receive on my social media.

It's nothing like the bullying I live with on a daily basis.

My feet carry me through the house and up to my room. In my bathroom, I shut the door and lock it. I need something, anything. Dad won't come up here, not for a while. If I don't show up for dinner, he'll come looking; whereas, my mother wouldn't be bothered if I didn't eat.

I find the bottle I'm looking for. The sleeping tablets my doctor prescribed to help me get some rest when my insomnia kicks in. Flicking the cap open, I fill my palm with the little white pills. These will have to do. I fill a glass of water and take them one by one. I want them to slowly course through my system, and shut down all the horrible thoughts that plague me.

Seeing as I'm not his daughter, my father won't miss me. And my mother, she should never have had children in the first place. Once my hand his empty, and the glass holds no more water, I set it down and go back to my bedroom.

On the bed, I lie back and close my eyes. It won't take long. Soon enough, these little pills will work their magic and I'll be gone. A smile of relief curls on my lips. Knowing that I won't feel the pain, I won't hear or read the vile words *anymore. It all culminates in my heart, and I'm finally at peace.*

Darkness shrouds my vision, and when I try to lift my eyelids, I can't. They're so heavy. Even when I do manage to fight the exhaustion, my room looks blurry. But it's not for long because, soon enough, I'm taken to the darkness where I'll forever lie.

I shake my head of the memory. I'm in the forest, alive and breathing, while Finn and Jarred surround me. They're like wolves, hunting with bloodlust on their minds. Adrenaline shoots through me when I hear a twig snap close by.

As long as I can get to the lake, I'll feel calmer. But the moment I step away from the tree that's been shielding me, an arm wraps around my middle and a hand shoots to my mouth before the scream lodged in my throat can escape.

I'm lifted into the air before the person carrying me makes his way deeper into the darkness. The scent of his cologne, the smell of his skin isn't familiar, and panic sets in. I swing my legs, trying to kick at my attacker, but it's not use.

Baring my teeth, my attempt at biting him only earns me a dark, sordid chuckle that sends fear racing down my spine. His hold on me is so tight, my lungs struggle to work. And when he finally sets me down, he spins me so fast, I'm dizzy. My back hits a tree trunk and that's when I come face to face with the dark mask that's peering down at me.

My mistake is to open my mouth, but nothing comes out. Instead, my kidnapper slides his thumb along my lower lip, dipping it onto my tongue and pressing down hard. He leans in, his body pressing mine against the trunk, causing it to bite into my back.

I bite down on his thumb, and another dark rumble vibrates through his chest. Either he can't feel the pain, or he enjoys it. My blood turns to ice when I look up into eyes that hold me hostage.

"Now what do we have here?" he coos into the mask before he tugs at the material and I'm met with a man who's breathtakingly handsome, but there's a sadistic glint in his eye. "I didn't think I'd find something so delicious when I came out for a run tonight."

He tugs his thumb from my mouth, and I let out a scream while praying Finn and Jarred hear me. "Do you always run with a mask?"

"Only when I'm hoping to find something delicious

to satiate my hunger," he says darkly, while his eyes trail over my face then to my lips, where they linger for a moment too long. There's no doubt this man must be Creed Haven.

"Let me go, please," I say, my voice breaking as fear takes hold of me. I know he's known Finn for most of his life, but Finn never said they were friends.

"Why would I do that?" he questions, while tipping his head to the side.

"I'm Finn's fiancée," I blurt out, praying with all I have that he considers the man I'm going to marry somewhat of a friend. Even if they don't like each other; hopefully, there is something human in him.

I'm about to make my case when I hear my salvation. "Creed," Finn's voice cuts through the darkness, and he appears like a mirage in the desert. "Leave her." There's a moment in time when I think Creed will refuse Finn. I see the war etched on his face. He wants me, but he knows that it won't end here. Finn will kill him. Of that I have no doubt. The two words linger in the air long after Finn spoke them.

I hold my breath.

My pulse spikes when Creed runs his index finger over my lips once more before he pushes away from the tree. He steps back and turns to Finn. "Good to see you again, Thorne," he says as he nears Finn. "You've got yourself quite a firecracker there."

"I do. She's mine." The possession in Finn's voice is nothing short of caveman-like. Both men stare each other down. Jarred stands to the side, but he doesn't come to me. It doesn't take long before Creed offers a wave and races into the darkness, his form disappearing quickly.

"So that's Creed Haven," I mumble, trying to break the tension.

"Did he hurt you?" Finn is on me in seconds. The fear that flickers in his stare is heartwarming.

"No," I tell him. "I'm fine. He scared me a little, but other than that, he didn't do anything else." *Thankfully,* I add silently.

Both men tangle their fingers with mine. "I'm taking you home," Finn says.

"I think you need a shower, and we can calm you down after that," Jarred promises, and my body reacts as my pussy pulses with the need to be filled.

"It was fun," I add, hoping to lighten the mood. Even in the dark, I can tell Finn and Jarred are tense. I'm sure it's because of Creed. They clearly don't trust him, but thankfully, they seem to be on speaking terms. If they weren't, tonight could have gone a lot differently.

"There's more fun to be had inside," Jarred says with a wink. But Finn is silent. He doesn't say anything else as we make our way into the house and to Finn's bedroom. It's in the shower that he pins me against the wall and grips my neck.

His long fingers wrap around the column, squeezing until I can no longer pull in air. His mouth is on mine the next second, and his tongue licks at my lips, his teeth grazing the flesh as he bites down hard on my lower lip. The sting of pain skitters through me, zapping every nerve-ending all the way down to my pussy, causing my clit to throb with desire.

And, once again, he makes the promise in a deep, husky tone, murmuring against my mouth, "Ours."

Finn

WHEN I REACH THE KITCHEN, I FIND DAMIEN and Cassian sitting at the table, both with a mug of coffee in front of them. The girls aren't here yet, but they'll be down shortly, and I needed to talk to my brothers in private.

"What's up?" I keep my voice light, but there is tension coursing through my veins.

"You're chipper for someone about to join a secret cult that Dad never told us about," Damien says, sitting back in his chair. He hasn't aged at all. He still looks like he's in his twenties. But there is a cool calmness that he has always exuded, and it's present

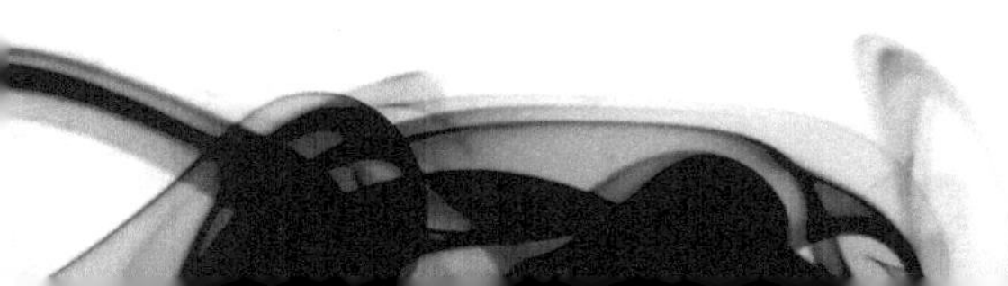

now.

"What can I say? I'm always game for anything," I tell them with a grin, putting on the mask I've worn around them for years. For all my life, if I'm being honest.

"How is your fiancée?" Cassian questions, his teal eyes on me. He's always been the quiet, silent type. One who observes rather than speaks.

"She's fine." I know I can't put this off any longer, so I slip into the chair beside Damien and flick my gaze between my brothers. "But there is something I needed to talk to you both about," I say, my voice tight with anxiety.

"Yeah?"

"I hope this has nothing to do with you leaving Thorne Haven. Dad mentioned that—"

"This is personal," I interrupt Damien. "I… There's been something I have kept from you both, and it's time you knew."

"Oh god," Cassian groans, leaning back in his chair and arching a dark brow. "You haven't fantasized about one of our women, have you?" For a second, I think he's serious, but then he laughs. "I'm kidding. What's up?"

I sigh, while rolling my eyes. Since he's been with

Kalyn, he's been a different man. "Well," I start slowly, "I've been seeing someone."

"Okay?" Damien's tone is filled with confusion.

"It's been going on for a while, and I haven't told anyone because I was afraid." Emotion clogs my throat, the lump suffocating me.

"Dude, spit it out," Cass tells me.

"I'm... I'm bisexual," I finally spit the confession out into the room. "I'm bisexual." I don't know why I say it again, but I do. And it feels good.

"Is that it?" Cass's question has me snapping a nervous gaze to him. "Brother," he says, "I don't care who you love, fuck, or want, you're still a Thorne. You're my brother."

"What he said," Damien tells me. "You're blood. Nothing you say or do can change that. We are always here for you."

"I was scared," I admit quietly. "I didn't think further than what I was feeling. It was difficult for me to admit it to myself, let alone you two."

Cass smiles. "Is it Jarred?" he asks, the knowing glint in his eyes tells me even though I've tried to be discreet, it's not worked that well.

I nod. "It is. I mean, it started innocently, but," I say, swallowing the lump of emotion that's threatening to choke me. "He's a good person. I fell so quickly; I didn't even realize it was happening."

"Or, you did know, you just couldn't stop it," Damien tells me with a supportive hand on my shoulder. "I get that," he whispers, and I realize he's talking about how he fell for Nesrin. It was monumental, it shook him to his core, just like Jarred stole my heart.

"All I wanted was to be me."

"And he allowed you to be," Cassian confirms as he watches me. His relationship was much the same with Kalyn. I had never seen my brother more at ease than when he was with her.

Once again, I'm surprised by how much they understand me. We've always been close, but we haven't allowed ourselves to show emotions, especially soppy shit like this. But knowing they love me no matter what, that lessens my anxiety when it comes to my future.

"I just wasn't sure how to even tell you," I finally say. "The fear held me back from so many things. From living my truth. My life. I didn't want to admit it," I confess as my heart thuds against my ribs.

"I understand that fully. It's difficult coming to terms with life in general, but to have emotions changing you and everyone around you, it can't be easy to admit." Damien's words settle my pulse, and I can breathe again.

"You know something brother," Cassian adds, "nothing in life is easy, but we will always be here for you. No matter what."

"I thought—"

"You're still Finn. Your sexual orientation doesn't change that," Damien assures me, and he pushes to his feet, before pulling me into a hug. The anxiety and tension that had coiled in my gut eases and I can breathe again.

"Don't ever feel like you can't tell us anything," Cassian says as he joins us, and that's how the girls find us moments later. Hugging in the kitchen, while my eyes burn with salty emotion.

Initiation.

A fucking crowning ceremony.

All four men are here from Tynewood—Ares, Etienne, Philipe, and Tarian. They're suited in black, with crisp white shirts and black ties. It's as if we're at a funeral. But this is my choice. I wanted to do it.

It's quiet as we each pull the raven-hued capes

over our suits, and the hoods over our heads. Silence hangs heavily around the dark cave-like structure that resides under the Thorne Haven cathedral. I've always seen the building, but never been inside.

Our family aren't religious in any way, so growing up, we never attended mass, so I haven't stepped foot inside, let alone beneath the church before. When my father made his way to the back of the grounds and took the small stone steps beneath the earth, I wasn't sure where we were going.

But the carved-out cavern is enormous. There is a concrete table that has a crown engraved into it, while the chairs, which were taken from the church, surround the structure.

"It's time," my father murmurs, and two of the hooded figures I noticed when we walked in go around the space lighting candles. The circle is illuminated with a soft yellow glow.

The older gentleman, who came along with Ares, steps forward and sets a black leather doctor's bag on the table. We watch as he removes the tattoo gun from the bag and sets it up.

I've never seen anything like it before.

"Sit," he orders, his dark eyes on mine.

I don't argue. Slipping into one of the chairs, he

waits for me to shrug off my shirt, then goes to work on my left shoulder. The symbol of the Sovereign is a crown, and I know that it will be with me forever.

"You will be a Sovereign," Ares says as the older man works. "This means you abide by the laws that rule us, and you do as we say."

"The only way you leave us," Philipe murmurs, then Etienne chimes in, "is in death."

"Vow your allegiance," Tarian commands. For a young guy, possibly in his early twenties, there's a darkness in him. Tarian Calvert is the fourth of the Gilded Sovereign. While Etienne Durand is the third. They make up the head of the society in Tynewood. Thankfully, I like them all.

I don't know what I would've done if they were bastards.

"I swear my allegiance."

"And I swear mine," Jarred suddenly says, stepping forward as he looks between us. "If he's a Sovereign for life, I take my rightful place at the table."

"Are you sure?" I ask, knowing this wasn't something he wanted in the past.

He nods. "I do." Then he looks at the men who hold the decision.

"Then we accept your choice," Ares agrees. "They

both join the Sovereign," he announces. "Please, Jarred, vow your allegiance."

"I swear my allegiance," Jarred confirms confidently before he settles in beside me. And I know that no matter what happens, we will always be together.

From this day forward, I'll have a connection to law enforcement, to politicians, to money that I couldn't spend in my lifetime. The Society rules over the country, but also different countries around the world. We can go anywhere, do anything we want, and they'll watch over us.

Yes, we may have to work on underhanded deals at times, but we knew that. The Gilded Sovereign have mostly cleaned up their act, but there are still times we'll come face to face with criminals.

At first, I thought I couldn't do it, but knowing that I'll be free, be able to travel with my wife and partner, I know I've made the right choice. I never wanted to be a businessman. I wasn't cut out for it, and this brings me the freedom I've always craved.

I smile as I take my oath.

One vow today, and another to take when I marry Zaria.

Finn

THE LIVING ROOM IS A FLURRY OF ACTIVITY AS I walk in and find Nesrin and Damien with Marcia. Dad is at the bar, pouring himself a drink. With Jarred busy, I only have Zaria with me. The blue eyes of my eldest brother lock on mine and I know he knows about Nesrin's father. The look he gives me is one of thanks, relief almost.

Nesrin, on the other hand, looks like she's about to be sick. I don't blame her. Finding out your father is now married to a woman who's going to be part of your extended family can't be easy.

"Finn," she greets with a smile.

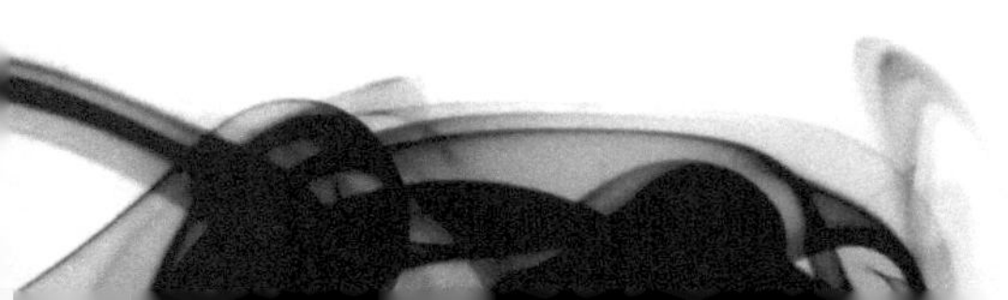

"Hey, sis." I pull her into a hug and hold her for as long as she needs. When she finally steps back, I say, "This is Zaria." The two girls smile, and it's then that I notice it. Something about them both is so familiar, it makes my chest tighten. I flick my gaze at Damien whose eyes widen for a second before his wife slips into the crook of his arm.

He saw it too.

Just then, the living room doors open and Zaria's mother walks in. Her back straight, head held high. There's a look of calm on her face, but the moment I step out of the way of my brother and his wife, Mrs. Abadi's face falls. Not only that, it's the man behind her who looks like he's walked into the lion's den.

Amira Abadi can't stop this any more than he can. Isaac stops dead, his gaze flicking over to the daughter he walked away from all those years ago. He was good to her from what she's told us, but then, one day, he just walked out and never returned. And now, he's here, married to another woman.

"Nesrin?" His voice is faraway, pained almost. "Marcia?" The confusion written on his face tells me he didn't realize his ex-wife would be here, let alone his daughter. It's the smile on Amira's face that confirms my thoughts are going in the right direction. She knew. She's always known.

"I think perhaps we should let father and daughter speak," she announces happily, as if her plan has finally come together. But when Zaria steps forward, she stares at Isaac. And there is no doubt in my mind that everyone can see it: the resemblance between father and his daughters. His genes must be strong because with them all in the same room, no lie can be told.

"You're...." Zaria's voice cracks, then she looks at her mother, whose smile falters. "Did you do this?"

I take Zaria's hand, and she lets me. But I don't stop her.

"He's my father. Isn't he?"

"What?" Marcia's voice cuts through the silence.

The bomb has been dropped and it's about to explode through Thorne Manor. Growing up here, there's never been a dull moment. Ever. And this is no different. I watch as realization dawns on everyone's faces. Damien's eyes lock on mine, and he nods. We need to get the girls alone with their father. Who knew I'd be marrying my stepsister's—who is also my sister in law—half-sister. God, this fucking town only gets more sordid by the day.

"Perhaps we should let Nesrin and Zaria talk to

Isaac," I suggest, and thankfully, Dad drags Marcia from the room who's shooting daggers at Isaac. It means that he cheated on his wife more than once throughout their marriage.

I press a kiss to Zaria's temple before I lead her mother from the room. "You should give them some space," I tell her, before she tries to fight me on it. I'm in no mood for this, so she won't get away. All I can do is hope my girl comes out of this unscathed.

Zaria

Shock.

It's the only thing that can even remotely describe how I'm feeling right now. Nesrin steps up beside me. It's as if we're going to war alongside each other, and I have to admit, it feels good not being alone. I know Finn left because I needed to do this on my own. But coming face to face with a father I never knew is daunting. He doesn't move as he takes us both in.

"Girls—"

"No," Nesrin says, fire lacing her words, "you don't get to look nervous, or guilty, or anything other than shamed." Her voice is so strong, so confident, for a moment, I'm not sure I can match her strength. She knew him as a child; I never did. I had a good father, but he wasn't my blood. Or I wasn't his. And that hurts more than I thought it would.

"I can't believe you couldn't come and see me," I tell him after a moment of silence. "You were there, at my birthday party." The accusation causes him to flinch. "I saw you talking to Mom."

He nods slowly. "I did. I wanted to tell you," he admits. "But the moment she saw me, she told me to leave. We had an argument and even though I wanted you to know who I was, your mother was defiant. She convinced me to leave."

"And you listened to her?"

He snaps his gaze to mine. "I did. She told me she didn't want you upset on your birthday," he murmurs. "And I didn't want it either. You were so beautiful—"

"You just walked out," I grit, fighting back the tears as I recall standing beside the man who I called father, watching my real dad walk out and leave, never looking back at me.

It shouldn't hurt so much, but it does. Nesrin's hand finds mine, and we tangle our fingers together. She's tougher than I am, because I feel like breaking down, like falling to my knees and begging him to stay. So hungry for the affection of my real father, I can't stop the lone tear from trickling down my cheek.

"I left two beautiful daughters because I couldn't be a father."

"You couldn't be a father because you're a lying cheat," Nesrin throws back easily. "You did it to my mother, and you did it to Zaria's father."

He can't deny it. There's truth behind her words, and I can't bring myself to speak because the lump in my throat thickens, choking me silent.

"You spent a few years with me, but I woke up one day and you were gone." This time, she releases me and steps closer to the father we share. "I hate you, for breaking my heart, for shattering my dreams, and for what you did to me, mom, and Mallory. And most of all, what you did to Zaria."

His gaze lifts to mine. "I'm sorry."

"That doesn't fix anything," I tell him after I've swallowed back my pain. "It doesn't fix the heartbreak or years of lies." I tip my chin up, trying to exude confidence I don't really feel. But I've spent my whole life faking happiness, so this time, I can fake the fire in my veins. "I spent my life portraying the perfect daughter," I say. "But it was all a lie. You forced me to lie to everyone, even myself. For so long, I thought something was wrong with me, but now I see it has nothing to do with me."

"I'm not a good person," Isaac says then. "I never have been. I tried for so long to do the right thing by Nesrin, but I knew you were out there. I left her, because I couldn't give one of my daughters something the other didn't have. Even though you had your dad, it wasn't me."

"So, instead of fixing it, you broke us both?" The incredulous tone of my voice makes him flinch. "I can't believe someone who claims to have thought of everyone but himself can ever be sorry. There's nothing that can make this okay. Why did you marry my mother?"

The question that's been dancing around in my mind for the past week has him staring at me with wide eyes. I remembered his face from the party, but now that I know who he is, it doesn't make sense that he would marry her now.

"There are things that–"

"Don't give us bullshit excuses," Nesrin interrupts. "Why did you marry Amira? Why did you suddenly come back into Zaria's life?"

"It can't be because you love my mother," I say suddenly. If he did, he wouldn't have given up on her. Clearly, they had a relationship, that's why I'm here. But it doesn't make sense. If he truly felt anything for her, he would have fought for her, asked her to leave Dad.

Unless.

"You wanted the one thing my father had that you couldn't get," I murmur as the realization hits me. It had nothing to do with my mother. She sent me away, not realizing the man who claimed to want her, didn't actually feel anything for her.

"He was a bastard all his life," Isaac admits in a confident tone as the truth finally hits me right in the chest. "I hated him and he hated me."

"It was my father's company," I say. "He built it from the ground up and you wanted to walk in and claim it as your own once the ink had dried on the marriage certificate."

The door bursts open and my mother strolls in as if she owns the house. "This is enough," she sneers angrily, her gaze bearing down on Nesrin. But it's not my half-sister my mother should worry about.

"You know he only wants Dad's company, right?"

Her gaze snaps to mine. But the cold, aloofness she regards me with is one of a stranger. The woman may not have been warm and maternal with me, but she was never so ice cold I didn't recognize her.

"I think you and your friend should give this up now," she tells me. "Your father was a good man, but he's dead." The callousness in her voice makes me flinch. The same man who gave her anything and everything she wanted is clearly nothing more to her than a forgotten memory. Just like me.

"How can you be such a monster?" I whisper, shock thick in my voice. The tears I'd been holding back burn my lashes, and as much as I try to fend them off, when I blink, they fall.

"Your father was a ticket to a better life," Mom says to me. "He gave me what I needed at the time. If it wasn't for him, you would have grown up in a one-bedroom apartment in a shitty neighborhood. You would never have had the education and life that he gave you. Is that what you wanted?"

"I wanted a mother who gave a shit," I bite out, anger taking over my frustration and hurt. My chest tightens when the woman I grew up desperately wanting approval from smiles. There is no love between us. I thought if I did this for her, if I married Finn, she'd finally care about me. Or show an ounce of love. But as she looks at me, I realize there's nothing left to say.

"I made sure your life was filled with everything you ever wanted. I've even given you a future that will ensure you'll never want for anything again." It was all one master plan to get rid of me, so she could live her life with the bastard who was nothing more than a sperm donor. "You can now live a life without worrying about me."

"Then consider me nothing to you," I tell her. "But I'm pretty sure you already do."

I thought it would hurt more. All my life, I thought that if I ever lost my mother, it would break me, but as I watch the relief wash over her expression at my words, I realize I'm stronger now. I lost my father, which hurt me more than anything I could have imagined, but with her, I no longer feel anything. I'm numb.

"You'll rethink that," she tells me. "Consider this your final offer," she says as she slips a folder onto the coffee table and turns for the door. Isaac doesn't follow immediately. His gaze flicking between

Nesrin and me.

"I want—"

"You know where the door is," Nesrin says before he can get another word out.

When he looks at me, I feel nothing. There's a plea in his gaze, as if he wants me to ask him to stay. But I can't. I don't want to.

"You heard her," I tell him as I take Nesrin's hand. We may not have known each other growing up, but we sure as hell have found our family now.

"I love you both," he tells us. "I always have. And if you ever need me..." He allows the words to turn to silence. And then he sets his business card on top of the folder before he follows his wife out the door.

Nesrin pulls me into a hug the moment we're alone. I don't know her. It's the first time I've ever met her, and yet, I feel as if we're kindred spirits. I hold onto her for a long while before stepping back.

"Do you want to see what this is?" she asks, picking up the folder.

Shaking my head, I say, "Not yet."

"Is it safe to come in?" Damien enters the room, making a beeline for his wife. Finn follows soon after, and his arm is around me, warming me with his body heat. I can't stop thinking about the fact that I now have a sister.

Two girls who grew up so differently, and yet, here we are.

And even though my mother has left me here, I know I'll survive.

I'm strong.

I'm no longer an Abadi; I'm a Thorne.

Zaria

MY HEART HURTS FOR EVERYTHING I HAVE lost. Even though I'm done with my mother and her diabolical plans for her future, I can't believe she would do something like this to me.

She hid my real father from me for so long. And now that I know the truth, all I want is lose myself in the familiar numbness. I hate her. I don't want her near me. Ever again.

Instead of telling me the truth, she sent me off to get married to gain more power, when she already had the world at her feet. The rooftop of Thorne Manor is exquisite. I recall Finn telling me that they

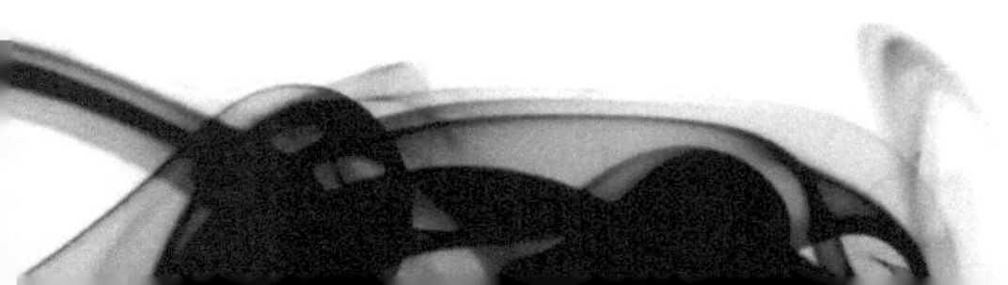

297

furnished it so that if you needed a place to hide, you would always be able to come up here and be alone. But now that I'm here, all I can think about is the darkness that used to swell like a tumor in my brain. It would take over until all I could envision was ending my life. With every taunt and tease the kids used to throw at me, I longed for total silence.

Knowing my father lied to me broke me. He was my hero and then he turned into my villain. It was a lot to take in, especially when I was already dealing with so many dark thoughts that took a hold of me. The bullying was almost as bad as knowing the man I looked up to wasn't truthful to me.

"A pretty girl like you shouldn't be alone." The voice comes from behind me, but I don't turn to face him. I can't look into those silver eyes. Jarred has a way of digging into the darkness and finding solace there. They bore into me whenever he looks at me, but I can't allow anyone else to delve into my broken pieces.

"Please leave me alone," I beg with my back still turned to him. There's heat behind me, a sudden rush of warmth in the nippy air. When I feel a second body step up to me, I realize that Finn is here too because his cologne envelops me in a blanket of safety.

"I hope you weren't thinking of throwing yourself from the roof," Finn remarks nonchalantly, as if he were talking about the weather. He has this way about him, a cool demeanor that could come across as uncaring, but he speaks with his eyes. Those almost black orbs hold so much affection, so many emotions; they're like a fountain of love.

I lean into them instinctively. Memories of our last encounter flood my mind, washing away the thoughts of pain just for a moment. If I can lose myself in them, in the pleasure they bring me, then perhaps I can overcome this need to leave. I wanted to run, to walk away from my obligations, but that would mean leaving Finn and Jarred, and I can't do that. Not now, not ever.

Even though we haven't said the word *love* yet, I can't deny that all my heart wants and craves is them. I didn't think I was capable of feeling something for a man I was practically sold to, but I've come to care about Finn. And I've grown attached to Jarred. My life has taken a turn, and it is the best thing that's happened to me in a long time.

Finn's hand tangles in mine, while Jarred trails his fingertips over my shoulder. It moves down, over my breast, taunting my nipple with a light brush before he grips my hip. Finn spins me around, while Jarred's hand follows my torso with his heated touch. The moment I face them, I'm breathless.

"You're not leaving us," Finn informs me.

"I didn't think you wanted me here in the first place," I tell him, remembering how our relationship started. We've come a long way since then, but there are moments, I wonder if what we have is only physical.

Finn stares at me for a long while before he says, "I didn't want you here. But I don't know why I can't let you go." There is honesty shining in his eyes as he looks at me. "You deserve someone who can give you everything you need," he tells me. "And I want to be that someone. We want to be that for you."

I glance at Jarred, who's watching me. Now that the truth about my mother has been revealed, and the contract torn up, I don't have to marry Finn. I could walk away. I have my freedom for the first time in a long while. I've deleted my social media accounts to start fresh.

I no longer see myself as Zaria Abadi, but as Zaria Thorne. It may be my mind churning out unrealistic thoughts, but I do want Finn. And I want Jarred just as much. That brings a small smile to my face.

"I want this," I whisper, flicking my gaze to both men. "I didn't think I would. It's not the type of person I am, but I feel as if I'm safe here. I feel like myself for the first time in so long. I can be honest with my feelings, show emotion, I can be real."

Finn captures my cheek in his palm. The touch is gentle, affectionate. "You are real," he insists. "We will never ask you to be anything other than yourself. I believe that is what a relationship should offer. But you also should be comfortable in your thoughts and feelings. You should have the confidence to love yourself before loving someone else."

"And if you ever feel as if you're going to step outside the path and lose yourself, then we'll bring you back," Jarred promises with a smile on his handsome face. I can't deny they make me happy. I want to see how we can grow, how we can turn our three hearts into one.

"Then show me," I whisper, my voice thick with the need to be with them again. This time, I want more than they taunted me with the first time. "I want everything. I want you both."

Finn takes my hand and leads me back into the warmth of the manor. Jarred is at my back. With the darkness left behind, I step into the light of Finn's bedroom.

It's the first time I have been in here, and I find my gaze flicking around, taking everything in. The room is decked in soft browns and gold. It's a rich color palette that shimmers with the golden light coming from the nightstand. The glowing bulb offers the space a warmth that no other room in this house has.

Finn stops with me beside the mattress. He tugs at my top, which comes off easily as I allow him to undress me. Once I'm in my underwear, the deep groans of both men skitter across my skin.

Jarred steps up to me, gripping my chin in his thumb and forefinger, and he pulls me closer for a kiss. The softness of his mouth against mine, the heat of his wet tongue dancing along my own makes my thighs squeeze together.

When he breaks the short-lived kiss, I turn to Finn, who has discarded his shirt. The smooth planes of his chest shimmer with the soft golden glow from the light.

"If you want this, show us," Finn orders. The deep gravel in his voice makes me shiver. A smile dances on my lips as I drop to my knees before both men.

The need inside me coiling like a serpent as I find my body responding to the lust coursing through my veins.

Jarred's shirt falls to the ground in a soft whoosh. I start with Finn's jeans, undoing the zipper with a loud hiss, before I turn to Jarred and mimic my actions. Once they're both only in their boxers, I tease my hands over their thick bulges, and my pussy pulses with the desire to be filled.

I tug at their underwear. Both cocks jut out, and I grab them gently at first, then I stroke along the shaft, my tongue darting out to tease the weeping tip of both men. Salty flavor bursts on my tongue, and I savor the desire coating my tastebuds.

"Fuck," Finn curses with a growl as I take him into my mouth, flicking my tongue over the piercing. His hand tangles in my hair, and I allow him to thrust deep until I choke. The feeling of submitting to his need causes my pussy to pulse once more. I want so much more from him. "You like that don't you?" He grunts as I squirm on my knees. Lifting my eyes to lock on his, I can't respond, but I hope he can see the desire burning in my eyes.

"Such a good girl," Jarred coaxes as my hand strokes his cock, his thickness feels smooth against my fingers, and the metal bars tickling over my palm. Each time I reach the base, I slide back up. When Finn pulls from my mouth, spit trailing from my lips to the tip of his cock, he takes the shaft and coats it with my saliva.

I don't wait for the order, before I'm taking Jarred into my mouth, just like I did Finn. His hips roll, thrusting toward my face as he fucks my mouth. The choking sounds echo in the room. Power burns in my veins as I look up at Jarred, taking in his inked skin which is a beautiful canvas.

His cock thick and violently fucking my throat, coating it in more saliva as he smirks down at me.

"I think it's time our princess took us both again," Finn murmurs as he moves away from me. He crawls onto the bed, before lying back and crooking his finger toward Jarred and me. The cock in my mouth pops out, and I'm pulled to my feet. My knees almost give out, I'm so turned on. My panties are soaked with the arousal dripping from me.

Behind me, Jarred drops to a crouch and tugs at my underwear. I step out of them and turn to regard him from over my shoulder. He lifts his hand, the material clutched in his fist as he brings it to his nose.

"You smell just like a blossoming rose," he whispers as he inhales my scent, causing my cheeks to heat in embarrassment. We've already done so much together, but seeing him smell my panties is on another level. He shocks me then when his tongue darts out, and he laves at the wet material. A groan of satisfaction rumbles in his chest.

"Jarred," I gasp in surprise. I didn't think seeing someone lick my panties would turn me on, but it does. More than I care to admit.

"Just getting a taste, Rosebud," he tells me with a wink before he helps me onto the bed. It doesn't take long for me to straddle Finn. But the moment my leg swings over his torso, his hands grip my ass and he pulls me to his mouth.

"Time for me to have a taste as well," he tells me before his tongue laps at my wet core. The sensation spirals through me, causing my body to shiver as pleasure zips down my spine. He doesn't stop. And when Jarred joins us, he doesn't touch me, but his mouth is on Finn, causing the man eating me out to growl, sending waves of vibrations through my pussy. My clit throbs with need while Finn devours my wet flesh.

My legs shake as my eyes fall closed. I don't think

I can stay like this for much longer. Finn dips two fingers inside me while he sucks my clit, then bites down hard, sending electric currents through my nervous system until I'm screaming his name.

He doesn't stop, though. My hips roll as I ride his fingers, his face wet and slick with my juices as he finger-fucks me into oblivion. Fireworks sparks at the back of my eyelids while my mouth falls open on another mewl of bliss. My body feels alive.

The gagging sound of Jarred taking Finn's cock sends me over the edge while Finn teases that spot deep inside me and I'm flying. Darkness consumes me, but this time, it's not scary, it's filled with pure, hot, and feral lust. I'm overtaken by it. The need to have both men inside me, the only thing I can think of.

"I... I...I need..." I can't form words as my body shudders from euphoria. It's like being high, or drunk. You have no control over your actions. How you feel is nothing you can hold onto. It's as if a tornado is ripping through every inch of you and all you can do is lie back and let it destroy you.

"We know what you need, Rosebud," Jarred murmurs behind me as his hands grip my ass, spreading me open to his gaze. His fingers delve into my wetness, coating his finger before he teases the tight entrance that causes me to whimper. He's right, I want them now, claiming me as theirs.

And I know that once they do, I'll never be able to leave them.

Ever.

Zaria

THE WHITE DRESS DOESN'T FEEL REAL. EVEN AS I stare at myself in the mirror, I can't believe I'm looking at my reflection. After spending my life knowing that my future would be planned out for me, I never allowed myself to think of a *dream* wedding. I was shocked when dad said he wanted me to marry Finn.

"You look beautiful," Nesrin says as she enters the room. I've asked her to stand by my side as my matron of honor. "The dress is perfect." She takes me in for a moment, from head to toe. My shoes have offered me some height, which puts us face to face.

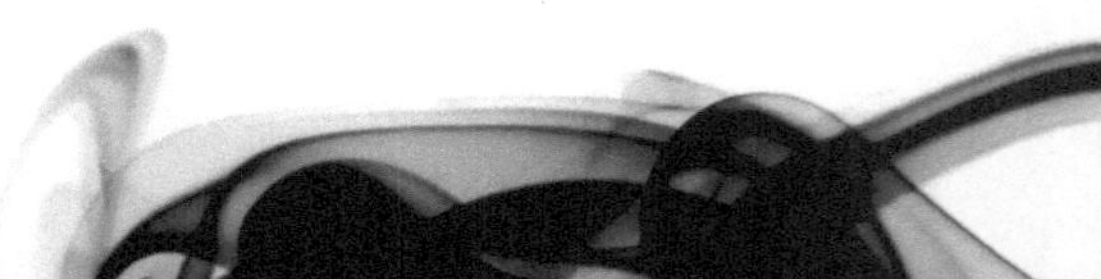

I still can't believe this girl is my sister. Well, half-sister, but that still counts. I thought I had lost all my family: first, my father, then my mother, but now, I've gained so much more.

"Thank you," I whisper, emotions holding me hostage. I opted to not wear a veil, so my hair has been styled in loose waves down my back. My makeup is a mix of natural with a smoky eye and a soft pink lip shade. "I wasn't sure if the shoes would go with the gown, but besides the nerves, I'm happy with how it looks."

"Nerves are normal," Nesrin assures me. "I remember when I got married. I was a mess." The way she holds my arm and offers it a squeeze calms me down somewhat. But there's still a twist in my stomach along with the flurry of butterflies that can't seem to leave me alone.

"I can only imagine," I tell her. "I mean, our guest list is far smaller than you had."

"It is. I think we had about four hundred people, and most of them I didn't know," she tells me. "They were colleagues and staff from Thorne Industries. To be honest, it would have been nicer if we had a more intimate setting. This is perfect." She gestures around the room, and I know that outside, we have about fifty guests waiting.

I let out a long breath as I glance at myself in the mirror. It's now or never. But I know that there is no way I can walk away from this. I'm in it. There are two men outside that I love more than I wanted to admit. At first, I found it difficult to even consider having both men in my life. But now, after the handful of months, I can't think of not having them right next to me.

"Are you ready?" Nesrin asks, her smile is infectious, and I can't help but return it.

Nodding slowly as I run my hands down my dress, I turn to my sister and smile. "I think so. There isn't anything that can keep me from getting married. I just need to calm the butterflies in my stomach."

She smiles. I know she knows how it feels. Then, she tells me, "Finn and Jarred are going to lose their minds when they see you walk down that aisle. A princess befitting of a royal ceremony."

I turn to her. She's married to Damien, Finn's eldest brother, and she's known Finn far longer than I have. "Do you think Finn is happy?" I don't know why I need to know this now, or why I'm asking her, but I trust her. She is my sister after all.

"He is," she tells me confidently. "If he wasn't, he

would never have gone through with this. One thing I've learned about Finn Thorne is that he never does something for the sake of it. Even if Bradford wants it. Mind you, all the brothers do what they want, following their own passions. They may love their father, but they're also very stubborn."

Interestingly enough, I believe her. I've seen that side of Finn, so I don't know why I'm nervous about walking out there and confessing my love in front of our family. I nod and take another deep breath.

"The only difference between your relationship and mine with Damien is that you have Jarred. But that just means you have extra love to account for." Her words are a salve to my worried soul.

Nodding, I say, "Thank you. I needed that."

"That's what family is for," Nesrin informs me before she takes my hand. "Now let's go and show those Thornes exactly what we're made of before Finn has a panic attack and thinks you're not coming." A shiver of nervous excitement causes me to tremble before I grab my bouquet and make my way out of the room.

We decided on having the wedding at the manor. It's been decorated in golden fairy lights that lead down the stairs, all the way to the garden. With every step along the white carpet that guides me to my future, there are large vases filled with white roses. Everything feels as if it' been set out in a castle rather than a home. But this place is like a gothic palace, because no home I've ever seen looks like Thorne Manor does.

With every step, I pray silently that I don't fall flat on my face. I'm used to wearing heels, but not when I'm shaking like a leaf in the breeze. The moment I reach the patio doors, my heart stutters in my chest. My ribs ache from the attack, and my lungs struggle to pull in air. When I glance up, I find Finn's gaze on me. There's a small, mischievous smile on his face as he stands alongside Jarred, Damien, and Cassian.

The four men are dressed in black tuxedos and crisp white shirts. Their bowties are black, matching their shoes. The guests rise as a song fills the space. It's not the typical wedding march, and I smile when I realize what Finn chose for me to walk down the aisle to.

"Eyes on Fire" by Blue Foundation haunts my ears as I move toward the makeshift altar that's been set up for the wedding. The moment I reach my two men, the tears I've been holding trickle down my cheek. I may only be marrying one of them, but they're both mine. As I am theirs.

"You're perfect," Finn whispers in my ear when he leans in to press his lips to my cheek. The wetness of my emotions comes away on his mouth, and I'm tempted to kiss him, just to taste it. But he turns toward the minister who also married Damien and Nesrin.

"Today, we're gathered here to witness the joining of not only two souls, but three," he starts, which has me smiling over at Jarred. "It may not be conventional, but the love these three hearts have found is special."

As the ceremony continues, we hold hands. All three of us. There's a special moment when the minister stops and asks us to recite the vows we wrote. Finn looks at me as if I've just walked out of his dreams.

"I didn't think we'd get here to be honest," he says, causing the guests to laugh. "But I'm so glad we did. Nothing in life is easy, it's messy, it's painful, and it's difficult," he continues with the corner of his mouth tilting upward. "However, with you, with Jarred, it's all worth it. I've never found love before. I've never wanted it. Somehow, I didn't just find one soulmate, I found two. And I'm the luckiest bastard in the world."

He slips the ring on my finger, and I turn to stand between both men. "Never in my life did I think that loving someone would be possible. I grew up sheltered from the normal, but also exposed to so much. And yet, when it came down to it, forever wasn't just the straight and narrow path I thought it would be. It's a twisted rollercoaster that has set my soul on fire. I love you both, more than I ever thought I could, and I want our forever to be a journey I'll never forget."

Nesrin steps up to hand me two rings as she takes my bouquet. Both matching silver bands were made just for Jarred and Finn. On the inside of each ring is a matching engraving of our tattoos: three hearts, one infinity sign.

I slip the rings on their fingers, which fit perfectly. But it's then that Jarred steps up to say his vows. He takes my hand gently as he slips a ring on my right hand. Then, he takes Finn's hand in his and holds us both.

"I spent my life running," he murmurs, but I know the crowd can hear him. "But the moment I walked into Thorne Haven, I knew I was home. There was no more running, even though fear had held me hostage. I didn't know why I was so at ease here, but then I found Finn," he says as he looks at our husband. "You showed me that love is possible, even for someone who's been hurt and left broken." Then, those silver eyes lock on mine. "And you walked in and shattered every illusion I had of a normal life."

The guests laugh once more, because we all giggle at that. There's certainly no normal around here. Especially when it comes to our relationship. I mean, normal is boring, right?

"But it's not what I wanted. I could never have a regular, old life because I would never be happy. I want the unconventional, I want the challenge, and I want the love of not one, but two perfectly imperfect people. We may be broken in our own ways, but those shattered pieces, they fit together to form a triad of the purest love I've come to know."

The emotional silence that fills the air has my throat thick with tears. I swallow back the lump as the minister continues his sermon. It's not too long, and soon enough, he's speaking the words that cause my stomach to somersault. "And I now pronounce you husbands and wife. You may kiss the bride."

Finn is the first one to pull me into his arms and steal my lips. The softness of his touch burns a hole right through me. I may as well be naked as he tangles his tongue with mine. The whoops from the crowd surround us, causing me to laugh as I'm released from the confines of his arms, only to be stolen once more, but this time, by Jarred, who kisses me by stealing my breath.

More cheers from the guests make me smile as finally, Finn and Jarred share an intimate kiss. It's short, nothing like the one they gave me, but there's so much affection in the connection between them, it's palpable.

"Time to party," Finn shouts as we make our way down the aisle toward the patio, where drinks and snacks have been set out. We decided on dinner in the dining room, but since the weather seems to be holding out, the pre-reception drinks were set up outside.

"Congratulations," Damien says while shaking his brother's hand, then slapping Jarred on the back. He takes my hand and wishes me all the best with the two troublemakers, which has all of us laughing out loud.

"Welcome to the family," Cassian says. He's been rather quiet since he and Kalyn arrived earlier, but he pulls me into a hug, which warms my heart.

"Thank you so much," I whisper before he lets me go. Kalyn smiles, giving me a quick hug as well. I grew up the only child, and now, I have a family, an extended family, and even a half-sister I never knew I had.

It's strange how life can take you on a rollercoaster ride, not allowing you to see what's up ahead. It's as if you're speeding through everything and suddenly, once you're ready for it, it drops you right in the thick of things.

Looking around at the loving faces and listening to the affectionate words, I know there's nowhere else I'd rather be. With my new family, in my new life, with my new name.

EPILOGUE
Zaria

One Year Later

THE DARK INK ON MY WRIST IS STILL BRIGHT with the tattoo that now adorns my skin. Three hearts, an infinity symbol entwined amongst them. A reminder that I'm forever their girl, and they're mine. Possession feels different when you want it. A deep ache in my chest reminds me that if I didn't have Finn and Jarred, I'd be alone in this world. Not in the literal sense, but because I told my mother I want nothing to do with her.

Walking away from a life I've known to a new, exciting home has its perks, but it also has the reminders of what I left. My past is riddled with mistakes that will always be memories, ones that can appear at any given moment. But I have learned to breathe through the heartache and come out on the other side.

My father couldn't do that. And even as I remember the anger I felt toward him for lying to me, knowing that I'm not his daughter, I'm thankful because he loved me. There are times secrets held are to keep those we love safe. And I realize now, that's what he did.

What hurts the most is that he couldn't live with himself anymore. He couldn't be with my mother, and instead of breathing through his pain, he went out and sought death. It was something I nearly did myself. And I realize, I took after my dad more than I thought I did. Even though we didn't share blood, we shared a connection. I almost ended my own life.

I'm thankful I didn't.

Even though those thoughts crop up now and then, I have a support system that no longer allows me to wallow in the darkness. Instead, we play there, we bask in it, and we don't let it drag us down into its full depths.

The sun has finally set and the stars twinkle above

me. The guys are on their way home from London while I've just returned to Thorne Haven from New York. We've all been rather busy, but with the patriarch of the Thorne family not doing so well, the Thorne brothers will all be under one roof again.

When I first came to the manor, I was angry. There was an immaturity that I never let go of and Finn saw it. There isn't a moment, since we met till now, that he doesn't see through my armor. Jarred was like a bonus love. He came along with the package I was forced into. At first, I didn't want it. My focus was on getting out of the marriage my mother signed me up for, but the more time I spent around both men, the more I knew they brought out the best in me.

Finn dug deep into my bones, Jarred hammered through all those hardened walls, and they found me. I found me. A sense of self took a hold of me and I realized I am strong. Even though I spent my early life swallowing bitter pills of bullying and vicious attacks on who I am, I'm still here.

"There she is," Finn says as he saunters into the room. He's still dressed in a suit, without a tie. He looks so handsome. His hair longer now, flopping over his dark eyes. The smirk that tilts his lips to the side makes me smile.

"How are you?" I ask, falling into his arms. It's not easy when you know your family is in distress. He rushed back while Damien tied up loose ends before he and Nesrin will return home.

"I'm okay," he tells me, before pressing a kiss to my head. More warmth curls itself around me and I realize it's Jarred. I'm sandwiched between them, and I wouldn't want to be anywhere else. "I needed you both," Finn murmurs into my hair as he pulls me closer. He's not always been the sweet, affectionate man I've come to know. When I first arrived, he was angry, rightly so. I wasn't easy to be around either. But we made it work.

Since the wedding, both Jarred and Finn have been attentive, affectionate, and more than I could ever have expected. Both men love me unconditionally, and I love them.

"He's not okay," Jarred whispers in my ear, and we both turn to look at Finn. The fear in his eyes dances like a flame in the breeze. We can't say anything that would make it better. There are no magic cures for heartbreak, but we'll be here for him, if and when, he needs us.

"I think you need to go see him," I tell Finn. His father refused to stay in the hospital, so instead, they've brought his care to the manor. The Cancer has hit him hard, fast. He hid it from his sons because he knew about the diagnosis months ago. With it being stage four, there's nothing more they can do.

Marcia has been rushing around, making sure everyone knows what to do, and even though she's very much a trophy wife, she's stood up for her husband. She hasn't left his side, and that is something I truly admire.

"I don't know if I can," Finn admits as he pulls away from us. I watch him unbutton his shirt, then shrug off his jacket before he turns to the bed. The clothes he discards land in a heap. "Facing him like that is not something I can handle, not right now." He doesn't look at us as he speaks, but the pain in his voice is apparent.

I cast a glance at Jarred, then back to Finn. I know that the pain will only worsen before it eases. From my own experience, I found being alone helped me, but that was because I grew up with nobody to comfort me when I was hurt. My father did his best, but I still felt as if I were a stranger in a place that I called home.

"I know it hurts," I tell him. Leaving Jarred at the window, I make my way to Finn. I gently place my hand on his shoulder; the tension in his muscles tightens then releases when I trail my fingers to his hand. With his warmth bathing me, and my affection calming him, I know he'll get through this. "You can be alone," I whisper. "But we'll still be close." It's a promise I make and intend to keep.

For a long, silent moment, we stand at our positions in the bedroom. And I wonder if Finn will allow me to burrow into his heart once more.

"Tell me about your father," I urge slowly. I found talking about happy times helped the pain. It brought tears, but it also allowed me to remind myself not everything was bad. "What is the one memory you have where you laughed, where you were so happy, so content, that you didn't think anyone could change it."

Finn's smile tilts his lips, which lights up his face in such a way, he looks so much younger than his twenty-eight years. The way his dark eyes flicker has my heart filling up with the need to put that look on his face every day.

"I was thirteen, a bit of a dick," he says with a chuckle.

"Nothing's changed then," Jarred joins us and the guys glare playfully at each other before they settle on the bed. Finn pulls me into his arms, and I fit between his spread thighs. He and Jarred sit beside each other, the heat of them both filling the room.

"He always knew when I was up to no good," Finn recalls with fondness in his voice. I've known this man over a year, and yet, I've never seen him like this. The tough exterior that he exudes is no longer there, not right now anyway.

It's refreshing.

"I was coming home from school when I got this great idea to play a prank on my brothers. Damien was excited for his new car, and I wanted to change the batteries in his key fob so that it couldn't open the doors."

"And your father found you?"

Finn smiles. "Of course he did. It was almost as if he had a tracking device inserted in my neck, so he could find out when I misbehaved." I can't help but smile along with my husband. "Anyway, he walked into the kitchen while I was opening the damn thing and stopped me before I could ruin it. I was grounded for two months."

"And did you stay indoors for those two months?" Jarred asks, but the laugh we get in return is the only answer we need. There's no way Finn would follow the rules. He doesn't do that now. I'm sure when he was younger, it was so much worse.

"You were quite a naughty little shit," I remark as I settle on his lap. His arm wraps around my waist, holding me close, while the fingers of his other hand tangle with Jarred's.

Finn nods. "I was. And it got worse when we made friends with the Havens."

"You still have to tell me all about your misadventures with them," I say.

"I don't know if that's a good idea or not," Jarred answers quickly. I've heard some of the rumors about the Haven boys. They're all adopted, so they're new to Thorne Haven in the sense that their lineage doesn't start in this particular town. But they've grown accustomed to their lives here.

"Well, Creed is the only one still around," Finn says. "I think Brody and Keirin have both moved. But they do come home every year." There are so many events that the founding families have, the annual Halloween and Christmas galas being two of the most talked about events. Then, there is the New Year's celebration, which I'm looking forward to.

"I suppose I should go see my dad," Finn finally admits. It's not easy, but at least he's getting to talk to his dad. I never got the chance to say goodbye. I never even got the chance to understand why he wanted to leave. There are so many ideas in my mind as to why he ended his life, but we will never know the truth. He took that with him to the grave.

"I think that's a good idea," I tell Finn, before pressing my lips to his. "If you need me, I'll be here." He nods slowly and sets me on the bed before he flicks Jarred's hair. And then he's gone.

"Do you think his dad will pull through?" I whisper, but I can't look at Jarred. Even though I'm married to Finn, I'm married to Jarred as well. It may not be official in the eyes of the church or the law, but he is part of our relationship, just as much as Finn and me are.

"I don't know," he answers. There is no need to say the words because I know the truth. As much as I want to pray for Bradford, I'm convinced, along with everyone else, that the illness will take him.

"We'll have to be there for him." My words are filled with pain. My throat thick with heartache for the man I love. Jarred takes my hand and holds it tight.

"We will. And you should know that we're here for you, too. This can't be easy to go through when you lost your father as well." His words are a salve to my rather fragile heart. The memories of what I went through have come crashing back in since I made the call to Finn.

We found Bradford passed out in his office. I nearly broke down the same way I did with my own dad. But I forced myself to be strong. I needed to be for Finn.

"You're only human," Jarred says as if he can read my mind. He has a way of doing that at times. It can be rather disconcerting, but I've gotten used to it. "You're allowed to feel."

"I know," I murmur with a nod. "I just didn't think that something like this would happen so soon after our wedding. I thought he would have more time, perhaps to see grandchildren." As I say it, the lump in my throat thickens, and the burn in my eyes blurs my vision.

Our children won't have any grandparents. Even though my mother is still alive, I want nothing to do with her. And she knows it. Any child that I bring into this world won't know his or her grandmother. It may be selfish, but I don't want any negativity around them.

"It's not easy losing anyone in your life," Jarred says, bringing my attention back to the present.

"But with the right support system, it can ease the burden."

I nod in agreement. "It can." We both have to be strong for the man we love.

And that will be the easiest thing I do, because when you love someone, you'll do anything for them.

BONUS SCENE
Finn

One year later

THE SUN SHIMMERS DOWN ON THE SWIMMING pool where Zaria and Jarred are playing with Holden. I can't believe I'm a goddamned uncle. Damien's son is almost two-years-old, and he looks like a mini-version of my brother.

Nesrin is settled in beside me as she sunbathes in her bikini, which I know Damien has already chastised her about. It's a bright blue two-piece, which matches the color of his eyes. But I'm certain it's the strings and tiny triangles that are causing him the most torment.

"You know my brother is going to have a heart attack if you continue wearing that," I inform my sister-in-law. "Also, when Creed arrives, Damien will lose his mind since the bastard is still single."

"Your brother needs to know that I love him. And I'm not about to cower to his demands, just because he can't handle a bit of competition." Her playful, yet fiery nature is the reason Damien fell for her in the first place.

"Oh, I'm sure he'll make sure you obey," I warn her, knowing my brother. The two of them have always had an intensity that outshone everyone else in the room. The summer vacation is well underway as Cassian and Kalyn arrive in matching green swimsuits. Kalyn has also opted for a bikini, which I can tell by the look on Cass's face he's not happy about.

I can't help but chuckle. Zaria exits the pool. She may be in a two piece, but at least it covers more than both my brother's wives do. Even though they're cavemen when it comes to their women, they know they're safe at home. But like I said, the moment Creed walks in, the fangs will come out.

Damien's best friend is well-known to be a playboy, just like I was. That is until Zaria and Jarred roped me into their orbit and now, all I see are those two. Zaria settles between my legs, her wet skin glistening in the bright sunshine.

"Holden is so gorgeous," she tells Nesrin.

"He's just like his dad, although, I can already see we're going to have our hands full," Nesrin says with a smile.

"Because he has his mother's fire," Damien informs us as he settles down on the end of Nesrin's lounger. "Hey, man," he greets Cass with a handshake. I reach mine out to fist bump my brother before I press a kiss to Kalyn's knuckles.

It feels good to have the family around us. After losing our dad, we've come to the realization that life is short and being apart doesn't work for us. Damien and Nesrin have decided to move back to Thorne Haven, while Cassian and Kalyn live just down the road.

We made a vow to always be close enough to help each other when needed. Blood is a strong bond. It's one that cannot be broken, even if you want it to be. Jarred's father has finally visited a few times, and they've slowly started a path to getting to know each other again.

"So, Cass," I call out, "when are we expecting a little

version of you running around?" The question is one I've posed before. One that has my brother rolling his eyes.

"Well," Kalyn pipes up, a shy smile on her lips. She's been through a fucking dark road, but she's come out on the other side. "There might be one in about nine months?" she tells us as her hand circles her stomach. There's no bump to speak of, but I am pretty sure it will be apparent soon.

Shock laces my voice when I say, "Really?"

"Yeah," Cass says with a nod. "We found out two days ago." The pride in his expression has all of us smiling as he kisses his wife.

"Congrats," I shout out, along with Damien. Just then, Jarred walks over with Holden in his arms. The sight of him with a kid makes my chest warm and my heart expand. We haven't started trying yet, but Zaria, Jarred, and I definitely want a family. We've said we'd like to fill the manor with the pitter pattering of small feet.

"Damn, we better get on it then," I tell Zaria, earning myself a swat to the leg. "Hey!"

"Don't be an ass," she bites playfully. "I don't go announcing when we're going to have sex to everyone."

"Yeah, we don't need to know that, brother," Damien informs me before laughing out loud.

I push up and pin him with a glare and an arched brow. "Oh yeah? While you and Nesrin were smooching like two teens all around the house, Cass and I had to put up with it."

"True story," Cass chuckles when Damien gives him a glare that forces him to laugh even louder. Our eldest brother wasn't the most private when it came to his feelings for our stepsister. And even so, I loved watching the cold-detached man become putty in her delicate hands.

"Okay, enough of that," Damien announces. "We're getting drinks. Holden," he calls to his son. "Do you want ice-cream?"

"Cleem!!" Holden shouts excitedly, causing us all to laugh. Watching my brother be a dad is new; I haven't been around him much since they were living in London. But now, having them here, I feel content knowing how happy he is. The two of them head off to the kitchen, and I'm almost certain it won't be long until Holden is in the pool again. The sticky sweets he's about to devour will ensure the place needs a good cleaning tomorrow.

I take in the happiness that fills our home, and I

can't deny, I'm finally content. My life hasn't been easy, and the road to a happily ever after has been filled with potholes, but we made it. Zaria leans back against me, while Jarred settles between her thighs. The three of us watching as Nesrin and Kalyn take to the pool for a game of volleyball.

My heart is full.

My life is perfect.

And my happiness is right here.

Jarred

Nine months later

I didn't think about life after leaving Tynewood. I never allowed myself to fantasize about happy endings because that's not how I was raised. But as I settle into bed beside Zaria and Finn, I know that my heart is finally home.

It's become apparent to me that happiness isn't what you have. Material possessions aren't what bring a smile to your face day to day. It's these moments of closeness with people who see you for who you really are. They're the ones who will forever be by your side when you need it the most.

Finn and Zaria are my home.

My hand circles her growing belly, and I can't wait to feel the baby kicking. We decided on two kids, one Finn's, and one mine. When we sat down one night, discussing a family, it was an idea Finn had come up with, and when we all agreed, it had become our plan.

The three of us have made something unconventional work.

Life may never be an easy road, but it's so worth it when you find happiness. I glimpse Finn's gaze on me. "What?"

"I'm just thinking that we're finally here," he says. "We made it and I honestly didn't think we would."

"Because of your fears."

He nods.

"It's also because you both are so damn stubborn," Zaria adds as she rolls onto her back. The fact that her tiny tank top no longer holds her full breasts makes my cock hard. I lean down and capture a nipple in my mouth, causing her to forget her chastisement of us, and instead, she moans as my tongue flicks over the hardened bud.

"Shit," Finn growls, and his mouth works her other nipple. Her hands tangle in our hair, and she holds us close. I skate my fingers over her body, down to her pussy, where I tease her clit with slow circles.

She's been a horny little wench since becoming pregnant, and we've thoroughly enjoyed teasing and taunting her. Her wetness coats my finger as I suck on her breast. When I finally look up, her pupils have dilated, the dark middle expanding as desire takes a hold of her.

"I need…" Her words fizzle into silence when I dip two fingers inside her pussy. "Oh god," Zaria moans out loud.

Finn moves down to where my fingers are, and his tongue darts out to taste Zaria's arousal as it coats my fingers. My cock is throbbing as he takes both digits into his mouth and sucks the juices from them. Our gazes lock for a heated moment before he goes to lap at her pretty cunt that's leaking her sweet juice.

I move to kneel, before I tug my sweatpants down to my thighs. My cock is thick and hard as Zaria wraps her fingers around the shaft and slowly, teasingly, strokes me until I'm groaning as pleasure zips through me.

Her mouth sucks the tip, the warmth of her

sending shivers down my spine as Finn moves until he's kneeling between her thighs. I lean over to kiss him. The flavor of Zaria's pussy on his lips as we share the sweet honey.

"Fuck," he groans as I suck on his tongue while he strokes his cock, slapping it on the smooth pussy that's dripping wet for us. With Zaria sucking me deep, I reach for Finn's cock and I stroke it until he's close to the edge.

His arousal coating my hand as I guide him to her entrance. With a slow thrust, he enters her pussy, causing her to moan around my cock. I'm so fucking close to coming, I focus on the pleasure that's taking a hold of my body.

Finn's movements are gentle as he pulls out and slides back into her body. The naughty girl plays with my balls as she takes me into her throat. The soft gagging sounds are enough to have me riding the line of orgasm yet again.

"I'm going to come," I warn her, but she doesn't relent. Instead, she grips the base of my shaft and toys with the piercings along the underside of my cock. Her tongue flicks against the bars, sending euphoria zipping through me like an electric storm.

My focus is on my dick as she swallows me deep

once more and then, she hums approval. The vibrations send pure lust through me and I lose all control, my orgasm rocking through me.

White sparks behind my eyelids as I groan in pleasure. The fact that we're all three lost in the desire that's perfumed the room has me jutting my hips until the last drops of my seed coat Zaria's tongue. When I glance down, she's smiling up at me, her mouth still filled with my release.

As I move, Finn leans down and kisses her. Watching them share my cum is a sight that has me needing more. "Fuck," I curse out through clenched teeth. "You two look so fucking hot." They toy with my release, before swallowing it. Finn's hips pick up their pace, and I know he's close. I reach for him then, my finger teasing his ass as I slip a digit inside.

"Oh fuck, you're going to make me lose it," he warns, which has me chuckling. I scissor him open, dipping two fingers in. I finger-fuck him faster as his hips slam into Zaria. It doesn't take him long to groan out loud. His body shuddering as his hands hold onto her hips, keeping her in place.

The moment he pulls out, I lean in and lick Zaria's pussy, enjoying the flavor of Finn and her mixed together like an elixir. I bring her to a screaming orgasm as I suck on her clit, biting down until my name is chanted over and over again.

And as we slowly fall asleep moments later, I can't help but do it with a smile on my face.

Have you met the other two brothers yet? If not, meet Damien in A Cut so Deep, or meet Cassian in A High so Sweet.

Do you want to know more about the game - The Burning Roses? Grab it for FREE right now!

Intrigued by the Gilded Sovereign and Ares? Keep reading for a sneak peek, or cgrab Cruel War on all major platforms!

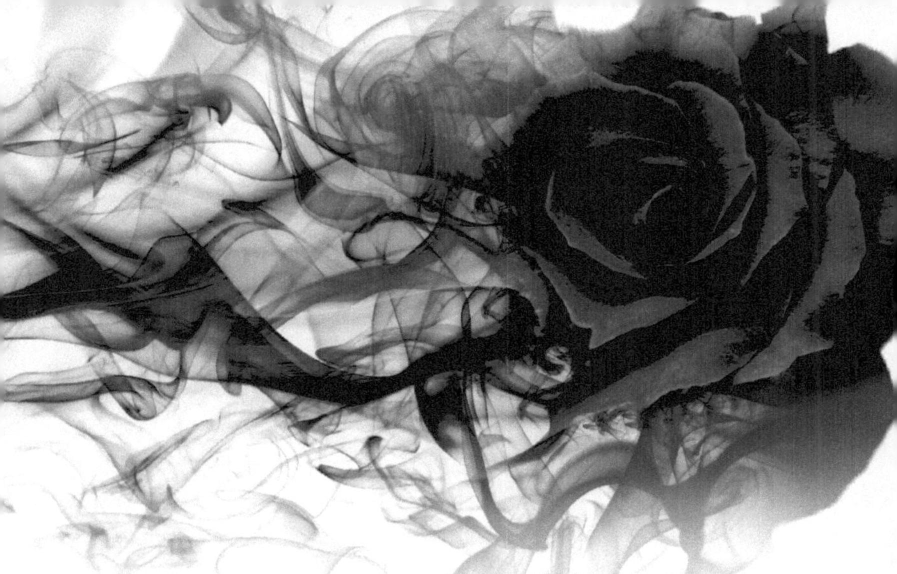

NEED SOMEONE TO LISTEN?

You are not alone

If you're struggling, feeling depressed, or thinking of harming yourself, please seek help. Below are a few places you can reach out to.

United States
http://suicidepreventionlifeline.org/

United Kingdom
https://www.nsphuk.org

Australia
https://www.lifeline.org.au

Canada
http://www.crisisservicescanada.ca/

Cruel War

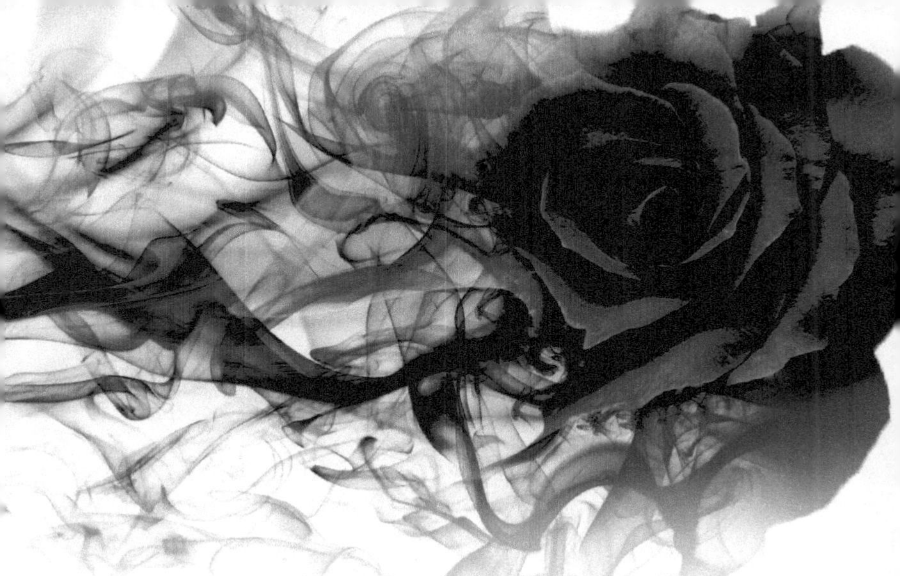

PROLOGUE
Abner

I'M PACING A PATHWAY IN THE CARPET OF MY office as I think about the future. My youngest son's sixteenth birthday is coming up, and I know I'm going to have to tell him about the Sovereign. But I have a feeling he already knows.

Glancing at the clock on the wall above the fireplace, I note it's almost midnight. My plan is in place for next week. It took me years to make sure I had the right people in my corner. And it's finally time.

My office door clicks open, and Philipe saunters in with a smile on his face. My eldest son, who is

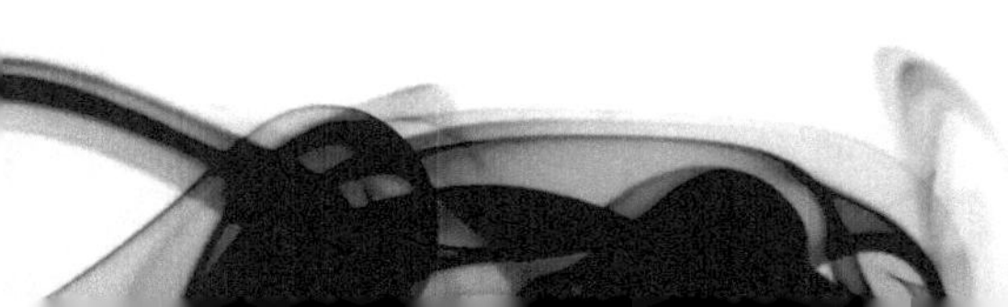

eighteen now, is like me: cold and ruthless, and he doesn't care for anyone outside our family. That's what a true Sovereign is, but Ares, I worry about him. I don't know if he has it in him to join us.

"The job is done," Philipe tells me, satisfaction on his face at the admission. The blood splattered on his shirt is evidence that he's finished the job correctly.

"Good," I nod, before turning to my desk to pick up the folder. Philipe will take over the head of the table from me when he turns twenty-one, but he's been doing odd jobs for me since he came of age.

Once he joins the Sovereign, he'll have all the power I ensured for him. This is our legacy. I hand him the manila folder and watch him flip it open.

"They voted this evening," I tell him. "You're taking my seat at the table, you'll only be sworn in when you hit the age set out in our history. Ares will be the second chair once he's old enough."

"I doubt Greg will be happy about this," my son remarks. The second eldest member of the Crowns, Gregory Birchwood, wasn't happy about two Lancasters at the table, but he can't do anything about it. His daughter isn't allowed to step up. Grecia Birchwood isn't meant to wear the gilded crown.

"He made his vote. There's no going back. The oath

was signed; blood was shed." I make my way to the armoire, which sits in the corner of my office and pour myself and Philipe a shot of whiskey. Handing a tumbler to him, I lift my own. "To the Sovereign and the rule of the Lancasters." I clink my glass on my son's, and a smile beams from his face.

It's uncanny how much he looks just like his mother. There's a soft golden hue to his light brown hair, and his eyes, the color of the freshly grown grass on a hot summer's day, match hers almost identically. I watch him take a sip before he narrows his gaze on me.

"I'm leaving," he utters. "I'm ready to go to New York. It's the one thing I've wanted, and it's time. I'll be back for my inking."

"I didn't think you'd stay, but remember, if we need you…" I allow my words to trail into the heavy silence in the office. He doesn't realize what being an Elder means, but he'll learn.

We still have time before Ares, Etienne Durand, and Tarian Calvert come of age, so Philipe will take the reins until the three younger boys step up and they form one entity.

Philipe swallows down the amber liquid before offering me a grin. "I'll be here whenever you need me."

"Go, I know you're itching to get to your girl," I tell him, shaking my head when he chuckles.

"See you tomorrow." He leaves me in the office with my thoughts. I've done things in my life that were needed to ensure my family are safe. Even though most wouldn't agree with my actions, it is my choice, and I'll never apologize.

My phone rings shrilly on the desk; when I pick it up, I note the name before answering. "What?"

"We found her. She's a crown," he tells me. I knew they would. The men I have around the country, around the world, would've tracked her down one way or another, and she knows it.

"Good, we'll keep an eye on her. The father?"

"He's around."

"Bring him in, the job I have for him is important. I want it done next week." Hanging up, I smile when I pour myself another drink and savor the burn of the whiskey as it travels down my throat.

I sit back and stare out the window. The full moon is high, reminding me of how small and insignificant we truly are in the grand scheme of things. But I also know that nothing can stop the events that will take place in the coming years.

My sons will rule the Sovereign with iron fists.

I gulp down the last of my drink as my office door opens, and my wife strolls in. She's my life. I fell for her when I was a boy, and even though she knows of the darkness that resides inside me, she hasn't run; she continues to love me even after all the shit I've put her through.

"Are you coming to bed?"

"I am. Philipe was just here to collect a docket," I tell her, crooking my finger to call her closer. "Ares will know about his new role in this household. I plan to speak to him tomorrow."

"I don't know if he's ready," she shakes her head, worry etched on her beautiful face. She voices my concerns out loud.

Sighing, I stand and go to where she's standing at the edge of my desk, pulling her into my arms. "He will be. He's a Lancaster, it's in our blood."

"This isn't some supernatural occurrence, Abner. He's not going to suddenly become powerful and grow wings," she bites out in frustration. Our son may not be something from a comic book, but there are things about the four new Crowns who will take over that nobody would ever guess.

Ares being one of them.

But what she doesn't know can't hurt her, which is why I'm not the one to complete the task I've set in motion. So instead of saying anything, I scoop her up and make my way through the house and up to our suite.

"I think it's time we made love again," I murmur in her ear, with my eyes shut, I pray she'll calm the fuck down. The darkness grips me when I think of the violence to befall us.

Her hands land on my shoulders, holding me away from her for a moment before she shakes her head. "Don't push me away and treat me like I'm fragile."

"You are fragile." I can easily overpower her, and she knows it. I could lift her with one hand, squeeze, and her breath will be stolen. I don't. I do allow her to glower at me though because that will ensure our night in bed together will be short.

"I'm not, Abner," she bites out, and I can see this night isn't going as planned. All I need, want, was a chance to feel her, but she's not having it.

I rise, turning away from her, and head into the bathroom. I don't need this. I really can't lose my shit so close to Philipe's inking. The moment my eldest son wears the mark of the Sovereign, I can take a back seat on the day to day running of the society.

"Don't walk away from me," she retorts, her voice shrill and angry.

"Darling, I suggest you go to bed."

"Like fuck, this is ridiculous. What are you not telling me? You've hidden enough from me over the years, Abner. The women, the killing, I see the blood on your clothes; I'm not stupid."

One rule of the Sovereign is to never speak of it with those outside the society. Even our partners. The only people who know about it are the children who will step up to the table.

No females.

No outsiders.

It may sound misogynistic, but that's what the ancestors wanted, and that's what they'll get. We observe their rituals, their way of life.

"Abner."

"Lilian. Go. To. Bed." My voice is low, a warning tone that makes her stop for a moment. I feel her. Every part of me knows what she feels because I can feel it, too. I sense every argument she has raging around in her mind.

I glance over my shoulder, meeting her questioning gaze before she shakes her head and turns away from me. I watch her slip under the sheet and curl into a ball. Her shoulders shake, but I don't go to her. I'm not that type of man.

Closing my eyes, I quell the urges inside me, and I calm my erratic heartbeat. My sons don't know about me; they have no idea who their father truly is, and I refuse to let them find out by me ripping their mother to shreds in a fit of fury.

Once I step down, my secrets will be safe.

I'll make sure of it.

AVAILABLE ON ALL MAJOR PLATFORMS

ACKNOWLEDGEMENTS
Thank you

Coming to the end of a series is always bittersweet. Knowing that you, the readers, loved the characters, and the world, is humbling to say the least. I've met so many new readers through this venture into New Adult Romance.

Thank you so much for all your love for this series, and even though the topics are tough to handle, you've been there with me through it all!

My Thorne boys will always hold a special place in my heart. And I have to start thinking about the Haven boys now. That's going to be one heck of a rollercoaster! I hope you'll be here with me through

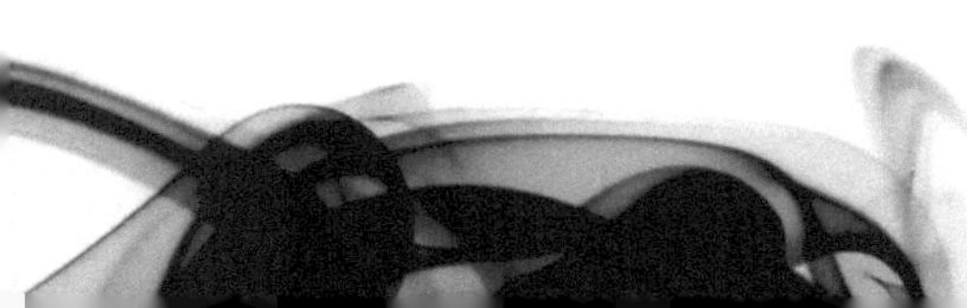

that ride!

To my editor, Rebecca Barney (Rebecca's Fairest Reviews), thank you for polishing this story and making it shine. Your advice and comments always ensure my book is eady for readers.

To my PA, Caroline, who keeps me in line when I go off the rails. Thank you so much for everything! I would be lost without you!

To my readers, the amazing ladies in my reader group, The Deviants, thank you for always being so incredible, and to my Captive Angels for pimping my ass out, you ladies ROCK!

And to the bloggers and bookstagrammers who were so excited to meet these characters. I truly hope the book lived up to your expectations. Thank you for always taking time out of your busy lives to help support and promote me. Your love is humbling.

Mad love,

Dani xo

ACKNOWLEDGEMENTS
Thank you

Coming to the end of a series is always bittersweet. Knowing that you, the readers, loved the characters, and the world, is humbling to say the least. I've met so many new readers through this venture into New Adult Romance.

Thank you so much for all your love for this series, and even though the topics are tough to handle, you've been there with me through it all!

My Thorne boys will always hold a special place in my heart. And I have to start thinking about the Haven boys now. That's going to be one heck of a rollercoaster! I hope you'll be here with me through

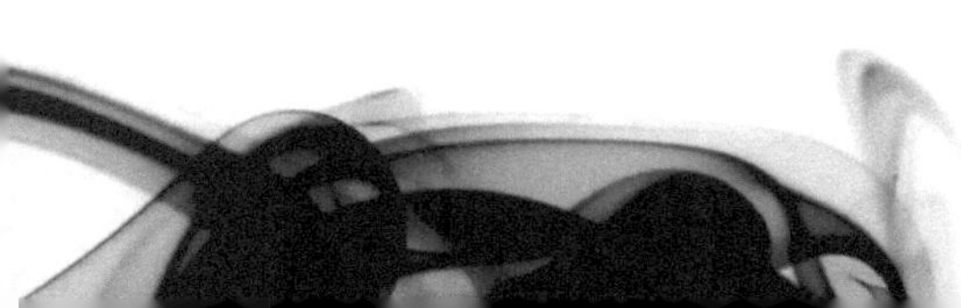

that ride!

To my editor, Rebecca Barney (Rebecca's Fairest Reviews), thank you for polishing this story and making it shine. Your advice and comments always ensure my book is eady for readers.

To my PA, Caroline, who keeps me in line when I go off the rails. Thank you so much for everything! I would be lost without you!

To my readers, the amazing ladies in my reader group, The Deviants, thank you for always being so incredible, and to my Captive Angels for pimping my ass out, you ladies ROCK!

And to the bloggers and bookstagrammers who were so excited to meet these characters. I truly hope the book lived up to your expectations. Thank you for always taking time out of your busy lives to help support and promote me. Your love is humbling.

Mad love,

Dani xo

ABOUT
the author

Dani is a *USA Today* Bestselling Author of seductive and deviant romance.

Her books range from the dark to emotional, but every hero is alpha, and each heroine is strong-willed, bringing the men down to their knees.

She now lives in the UK, after moving from Cape Town, with her better half who does all the cooking while she writes all the words.

When she's not writing, she can be found binge-watching the latest TV series, or working on graphic design. She has a healthy addiction to reading, tattoos, coffee, and ice cream.

www.danirene.com | info@danirene.com

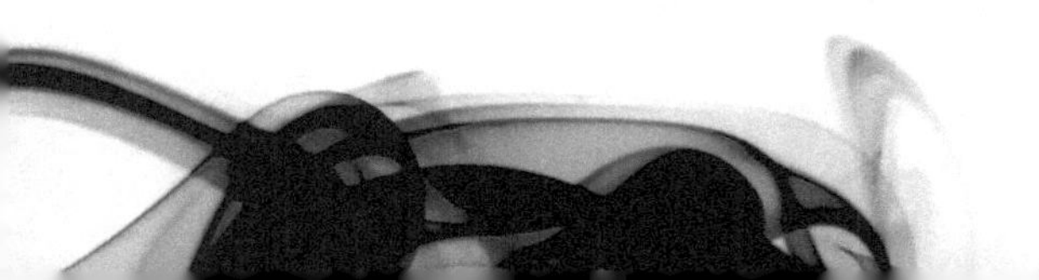

OTHER BOOKS
by Dani

Head over to my website to find all my titles!

https://danirene.com/books/

You can also find me on Kiss, Radish, WattPad